Conspiracies AND CHEMISTRY

CONSPIRACIES AND CHEMISTRY

A WORKPLACE AGE-GAP ROMANTIC COMEDY

40 AND FABULOUS

BOOK 3

MICHELLE MCCRAW

CONTENTS

JOIN ME!

Hey, reader! This is your personal invitation to join my VIP newsletter, where you'll get bookish news, freebies, sneak peeks, and, I'm not gonna lie, TONS of puppy pics.

Visit michellemccraw.com/joinme to get on the list!

BOOKS BY MICHELLE MCCRAW

40 and Fabulous

Fashion and Passion

Frenemies and Lovers

Books and Hookups

Conspiracies and Chemistry

Advances and Retreats

Marriage and Trouble

Sugar and Spice

Synergy Series

Work with Me

Friend Me

Trip Me Up

Boss Me

Forget Me

Tempt Me

For the nerds.
Own it, y'all.

AUTHOR'S NOTE

Readers, this story includes cancer and endometriosis as healthcare topics. Although none of the main characters have cancer, in their backstories, their loved ones have died because of it. If you're sensitive to this, please take care of yourself and consider if this is the right book for you to read right now.

On a lighter note, I've sprinkled in some conspiracy theories, some "real" and others made up, throughout this novel as a comedic element. The research was fascinating, but I don't believe in any of these, and I encourage you, my reader (and any FBI investigators), to take them as merely the fun storytelling elements I intended.

Though, if you'd like a copy of my manifesto about how dogs and cats have collaborated to domesticate humans and become the master species on the planet, contact me through my website, michellemccraw.com.

1
———

ICOSAGON

Icosagon: A twenty-sided polygon. Icosagons can be used to represent the twenty amino acids in modeling protein sequences.

OLIVER

"Guys, I think we've achieved pinnacle nerd here."

My buddy Andrew froze with the twenty-sided die cupped in his hand. He leaned back in his chair at their dining room table and gazed up at his fiancée, who rested her manicured hands on his shoulders. "What do you mean?"

"Um..." Carly looped a lock of Andrew's hair around her finger, one of the shaggy bits that poked out from underneath the brim of his purple wizard's hat. "I mean, I love our game nights. But this one is a little...extreme?"

"What?" I picked up the plastic kraken figure and twirled it, its long tentacles whipping the scent of garlic into my nostrils. Andrew had over-seasoned his baked ziti again, and the air was pungent with it. I could feel it seeping into my pores. (Days later, I'd still be able to smell it in my sweat.) "I called in a favor to get this advance copy of *Forge of Destiny.* It's the next huge tabletop RPG...um...roleplaying game," I added, since Carly didn't know a sorcerer from a paladin. "You won't be able to find it anywhere at Christmas."

The corners of her mouth twitched. "I'm honored. But maybe I should sit this one out. Leave space for the serious gamers." I'll admit it: the hat and the board game looked out of place in their sleek, leather-and-glass dining room, and Carly was a good sport to host this meetup for Andrew's friends, who were all a decade younger than her and the opposite of the cool celebrities she usually hung out with.

Andrew's lip stuck out like she'd killed his favorite character. "It'll be more fun if you play."

"It's true," I said, "it's better with more players, even if they're noobs." Andrew scowled at me, so I flashed his fiancée a smile and tapped one of the jingle bells on my jester's hat. "I thought you'd like the fashion aspect of this one, Carly."

She raised her eyebrows. "That's what you consider fashion?"

My friend snatched off his wizard hat and tossed it onto their dining table. "You like Texas Hold'em. I'll get another card table from the garage."

I couldn't lose methodical Andrew to poker. He was the best RPG strategist I knew. Almost as good as Simon used to be. "You still have to finish your character."

"I don't know..." He traced one of the stars embroidered on the silky purple fabric of the hat, his gaze on his fiancée. He was a total simp for her.

Not that there was anything wrong with that.

I wanted good things for my friend. But game night used to be our thing, with whiskey and pizza and no one judging us for being nerds. Now, there was wine—though none for me—and charcuterie and homemade pasta, not to mention the barely-disguised mockery.

And kissing.

I looked away as Carly pressed her lips to Andrew's. She murmured, "It's all good. I'll go check on Chanel. She might need some quiet after meeting all these new people."

"Need me to take her outside?" he asked.

I centered the kraken on its spot on the board. I would *not* roll my eyes about Andrew's purse dog. So what if he sometimes seemed to care more about the dog than me? Chanel made Carly happy, and that made Andrew happy. I needed to get over myself, hard as it was with the shit going down at work. I needed my friend.

"No, we're fine. You boys play your game." Carly's hand lingered on his shoulder before she glided away.

I grabbed the deck of cards and shuffled them aggressively. "Who else is in?"

I looked up to see which of our friends would sit down to play, but a swoop of russet hair in the foyer caught my attention. My throat went dry, and I grabbed the edge of the table to keep my fingers from trembling.

"You didn't tell me *she* was coming." I meant to say it softly, but my vocal cords seized up, and it came out as a too-loud wheeze.

And, shit, she heard me. Those eerie light-green eyes of hers locked onto mine. Her soft-looking lips tightened, then she turned her back to me as she accepted a hug from Carly.

"I didn't know," Andrew muttered. "Carly's been trying to get Tessa to come to game night for months. She's basically a hermit."

If I'd known she'd be there, I might have stayed home. My crush had already made me embarrass myself, and it was highly likely I'd make it even worse as the night went on.

Like he could read the thought on my face, he said, "Can you try to get along? I know you two are like cats and dogs, but—"

I scraped my chair back and accidentally bumped the table as I shot to my feet. The plastic figurines shuddered, and the kraken skidded off the edge of the board. My hat rang out like sleigh bells. I yanked it off and tossed it on my chair. "I'm going to get a drink. Want one?"

He glanced at my almost-full seltzer. "I'll come. Tessa, what can I get you?"

"Whiskey?" She turned her gaze on Andrew, and I wanted to leap in front of him and capture it all for myself.

"Neat?" he asked.

"Please." Her husky voice teased like a caress along my spine.

My glasses were fogging up. I ripped my gaze off her tight black turtleneck hugging the curves of her breasts and strode into the kitchen. As I flung open the refrigerator door, the beer bottles in the door rattled. I stuck my whole face inside, pretending to read the labels as I let the frigid air chill my hot cheeks.

"Look, I'm sorry." Andrew's voice came from behind me. "I thought she'd flake on us again. Can't you..."

I slammed the refrigerator shut. I didn't want a beer. I never wanted anything to dull my wits, not anymore, and especially not with her around. "Can't I what?"

"Be nice?" His smile was bright with hope. "For my sake. You're my best friend, and she's one of Carly's gang. They do everything together, and it'd be amazing if I wasn't the only guy tagging along." But we'd tried that before.

Last month, at Andrew and Carly's engagement party, the second I'd seen Tessa, I'd approached her, determined to impress her with my sparkling wit and sophisticated conversation and get her to finally notice me. But when I was close enough to count every freckle, my brain blue-screened. I couldn't think of a single word to say to the brilliant, gorgeous, worldly woman. She'd looked down her nose at me like I was a gangly teenager and not someone who was only ten or so years younger than her, then turned and walked away.

I wiped my sweaty palms on my jeans. "I don't think so. I'm dealing with a lot of bullshit at work." Which was true, even if it wasn't the real reason I couldn't be Andrew's extraneous wheel.

"Hey." His forehead furrowed in concern. "What's wrong?"

I leaned against the stainless-steel refrigerator. "The CEO's breathing down my neck about the numbers because the board's breathing down *her* neck. Apparently, we haven't released a new product since January, so ten months, and revenues have been dropping ever since." I waited. Andrew was a former banker and the smartest guy I knew with financial stuff. He had to have an answer for me.

"Makes sense."

"That's it? 'Makes sense'? Don't you have a strategy for me?"

"Yeah." He smirked. "Release a new fucking product. How close are you guys?"

"I don't know. Not close." The tasks piled up in my imagination like a stack of Jenga blocks.

Assay design.

Simulations.

Validation.

If one of those went wrong, the whole tower would topple, and we'd have to start over. We'd set a daunting challenge: a noninvasive biomarker test for ovarian cancer. It had never been done, but I knew with enough time and resources, our team could do it.

I'd watched someone I loved waste away with it, and the last thing I wanted was to rush a product to market that would give people false fear—or hope. It had to be accurate. Ninety percent would be good. But one hundred percent was my target.

Our CEO, Dr. Perrell, was far more interested in profit than accuracy. "I don't know if I can do this without him." Simon used to know how to talk to her.

Andrew palmed my shoulder. "Of course you can. He had faith in you."

"Did he?" I looked down at the toes of my sneakers. "He shielded me from so much I didn't even know about." Our competitors' schedules. Pressure from the board. And visits to my lab from Dr. Perrell.

"He did it so you could do the work. You need someone to run interference like he did."

Kraken tentacles squeezed my heart. No one could replace Simon. I wasn't sure I wanted someone to sit in his office and do all the things he loved to do and pretend to be him.

"An insufficiently validated test will do more harm than good. The board doesn't understand the risks they're asking me to take. We'd lose everything Simon and I worked so hard to build."

"Tell them that," my friend said. "Besides, you've still got enough voting power to control the company's destiny."

I forced a smile. I did, as long as I could sway a couple board members to my side. But was it the right thing to do?

Simon used to challenge me when I was moving too slowly. It was how we'd built the company from a tiny corner of our bioengineering lab in college to an entire building in Silicon Valley with thousands of square feet of dedicated laboratory space. I could never have done it on my own.

As much as I hated the idea of replacing Simon, I wasn't sure I could continue alone, either.

"Speaking of destiny," I said, "should we get back to the game?"

"Yeah, in a sec." Andrew hunted through the bottles on the kitchen island until he found the Jameson. He poured two fingers into a glass, then held up the bottle to me. I shook my head. To give myself something to hold onto, I grabbed another bottle of seltzer from the ice bucket on the counter. Then, taking a deep breath, I followed Andrew back into the dining room.

Tessa sat at the table. Her long, red hair stuck out of the bottom of a warrior's helmet as she perused the player's guide. My heart stopped when she turned her gaze up to mine.

"Let's play," she said.

~

Victory was mine. I fingered the stack of gold-colored plastic coins that represented my treasury and smiled. Through steady progress and strategy, I'd worked myself up from a lowly bard to a king.

"It's over, Tessa," Andrew said. He was the only other player left. The rest had been bankrupted or defeated in battle, so they'd slunk away to join other games. "Give up now, and we can try to win back our dignity at poker."

"You're only bitter because you flamed out three turns ago," she said, surveying the board. Her stack of coins was much smaller than mine, plus she'd taken a hit in health points thanks to Tyler's sneaky raid before she'd defeated him.

"How was I to know I'd draw the zombie attack card?" Andrew whined. "Zombies don't belong in a game with wizards and bards."

"Zombies belong in a game like this. They're a lot like Tolkien's Uruk-hai—" I began.

"Saruman created the Uruk-hai," Tessa said at the same

time. When she glared at me, her eyes narrowed to jade-colored slits. "The game is called *Forge of Destiny*. The zombies come from the sorcerer's forge," she finished.

Andrew's gaze darted between us. "Creepy."

I didn't think he meant the zombies.

"Come on, Tessa," he said. "Put us out of our misery. Roll so you can finish your turn and end the game."

"I'll take a chance on a card," she said.

"What?" I yelped. "Those cards have been nothing but bad luck for everyone. You don't need to go easy on me. I've got this game in the bag."

She tilted her head. "Do you?"

She pulled a card, scanned it, then showed it to us. It had an illustration of a warrior standing on a pile of skulls. "'A rout,'" she read. "'Warriors'—which I am—'with at least five pieces of gold'—which I have." She tossed all but one of her plastic coins onto the board. "'Can take the stronghold of an opponent and all treasure within.'"

I stared at Andrew, whose mouth gaped open just like mine.

"Thank you, Oliver," Tessa said. "I'll take that pile of coins off your hands."

My mind spun. "How did you... How could you..."

Tessa's long, freckled fingers stretched across the board and raked every hard-won coin from my side of the board to hers. Then she plucked my prize, a card that depicted a long blade with a jeweled hilt, from its spot in my keep. "With Worldforger, I hereby destroy the rest of your strongholds." She folded her arms, her eyes glittering like Worldforger's gems. "I win."

"How the fuck did you know that card was up next?" Andrew said.

"Simple probability." She shrugged. "Surely you took statistics in college?"

"But—" I snatched the next card off the deck. "How did you

know it wouldn't be 'Utter ruin: Give 90% of your treasury to the opponent to your right'?" I showed her the illustration of a king with a sword pressed to his throat.

"I didn't. But as Victor Hugo once said, 'Oser. Le progrès est à ce prix.'"

In her husky voice, French sounded like sex. I cleared my throat. I hated—*hated*—to ask, but I couldn't resist. "What's that mean?"

"'Daring is the price of progress.' Loser gets me a slice of chocolate cake."

"I'll get it." Andrew stood.

"No," I said, "I'm the loser. I'll get it." I heaved myself from my chair. My ass felt flattened from the hours we'd sat playing. So did my spirit. I'd been *this close* to showing Tessa I was a worthy opponent and getting her to think of me as more than Andrew's too-young, dorky friend. And then a chance pull of a card shot me right back down. She'd never think of me as anything more.

"No," she said. "Andrew will get it. You're likely to spit on it."

My friend howled with laughter. "One hundred percent."

"I'm leaving anyway," I grumbled. "See you next weekend."

"Okay," he said, "be safe."

I grunted and started tossing game pieces back in the box.

Tessa gathered the cards and slid them back into their carton. "It's a good game," she said. She lifted the helmet from her head and shook out her hair like a model in a shampoo ad. It glinted with a dozen shades of red, from rose gold to auburn. A few strands of silver glinted above her left temple.

I shook off the urge to touch the moonlight in her hair. "I don't know. I don't like the balance of strategy to chance."

"You don't?" she asked. "You started a business. Building a tabletop empire is a lot like that."

"Our business was successful because of a solid strategy. We left nothing to chance."

She lifted her chin. "I guess it doesn't feel as risky when you've got family money to fall back on."

And we were back to all the reasons I wasn't good enough for her. I'd never thought my family's money would be a liability, but Tessa Wright seemed to have strong opinions about men who'd started out halfway up the ladder, men who hadn't built their fortunes from nothing. So, as usual, I went on the offensive.

"What would you know about not having an emergency fund?" I asked. I could tell by her clothes and the car she drove that she had money too.

She took a deep breath like she'd let me have it but then she clamped her mouth shut. "Nothing, I guess."

"Thought so." I drew myself up. "Goodnight, Tessa." I shoved the lid on the box, tucked the game under my arm, and with a wave at Carly, sailed out her front door. I may have lost the game, but I'd won the more important battle against my ridiculous feelings.

2

PRINCESS DI FAKED IT

From Barry Wright's manifesto:
The one percent doesn't have to follow the same rules as the ninety-
nine percent. Like when Princess Diana got tired of living in the public
spotlight, she faked her death. She and that boyfriend of hers now live
in a fancy compound in Thailand.

TESSA

I shifted my gaze from the upturned faces of the audience to the slide on the giant screen behind me. It displayed only the highest-level statistics for the potential donors:

- One in seventy-five women will be diagnosed with ovarian cancer;
- Seventh most common cancer;
- Fifth highest cause of cancer death among women in the US.

I'd lovingly compiled rows and rows of data to back it up, but

I'd also learned that few people cared about the data. They wanted it distilled into the purest, most digestible drop of truth.

"With more accessible testing and earlier diagnosis and treatment," I said, "we could reduce the mortality rate by as much as thirty percent." A woman wearing an expensive pink tweed suit in the front row leaned forward, her red velvet cake forgotten on the banquet table. Maybe my message was sinking in. Maybe her mother had cancer, too.

Time to bring it home. I flashed up the final slide, a stock photo of a mother cuddling her daughter. It represented both the history I wished I could rewrite for myself and a hopeful future for the living ovarian cancer patients.

"I hope you'll join me in supporting this valuable research. Thank you." As they applauded, I scanned the crowd. The audience was mostly women, some of them already reaching into their Prada bags, I hoped for their checkbooks and not their keys. Most of the younger women had their phones out. If they were making an online donation, I'd done my job.

But I couldn't leave something this important to chance. I made eye contact with the pink tweed suit donor and stepped toward the stairs. I'd feel her out about adding a zero to her donation. Before I made it to the side of the stage, a white man in a gray suit caught my attention. He peeled himself off the back wall of the ballroom and sauntered toward me. My stomach clenched. I knew that lazy, overconfident walk.

Closing my eyes, I slowed my breaths. In. Out. *Stay focused. Don't lose control.*

I hurried down the metal stairs. The last thing I wanted was to be caught sweltering in the spotlight while Harry Boseman mocked me.

My friend Bridget who, as chair of the philanthropic organization, had been sitting at the closest table, near the woman in the pink suit, met me at the bottom. Her dark hair was pulled back into a bun with waves escaping artfully in the front to frame her pale jaw. "Great job, hon. I have someone who wants to meet you. Dr. Maya Perrell."

A petite woman with a gorgeous mane of salt-and-pepper hair stuck out her hand. "A compelling speech, Ms. Wright."

"Thanks, and please call me Tessa. You think it landed with the group?"

Bridget checked her phone. "Donations are at 40K and climbing." I nodded. I'd promised to match the final number with my own donation.

Dr. Maya Perrell said, "I was impressed by your knowledge of the subject. Do you work in biochemistry or biomedicine?"

"No, but my degree is in biology with a minor in computer science. I—"

"Tessa intended to go to medical school, but she was… distracted," a too-familiar voice said. "Weren't you, love?"

I took another measured breath. Harry's posh British accent was what drew me to him twenty years ago. I'd first heard his voice in a hotel ballroom not unlike this one. But twenty years ago, that ballroom had been full of tech bros, and I was one of them. Flush with cash, cocky, and positive I'd make a difference in the world with my business. His rich drawl was a novelty in that room, and when his beautiful blue eyes met mine, I stumbled.

I should've taken it as a sign.

Here, he cupped my elbow and pulled me in for a double-cheek kiss. "You remembered to focus on the message, not the data. You've come so far, darling." His smug smile turned sensual. "It's been a while."

"Not long enough," I muttered, tugging out of his grip.

I didn't think Dr. Perrell heard our exchange, but her gaze sharpened on me. "If you're not a Ph.D., I'm doubly impressed by your presentation. What do you do now?"

Harry drew himself up. "Surely you remember Tess founded—"

"Go away, Harry." Bridget pushed her way between us. "The grown-ups are talking."

I flashed her a grateful smile. Talking about my former business always threw me off my game. Regret had a way of doing that.

He looked like he might protest, but when Dr. Perrell ignored him, he said, "We should catch up sometime. I'll text you, Tess."

Too bad I blocked you years ago.

After he strolled away, hands in his trouser pockets, Dr. Perrell spoke. "You have such a passion for the subject. I'm impressed with how you conveyed the technical information in a way these people could understand." She swept a hand toward the audience.

Some, like Bridget, were businesspeople who lived in a world of research and development, profit and loss, debits and credits. Others were artists or stay-at-home spouses or heiresses. They'd all come together to fight cancer, and I'd brought my A game.

"Thank you," I said. "When Bridget invited me, I couldn't resist a chance to present my personal research to this group of philanthropists."

A calculating gleam lit Dr. Perrell's dark-brown eyes. "Tell me, Tessa, what do you do when you're not presenting to a group of two hundred people?"

Despite the pit that hollowed my stomach, I forced a breezy tone. "Mostly research, when I'm not supporting my favorite causes through volunteer work." I sounded exactly like the retirees and ex-trophy wives in the room. I didn't need to elaborate that I used research to battle my crushing boredom or that I could only volunteer on days when my pain was manageable or that for years my cats had been my only company. Like in my presentation, sharing too many details was dangerous.

Dr. Perrell stepped closer. "I'm the CEO and chairperson at Discovery Diagnostics. We've...we've hit a plateau with our research. We could use someone like you."

Why did that company's name sound familiar? But the usual words came automatically. "Oh, no, I—"

"Why not?" Bridget asked. "You've been looking for an opportunity for a while."

"Oh, have I?" I let a note of warning seep into my tone. She was right. I'd been looking for my next career move for over a dozen years, since the euphoria of selling my company for a billion dollars had soured over what happened next.

But nothing I'd tried held my interest. At least, that's what I told everyone. They didn't have to know that I'd developed a weird sense that warned me before someone was about to betray me. I raised my eyebrows at my soon-to-be *former* friend.

"Come on," she persisted. "You must have come across Discovery Diagnostics in your research. They're a leader in what you talked about today: biomarker testing for cancers and other conditions."

"Sign an NDA, and I can tell you exactly how close we are to developing a groundbreaking test for ovarian cancer," Dr. Perrell said.

I swayed back like she'd poked me. There was no way she could know about my mom, was there? I knew enough about cybersecurity to lock down my background online. Every time someone tried to create a wiki page about me, I had it nuked.

"Wh-why would you need me? I'm no biomedical engineer."

"We have biomedical engineers," Dr. Perrell said. "What we need is a person who knows business. Someone who can translate our scientists' discoveries into a language the market understands. A person who understands industry pressures and can encourage our team to deliver according to those demands."

"You mean you need someone to give your scientists a push," I said. I knew exactly what she was talking about. It was how I'd grown Red Rover from a group of college kids to a business valued at a billion dollars. My heart thumped. I could do this. And maybe save some other little girl the emotional pain I went through.

My mind spun with possibilities. Biomarkers could indicate a variety of conditions and determine the best course of treatment for them. With the right technology, I could save someone from physical pain too.

"Come to the office on Monday." Dr. Perrell extended a business card. "I'll give you a tour of the labs, and we'll talk."

I took it from her. "Okay." A tour and a talk wouldn't hurt. Plus, it would get me out of the house on another dull Monday.

"Thank you," the CEO said. "I've got twin daughters having destination weddings this year—separately. A little juice to the company's valuation could help me avoid a second mortgage." She chuckled nervously.

Bridget squeezed my arm. "This is going to be fabulous. I love a win-win."

Win-win sounded too much like what Harry had sold me. Except no one won but him. However, I'd give Dr. Maya Perrell a chance if she had the inside track on detecting the disease that took my mom from us.

3

———

BIOCOMPATIBILITY

Biocompatibility: *The ability of a material to interact with a living system without causing harm.*

OLIVER

I set the box of donuts on the counter in the breakroom and checked my watch. I always avoided I-280—too many people on their phones or speeding, or both—and although my alternate route took me past the best donut shop in Silicon Valley, today, I'd hit a snarl of traffic, and it was after nine. Which made it doubly weird that no one was waiting for a donut. Was I the first one here? If so, I was going to have to give the team a lecture on punctuality.

In my office, I set down my satchel and hung up my jacket. Then I strode past the breakroom, where the donuts still sat undisturbed. I scanned my ID badge and pushed through the lab door. My hand froze, mid-reach for my white coat, when I saw something completely out of place in the center of the room.

Tessa Wright.

She stood at the center of a circle of my white-coated lab employees seated on metal stools. Her long hair hung over one shoulder of her black silk blouse, halfway to the high waistband of her black slacks. She made a sweeping gesture with one freckled arm. The bluish LED overhead light made her skin look even paler than usual. Why the fuck was she in my lab?

It had been ten days since I'd seen her at game night. Not that I was counting. And she hadn't said a fucking thing to prepare me to meet her at my goddamn place of work.

I shrugged into my lab coat and stalked toward her. When she caught sight of me, she faltered, then she continued, "And I'm so looking forward to working with you all."

Sadie clapped, then the rest of the group joined in.

My employees were clapping for an unauthorized person in the lab.

"What is going on?" I asked. On the surface, the words were perfectly reasonable. But they came out in a roar that bounced off the hard surfaces in the lab.

"Hello, Oliver," Tessa said in a much quieter tone. "I'm sorry, I didn't make the connection that Discovery Diagnostics was your company until..."

"Until you saw my name on the door?" I'd managed to lower my voice, but it still came out sharp as a hypodermic needle.

"Exactly." Her shoulders lowered, and she smiled.

"What are you doing here?" All our trade secrets were inside the lab. Hence the flipping security scanner on the door. Suddenly, I noticed the white badge clipped to her belt loop. It had her name and photo on it.

What. The. *Fuck* was she doing with an actual ID badge? Was this a prank? I scanned the room for Andrew, but then I remembered not even my best friend had ever been allowed inside my lab.

She tossed her hair and planted her hands on her hips. "I work here now."

"In *my lab?*"

"At Discovery. I came into the lab because this is where the magic happens."

"It's not magic. It's science. And unless you're hiding a PhD under all that"—I waved my hand at her red hair—"then you don't belong in here."

She drew herself up. "That's not what Maya said."

"Maya? You mean Dr. Perrell?" We were supposed to meet on Friday, but I'd been in the middle of an assay, and besides, I could do without the pressure she always put on me. The reminder of her twins' expensive weddings and how much she needed the performance bonus. So I'd asked her admin to reschedule. Was Tessa the reason she'd scheduled the meeting?

"I'm your new chief operating officer," Tessa said.

"No, you're not." The words rushed from my mouth like they could make it true. Simon was the COO. And even though he'd been gone for two years, not just anyone, and certainly not Tessa Wright, could take his place.

She squared her jaw. "Maybe if you got to work on time, you could keep up with what's happening at your company."

My cheeks blazed. Although most of my employees had moved to their stations, I knew every one of them was listening. "I bring in donuts on Monday," I growled. Then, louder, I said, "Hey, everyone, donuts are in the breakroom."

There were a few cheers, then a stampede to the exit. Only Sadie lingered, a line between her blond eyebrows as she watched us, not bothering to pick up the tray of vials in front of her. "There's a gluten-free one in the small box, Sadie. Go grab it before someone else does."

She couldn't ignore a direct order, so she walked out. When

we were alone, I said, "Don't get comfortable. I'm going to have a talk with Dr. Perrell."

Tessa crossed her arms. "Can't wait."

"Until then, if you're going to be in the lab, you have to observe the safety protocols." I pointed at the sign on the wall and read out the words. "'All personnel *and visitors* must wear protective equipment at all times.' That means put on a lab coat. And also, 'Tie back long hair.' So do something with that." I waved at her hair again.

Deliberately, she tugged an elastic from her wrist and pulled her hair into a ponytail. "Happy?"

"Coat," I said.

"Don't worry. I'm not staying. I only came in to introduce myself. I have other departments to visit."

When she brushed past me, I caught a whiff of peppermint and something herbal that cut through my jumble of thoughts. I knew what I had to do: clear up this confusion with Dr. Perrell and get Tessa Wright out of my lab and off my campus.

She was a distraction I couldn't afford.

~

*D*r. Perrell was on the phone when I knocked on her office door, but she held up two fingers, then beckoned me in.

"I don't care what Piper said. It's two hundred people. I can't spend two-fifty per person on lobster."

I sank into the chair closest to her massive mahogany desk and checked my phone. I answered a text from Yujun about which micropipettes I wanted him to order, then a text popped in from Sadie.

SADIE

You okay?

No one in the lab could've missed my argument with Tessa, but Sadie would've figured out why Tessa's invasion hit me so hard. Like her brother, she was empathetic. Though I hoped she hadn't picked up on *all* the reasons Tessa's unexpected appearance had thrown me off.

I'm fine. Are you?

I never actually worked with him, so it doesn't feel strange to me that she's taking his place.

She was right. It was one hundred percent a me problem. I still didn't like it.

Dr. Perrell wrapped up her call exactly two minutes after she'd beckoned me in. She was like that: precise and predictable. Nothing like Simon, whose every decision had come from his gut and who'd walk straight out of a room if it had the wrong vibe. No, she was like me, a scientist through and through, focused on data and results. We should have gotten along great.

"I know you're surprised," she said. "I'd hoped to talk to you about it last week."

I crossed my arms. "You mean after you'd already hired her?"

"We've been trying to hire a COO for over a year, Oliver. You haven't liked any of the candidates."

Because they weren't Simon. "So you didn't bother to consult me?"

"I saw an opportunity, and I took it. Tessa is passionate about our research, and she has a background in entrepreneurship."

"Oh, does she?" I was being a dick. But a switch had flipped inside me when I'd passed Simon's old office next to Dr. Perrell's and seen the new sign with *her* name on it.

"She founded Red Rover. Do you know the company?"

"She did?" Everyone knew Red Rover. Their signature red insulated bags showed up in our breakroom at least once a week with pizzas or Chinese food. Once, when our regular shipment was delayed and we'd run out of stubs for our electron microscope, Red Rover had brought us a box just in time to continue our assay. And during the pandemic, they'd been the only place in town you could get the good toilet paper—at ten times the regular price. Someone must have sold their soul to get a steady supply and made a mint on it. Was it our new COO? Simon was brilliant at business, but he'd never have done anything predatory. Simon would—

"Tessa has exactly the experience and energy we're looking for," Dr. Perrell said. "We're lucky to get her. And we need her, especially now."

"Why especially now?"

"Oliver." She pulled off her black-rimmed glasses and set them on her desk. Pinching the bridge of her nose, she closed her eyes.

I straightened my glasses. Whenever Dr. Perrell did that, she was about to hit me with a truth bomb.

Her dark eyes flew open. "You are running late. We were supposed to have started the clinical trials for our ovarian cancer biomarker test by now."

"It's not ready," I snapped. Like I didn't know I was late. The board reminded me every quarterly meeting, and Dr. Perrell responded to each of my monthly status reports with another reminder. She didn't have to add to my burden of guilt by bringing up her daughters' upcoming weddings. "You know the risks of going to trial too soon. Of rushing a test to market."

"There's also a risk of never releasing a product," she said.

"I'm not saying we'll never release it," I argued. "We're doing everything we can to meet your timeline. We pulled everyone off their other projects to work on this."

"Which only means that everything is riding on your success. Look at this." She swiveled her monitor so it faced me.

She'd pulled up a press release, dated today. *Greenwich Biomedical Announces Ovarian Cancer Treatment.*

I scanned the article, then leaned back in the chair. "Good that they have a treatment." Maybe it'd work better than what they gave Grandma Vee.

"The market is hungry for tests like ours. It's only a matter of time before someone else makes it to market with one. And if they beat us, we become irrelevant."

"If we release a faulty test, we're worse than irrelevant," I growled. "We can't risk launching before we've thoroughly tested and achieved the certainty we're looking for."

"We're looking for strong results, of course, but certainty? That's unreasonable. And expensive. Plus, we don't have that kind of time. We have to launch by the end of next year, or you won't like the consequences."

That gave us a little over a year to work. It'd be tight, but if we worked very hard, we could hit our quality targets. "We'll get the work done," I promised.

"I feel more confident about it now that Tessa is here," she said.

I wished I agreed with her.

4

___

BIG PHARMA PROFITS FROM CANCER

From Barry Wright's manifesto:
Big pharmaceutical companies developed the cure for cancer years ago but never released it. Why? So they can profit from selling us poor saps their expensive "treatments."

TESSA

The naproxen finally kicked in, and I sank deeper into my cloud-soft sofa. Rain pattered against the window, blurring my view of the camellias, and my eyelids drifted shut. For once, my pain had conveniently waited for an obligation-free weekend when I didn't have to fight it at work. Thank the universal power it had been only a dull ache Friday at the lab. Though my anxiety over what it might become had led me to rashly promise Maya Perrell that I'd mentor Oliver.

What had I been thinking? When we'd met yesterday in the lab, I'd been relieved to find that they had already identified and validated some key biomarkers and developed an assay. (I'd crammed the night before to learn the terms so I'd be able to talk intelligently with him.) Then he'd walked me through his convoluted preclinical testing process. Despite all my arguing, I couldn't convince him to skip even one step. And we'd have to skip a lot of steps if we were going to meet our timeline.

Something punched my stomach. "Oof," I muttered, cracking open an eye.

A pair of yellow eyes stared back as my red tabby cat kneaded the heating pad over my torso.

"That's for me, you know, Hedy," I said. "You should be thankful the vet removed your reproductive organs. They're more trouble than they're worth."

Hedy rotated on the heating pad, turning her back to me. Her striped tail flicked against my nose.

"Fine. Be that way. I'm not sorry." A dull pain flared in my abdomen, but with the medicine and the heating pad, it was manageable. The cat helped a little too.

I closed my eyes again and matched my breaths to the rhythm of her purrs.

The buzz of my phone startled me awake. Hedy was no longer on my stomach, but Anita was wedged between my feet, her slate-gray fur soft against my ankles. From the stickiness of my eyelids and the bitter taste in my mouth, I must have slept for at least half an hour.

My phone buzzed again, and I shifted my hip to pull it from the pocket of my leggings. The display read, Discovery Diagnostics.

Who would call from the office on a Saturday?

I cleared my throat and took a deep breath. That was a mistake, it turned out. My stomach pulsed with a sharp stab. *Shallow breaths,* I reminded myself.

"Tessa Wright," I said as crisply as I could while lying flat on my back.

"It's Oliver. Sorry to bother you on a weekend."

I scooted upright, untucking my feet from under my cat and

ignoring the punch of pain. "Is something wrong with the assay?"

"No, nothing wrong. I was checking some things, and I had a thought..."

I'd been that founder. The one consumed by ideas for my business at all hours of the day and night. The one who worked seven days a week and called people on the weekends like they thought about work as much as I did.

Oliver hadn't yet learned that no one loved his business like he did. That others saw it as a machine that turned straw into gold. All they cared about was the gold. Either they'd run the machine until it failed, or they'd tinker with it to make it churn out the gold faster and faster until it wasn't even gold anymore but lead, and they didn't care.

But I cared. I saw the potential in Discovery Diagnostics. It could help so many people. People like my mother. People like me.

I tugged my knees to my chest.

"Actually," he said, "could we talk in person? You probably don't want to come here, but I could come to your place..."

"No." The word was out of my mouth before he'd finished asking the question. No one came over. Not even my friends, hardly even Bridget, who'd known me before Red Rover. Since everything went down years ago, only people I trusted were allowed inside my fortress. Right now, that list was limited to my housekeeper—paid handsomely, background-checked, and with a signed nondisclosure—Bridget, if she called first, and my cats. Maybe I'd invite my other friends over someday, but Oliver was not on the list.

Why would he ask to come over? He was too young to remember what had happened, but had someone told him? Did he want to observe the beast in her natural habitat? I wrapped an arm around my shins.

"Okay," he said. "We could meet somewhere. Coffee?"

The thought of putting on real pants and going out in public when the pain could crumple me at any moment sent a chill through me. I'd never let anyone see me like that—except Harry, and we all knew how *that* had turned out.

"I can't," I said. "What is it you need to talk about?"

There was a beat of silence on the line so long that I pulled the phone away from my ear to check we were still connected.

Finally, he said, "I think we need some boundaries in the office. Si—your predecessor—left the operations of the lab to me. Dr. Perrell wants us to work together, but we could benefit from some separation. How about you do your work in the executive suite so we can focus on the research?"

"So *you* can focus on the research," I said flatly. "You're saying I have nothing to add." That hurt, but I'd rather let Hedy use my arm as a scratching post than let him see it.

"No, I'm saying your skills would be better used clearing roadblocks and ensuring we have the resources we need to move quickly. That's what...that's what your predecessor did."

Pain sliced through my abdomen. The naproxen was wearing off, as was my patience. "My *predecessor* must not have done their job very well, or they'd still be here, and I wouldn't."

The line went silent, and I used the respite to dial up the heating pad. Sitting upright wasn't working out for me. I wished I could lie down, but he'd sense my weakness.

"You're here because Dr. Perrell wants you, not me," he growled at last. "I need you to leave me alone so I can do my work in the lab. Find something else to do and stay out of my way."

If I weren't so miserable, I'd have snorted. The kitten had bared his little teeth, pretending to be a lion. It was almost cute. And not fighting him might play in my favor.

I'd probably still be miserable on Monday, so I could give the appearance of ceding the field to him. Besides, I had an idea for a side project I could kick off while he was distracted.

"Okay," I said.

"Okay?"

"I'll stay out of your way next week. You can come to my office Friday and deliver a progress report. If you've made advancements in line with the schedule, I'll continue to let you run the project without interference. Sound fair?"

I could almost hear him choke on my offer to let him run his own lab. I was no baby-faced company founder anymore. But he was.

"Fine," he said, his voice gritty as sandpaper.

"Great. See you Friday." I disconnected the call. I reached over the side of the sofa for my laptop, groaning as the stretch strained my sore muscles. After a quick check of my security cameras, I flipped over to the company's email program and scheduled a video call for Monday with the lab manager, Yujun. If Oliver didn't want to work with me, fine. I had a pet project to spin up.

I'd show him who was *really* in charge.

5
___

BIOMARKER

Biomarker: *A measurable substance in an organism that indicates a
condition such as disease or infection.*

OLIVER

"So, Oliver, how is work?"

It was the question I'd been anticipating, and
dreading, since we'd sat down at my grandparents' Thanksgiving table. My grandmother, who'd asked it, turned her sharp
gaze on me. Three other heads—my grandfather's, my mother's,
and my father's—swiveled to face me.

Snow shushed against the window behind my parents. I
could still see the stand of maple trees that lined the front of my
grandparents' property, but the flakes were getting bigger. It gave
no signs of stopping anytime soon, which meant I was trapped
in Dover, Massachusetts, a town without as much as a bar,
tonight. And from the sharp gazes directed at me, I was going to
want something stronger than sauvignon blanc.

With the ornate sterling-silver fork, I pushed the dried-out stuffing to the edge of my Wedgwood dinner plate. Faded blue flowers peeked out from under the pool of cranberry sauce.

"It's going okay, I guess."

"'Okay?'" My father's eyes were blue and wary, like mine. "What's that supposed to mean?"

I set down my fork. "The new test we're working on is promising. But I'm getting pressure from the board to speed up development. Which, as you know, creates risk."

"Risk?" He grimaced. If anyone understood risk, it was my dad, a former executive at a top insurance corporation in Boston. Even in his retirement, he worried about everything from his house's pipes in winter to the Pats' quarterback's rotator cuff. "Is that something you can afford to take on in your business?"

"Exactly!" I leaned back in my chair. Finally, someone understood.

"Can you afford *not* to take a risk?" my grandfather said. Before retiring, he'd worked in banking. "No risk, no reward."

"It's not just money I work with, Grandfather. It's people's health. Their lives."

"*Just* money?" he and my father said at the same time.

"Without money," my grandfather said, "there'd be no funds to invest in your laboratory. How would you hire people to develop your products?"

"Without money," my father said, "how could medical insurers pay for tests and treatments?"

I put up my palms. "I understand money is important. It's why we brought in investors and a board of directors." I nodded at my grandfather, who, as one of our first investors, sat on the board. "Their responsibility is fiduciary. My responsibility is the science and the patients. People we can help with our tests." I glanced at my mother, who'd been uncharacteristically silent. "People like Grandma Vee."

She pursed her lips. "My mother couldn't have afforded your tests. She didn't have health insurance."

"But if this test is successful, it'll detect cancers like hers earlier, noninvasively. Cheaply, even," I argued, glancing at the two financial experts in the room. "It's a cost-effective way of detecting disease and determining the most efficacious treatment. Insurers will love it. And we're getting close." We'd already run the initial assays, and I had some ideas for improving it. If only Tessa would stop riding me about the schedule.

"Impressive," my father said.

"You were always a smart boy," my grandmother said.

"If you believe in your product," my grandfather said, "you must balance the risk of making it the best it can be against getting it to market quickly. What's the problem?"

My shoulders tensed. "That's my problem. Balancing quality with the schedule. Plus, the CEO brought in an outsider to fill *his* role."

A tightening around my mother's eyes was the only acknowledgment of Simon, who'd been my best friend since I was old enough to eat in the dining room instead of the kitchen with my nanny. He'd sat at this table almost as many times as I had.

"Tell us about this outsider," my father said.

"She founded Red Rover, but she's not there anymore. She's not a scientist, though she knows enough to be dangerous. She's been there a month, and she's already making changes. Last week, I walked in on her asking my lead scientist to show her how to use the microplate reader. But," I added grudgingly, "she's smart about business. She got us a twenty-percent discount on microplates. Yujun, my lab manager, already worships the ground she walks on."

So did Sadie.

I'd caught the two of them coming back from lunch together. Sadie was decent enough to look embarrassed about it while

Tessa tossed her gorgeous mane of hair and looked down her freckled nose at me. But I couldn't mention Sadie here. I hadn't even been able to say Simon's name, not when my emotions bubbled so close to the surface. My family would've recoiled in horror if I'd let so much as my lip tremble. Only Grandma Vee had welcomed emotions, and she'd been gone for more than fifteen years.

But if I could get the test right, we could save someone else's grandma or mother or sister so she could have another year at the Thanksgiving table. "I think," I said cautiously, "we could start clinical trials by the end of next year."

"That's wonderful, son," my mother said. "We were concerned when you opted out of finance to pursue science, but you've done the family proud."

"Hold on," I said. "It's too early to call it a success. We're not even out of development yet."

"It sounds like your new COO can get you across the finish line," my father said. "With her business acumen, she's an asset to the organization."

Maybe to the organization, but she was a distraction to me. Every time she said something brilliant, every time she hit me with that intelligent, no-bullshit, green-eyed stare, I forgot we were adversaries. I shook the image of her face from my brain. "It's her job to push me to meet the deadline the board has given me. But I'm afraid she'll do it by any means necessary."

My grandfather nodded, gazing at his phone. "Any means necessary may be right." Although my grandmother didn't allow them at the table, he was addicted to Google. "Tessa Wright is your new COO?" He waited for my nod. "Looks like she threw her employees under the bus when she sold Red Rover."

"What?" My muscles locked.

He scrolled on his phone. "Didn't you look up your new COO?"

"I've been a little busy."

"I thought I remembered something off about that sale," he said. "You'd have been a teenager, too young to pay attention to such things. Plus, you were more interested in your microscopes and textbooks than in finance or business. But her employees complained that she built the company on their backs, then abandoned them. They lost their health insurance and paid time off when Red Rover converted them from employees to independent contractors."

"Gig workers had benefits?" my father asked.

"Exactly." My grandfather's white eyebrows rose. "Not very savvy, but when she took the benefits away, there was an uproar. By then, Ms. Wright was long gone."

Saving twenty percent on some supplies was one thing. Taking away people's health insurance was another. Was that what she planned to do at Discovery Diagnostics?

Did Dr. Perrell know what Tessa had done? She couldn't. Otherwise, she wouldn't have hired her. Integrity was one of our core values. Though if my grandfather could easily find Tessa's history, how could Dr. Perrell have missed it?

"It sounds like a public relations nightmare. Can your business withstand a scandal like that?" my grandmother asked.

Could it? Simon would've never let anything like that happen. "I don't know."

"You need to stand up for yourself, son," my father said. "Rein her in, or she could take the whole enterprise down with her."

"You're right," I said. Simon was gone, and wishing wouldn't bring him back. I had to fight my own battle. "You're one hundred percent right."

6

THE THANKSGIVING
INDUSTRIAL COMPLEX

From Barry Wright's manifesto:
Did you know that a single agribusiness, run by a billionaire, provides most of this country's favorite Thanksgiving food items, from turkeys to table salt? What could a company do with that much power over the food supply? That's why I'll never eat a supermarket turkey again.

TESSA

*M*y electric SUV slid silently to a stop in front of a two-story home in suburban Sacramento. It wasn't the one that interested me. I glared at the nearly identical house next door, the one with two cars in the driveway and another three on the street in front, including a red Porsche convertible.

Yet my friend was inside, alone.

The four of us had met a little over a year ago after we'd walked out of a self-help seminar, and now, they were among my closest friends. I'd do almost anything for them. Which was why I was in Sacramento on Thanksgiving, which I usually spent with my cats, being thankful my father didn't believe in the holiday.

I took a moment to scroll up to today's first group text.

Goddess Gang

SAVANNAH

Can I vent for a sec? Jason invited *work colleagues* to Thanksgiving without telling me! The worst part is - they're here, and he's not.

CARLY

Oh no! Do you have enough food? Need me to Red Rover something?

LUCIE

Why are you even there? I should've invited you to Danny's mom's. There's like 50 people here. They wouldn't have noticed one more. It's a lot, but at least your soon-to-be-ex isn't here.

SAVANNAH

My sons are home. I thought we could have one last family Thanksgiving.

That had pierced even my cold heart. I knew about wanting things my family couldn't provide. I'd started to respond, but then Savannah's next text had come through.

SAVANNAH

Scratch that. The worst part is now Jason's here…and so is his girlfriend.

I'd almost flamed up at that. Before I knew it, my keys were in my hand.

> @Savannah, go someplace public and safe. I'll pick you up.

SAVANNAH

> No! Don't go to the trouble. I'm fine, just venting.

> Be there in two hours

There was more after that, mostly Savannah trying to take back what she'd said and our other two friends trying to convince Savannah to leave (Carly) or to tell off her husband (Lucie). But like I'd promised, I was on the road.

The situation was untenable. Savannah had been a stay-at-home mom for the past twenty-plus years and had no separate funds to speak of. She thought she had no choice but to remain in the home she shared with her husband and put up with whatever bullshit he served up until their divorce was final and she got her half of their property.

She was wrong.

When I parked in front of the house next door, I sent a final text.

> I'm here. Be ready.

I exited my car and stalked up the front walk. I knocked on the door but didn't wait for an answer before I tried the latch. It was unlocked, so I let myself in.

The sunny foyer was spotless and pine scented. It emptied into an open-plan living room, dining room, and kitchen. When they bought the place, my optimistic friend must have imagined cooking meals while her family chatted with her from the cushy upholstered stools at the peninsula that divided the kitchen from the living room. Or that her family would be drawn into the airy kitchen to help.

But that wasn't happening today.

Four men lounged in the living room, roaring at the football game. One propped his feet on the coffee table. Another wore a backward baseball cap and a mulish expression. A third clicked through his phone like he was wishing he were anywhere else. The one facing me jumped when he saw my expression and dropped his bowl of popcorn, spilling kernels across the carpet.

A woman perched on an armchair halfway between the guys in front of the television and the kitchen. She was younger, in her early 30s, with long brown hair curled into waves. She wore a silk dress the color of rust, heels, and a string of pearls like she'd somehow ended up at the wrong party. When she saw me, hope blazed on her face.

I shrugged. I wasn't here to save her. I strode into the kitchen. Savannah had her back to me as she aggressively buzzed an electric knife into the golden-brown turkey.

"Dinner's almost ready, Jason," she said. "Could you turn off—"

"Savannah," I interrupted her, loudly enough to be heard over the drone of the knife.

When she startled, the knife rumbled against a bone. She flipped it off and wiped her hands on a towel. "Tessa! You shouldn't have come. I'm fine." Then, lower, she mumbled, "I was only venting."

I tilted my head. "It sounded like a cry for help to me."

"I—"

"Who the hell're you?" a male voice slurred behind me.

It was Backward Baseball Cap. I asked, "Are you Jason?"

"This is my house, and I ask the questions," he said, louder.

"Jason." The girlfriend put a hand on his shoulder.

"Do you?" I said. "I've got some questions of my own. What gives you the right to think Savannah wants you and your friends here at all? This is her house too. Shouldn't she be consulted on the guest list? And finally, if she's graciously offered to cook, isn't it only polite that you help?"

"Help?" he snarled. "It's her job. I bought this house. I keep the lights on. I support her."

Anger flashed through me like lightning. "Maybe that was your arrangement while she was having her emotional needs met, if that was ever true, but now you're two people sharing space. She owes you nothing."

"Screw that. Tell'er, Savannah. You wanted to host Thanksgiving. And I can invite who I want to my house."

"I..." My friend's eyes looked ready to pop out of her face.

"Come on, Savannah. Pack a bag. Let's go." I waited, half hoping she'd fight me, fight him, do anything but cave again.

She ducked her head, refusing to meet either of our stares. "Okay." Leaving the half-carved turkey and the greasy knife on the counter, she washed her hands and walked up the stairs.

"Maybe you two would like to take over here?" Glaring at Jason and his plus-one, I gestured at the half-carved turkey, flesh still clinging to its ribs on one side.

The woman grimaced. "I'm gonna go."

"Baby, don't—" He swayed toward her.

Their drama was interesting, but my priority was my friend. I jogged up the stairs after her.

The front door slammed.

A few seconds later, I heard footsteps behind me on the hallway carpet. "Hey! What about dinner?"

I wheeled and Jason's momentum carried him almost into my chest. We were the same height, and I stared him in his bloodshot eyes. "You're a grown man. Are you incapable of feeding yourself?"

"No, but I...what about the kids?"

"Kids?" I glanced over my shoulder. Where *were* her kids?

"I'll say goodbye to the boys," she said from behind me, her voice low. "Abby's at her boyfriend's. I'll text her from the car."

That made me even more furious. Her kids had left her alone with her soon-to-be-ex and his girlfriend? What kind of children had she raised? If I had the kind of dad who'd make Thanksgiving dinner, I would've stood at his side. I'd have even listened to his screed about the Thanksgiving Industrial Complex.

I folded my arms and stared Jason in the eye. He took off his baseball cap, scratched the sweaty wisps of hair on top of his head, and jammed it back down. Behind me, a door opened, and electronic blaster fire boomed. It stopped as Savannah murmured something. She was answered by a couple of low voices. After a minute, I heard footsteps on the carpet.

"Excuse me." A pair of gangly young men brushed past me. Both appeared to be about college age. One was an inch or two taller, but the other was stockier. "Let's take a walk, Dad," the taller one said.

"What's she doing?" Jason peered around me.

"Leaving." The stocky one grasped his arm. "Now, let's give her some space."

"What if she takes something that's mine?" Their father's voice was petulant.

"Mom wouldn't do that."

"She stole my car once," he argued.

"California is a community property state. It's her car too." The taller one's face was kind like his mother's, but his jaw hardened.

"Come on," said the other one. "We can go for a ride. I'll drive."

Jason glared at me. I lifted my chin. After a long beat, he let his sons guide him back downstairs. I turned and went the direction I'd seen Savannah go.

There was a crash followed by a shattering sound. "Crap!"

I followed the sound of her voice and found her in a bathroom off a good-sized bedroom, her ankles and the tiles splattered with something peachy pink. She looked at me, an expression of devastation turning down her lips. "I dropped my foundation."

"It's fine. We'll get you a new one. In fact, leave everything except the things you can't live without. We'll replace the rest."

She bent to pick up a piece of the broken bottle. "I can't ask you to do that."

"You're not asking me to do anything." When I stepped toward her, a piece of glass crunched under my boot. "Leave it. We're going, and you don't need to worry about anything."

"But I..." She looked up at me, then nodded and stood, her knees creaking. "Okay. Just a sec." She stepped over the mess in the bathroom and walked across the hall to a room decorated with K-pop posters and a couple of movie posters that looked like romantic dramas. She scooped four paperbacks off the nightstand and dumped the contents of two drawers into a duffel bag. She plucked three framed photos—the kind-faced boy in a cap and gown, the stocky boy looking strangled in a redstriped tie, and a young woman with Savannah's blond hair leaning artfully against a brick wall—from the dresser. She laid them on top of her clothes and slung the bag over her shoulder. "Ready."

That went better than I'd hoped. "Great." I led the way downstairs, past the three men still entranced by the game on the big screen, to the front door. I was thankful Jason and his girlfriend were gone. But when I put my hand on the door latch, I realized Savannah wasn't behind me. She was in the kitchen, staring sorrowfully at the copper-bottomed pans hanging over the peninsula. "Give me two minutes, and I'll box these up."

"No time," I said. Who knew how long her sons could distract their father. "Besides, there's no space for them at my place. I've got a cabinet full of pots you can use."

She gave the rack a longing look. "But these are... Okay," she sighed.

Outside, I breathed easier in the fresh air that didn't smell like turkey and obligation. I'd never been gladder that, since Harry, I hadn't let anyone trap me into a relationship, much less a marriage that would end in shattered trust and abandoned saucepots.

7

———

RECOMBINANT DNA

Recombinant DNA: *The laboratory technique of joining DNA molecules from different sources to create a hybrid.*

OLIVER

The Monday after Thanksgiving, I was already waiting in Dr. Perrell's office when she arrived. The gym bag slung over her shoulder told me she'd done her morning workout in the fitness room in the basement.

"Oliver. Good morning." She slid open a deep drawer in the credenza behind her desk and dropped her bag inside. She pulled her laptop from her satchel, plugged it in, and powered it on. Finally, Dr. Perrell eased into her chair with a wince. "Leg day," she muttered. She took a long pull from her water bottle. She looked at me expectantly. "How can I help you?"

"Did you know Tessa Wright ended her employees' benefits when she sold Red Rover?"

The CEO waved a hand. "I'm not sure that was Tessa's decision. Besides, disgruntled employees will say anything. People don't like change."

Of course not. Change sucked. "I don't want her making changes like that here."

"Employee benefits are not her focus. Although West reports to her, they've agreed that he'll handle human resources while she concentrates on product development."

"Okay, then, I have an idea." I leaned forward. "I'll promote Sadie and Yujun. We don't need an outsider shaking things up. They'll keep us on track, we'll save whatever we're paying Tessa, and the lab will finish developing the test by the end of next year. This way, I can focus on what's important and not be..." *Distracted by the COO* sounded like the title of one of the dog-eared romance novels Grandma Vee used to keep on her bedside table. "Not be...not waste time educating a noob about the business," I finished smugly. I rarely was able to think on my feet, but that was the perfect excuse, worthy of Simon. I reclined in her guest chair.

Dr. Perrell leaned forward. "I'm not sure you understand the gravity of the situation, Oliver. Even if Yujun and Sadie were qualified to take on leadership roles, if you promote them, we'd have to hire someone to perform their current duties. Hiring and training people takes time."

She folded her hands on the desk. "Also, it appears you've misunderstood the timetable. You don't have until the end of next year to develop the product. We need to announce the successful test by then. Your development must be finished in time to start clinical trials no later than this spring if we have any hope of completing them this summer and starting the approval process. It's an aggressive schedule. If we fail, we'll have to seek a buyer." She rested her chin on the backs of her fingers. "At the last conference I attended, Greenwich Biomedical expressed interest."

My mind spun. Greenwich had recently announced their ovarian cancer treatment. With our early test, they could snag a significant piece of the vertical market. Of course they were interested. But Simon and I hadn't started our own company only to end up working for a soulless biomedical conglomerate. "I'm not interested in selling."

"Then we might have to dissolve the company."

"Dissolve?" My voice came out as a rusty squeak. Had I really managed to run Simon's company into the ground only two years after his death? Simon would never forgive me if I let that happen. He'd haunt me from the afterlife. He'd make sure in *Forge of Destiny,* my wizards always ran out of magic and my electric car would stop holding a charge and leave me stranded in the middle of the freeway. Worse, Sadie and the rest of his family would never forgive me. Hell, I'd never forgive myself.

"Obviously, selling would be a more attractive option. Most of our people could retain their jobs if we attract the right buyer."

"*Most* of our people?" Panic boiled in my chest, and I stood. "It's our fucking company! We built this place. Along with everyone who works here. Who are Greenwich to say who stays and who goes?"

More gently, she said, "That's the nature of a buyout. The buyer makes the decisions. And it's better than the alternative, where everyone loses their jobs and the company's value plummets to zero. My job is to protect the investors, including you and me, and if we can't get that test out in time, it's in our best interest to sell."

I gripped my hair and tugged to focus my thoughts. "Just so I understand, you're saying we have to go to clinical trials this spring. Or risk being acquired or going bankrupt." Tasks and checkpoints stacked up in my vision. I sent up a wish toward whatever plane Simon was currently on. "We can get the test to trial by June."

"March," Dr. Perrell said.

I thought at first she'd commanded me to leave. Then the meaning hit me like a fist. "March? As in March first?"

Smiling like a teacher whose student had passed a test, she said, "Exactly. And the best way to meet the deadline and avoid any unpleasant consequences is to work with Tessa. She's intelligent, experienced, and focused. But please don't mention the potential buyout to her."

"She doesn't know?" I asked. Wouldn't Dr. Perrell have given her the full picture when she hired her?

Dr. Perrell took another sip from her water bottle. "Tessa can be...sensitive. This needs to stay between us. If the employees were to find out, they might seek work elsewhere and then we'd never finish the test on time. I've only mentioned this to the board and to West, who was with me in the conversation with Greenwich."

Finally, I knew something *she* didn't. I felt a bitter smile twist my lips. "Understood."

But like any good clinician, I needed a second opinion.

~

When I left Dr. Perrell's office, I turned right and knocked on West's always-open door. His office was smaller than the CEO's and about the same size as mine. He'd decorated it in soothing shades of blue and beige that evoked a beach cottage. He even had a half-finished puzzle on a side table, which he welcomed employees to work on whenever they needed a break.

Sitting behind his desk, he looked up from his screen.

"Morning, Oliver. Good Thanksgiving?" He jumped up from his chair and strode across the room to pump my hand. Only a few years older than me, he was young to be a vice president of human resources. Simon hired him a few months before he died, and he had a similar energy, confident and exuberant, though without Simon's desperation.

"The usual. I went back home to Massachusetts."

"Brr." He shoved his hands into the pockets of his jeans. "Glad you were able to take a break. You work so hard."

I shrugged. "We're all working hard right now." I closed his door. "And Dr. Perrell told me if we don't succeed, we might have to sell or"—I swallowed—"close."

He grimaced. "She swore me to secrecy, but I hoped she'd tell you. Want to talk about it?" He gestured to a pair of powder blue upholstered chairs. The color was calming, and the chair was the perfect balance of firm and soft. The cushion was like an embrace, while the sturdy frame provided enough support that I didn't sink to the floor.

I tugged a tan pillow from the backrest and hugged it like a shield. "So...what happens if we sell?"

He settled into the other chair and set his hands on his knees. "It depends on the buyer. Assuming they're acquiring the company for our intellectual property, most of the key scientific personnel will keep their jobs. But some of the less experienced scientists might not be needed."

I thought of Sadie. She was flunking out of her master's program when we hired her eighteen months ago. Her brother's death had hit her hard, and I knew from experience college wasn't the ideal place to heal from grief. An undergraduate degree in biology and a semester of graduate-level classes didn't get you too far in today's job market, and I'd taken her in because she was family. I'd planned to encourage her to start taking classes toward her Ph.D. using our tuition reimbursement program because Simon would've wanted that for his sister. But if we sold the company, would there be a tuition reimbursement program, or even a job for Sadie?

He continued, "Those who are let go will receive a severance package in line with our HR policies. In operational departments like mine, there's often a fair amount of overlap, so cuts would, unfortunately, be significant. I'd probably lose my job." He chuckled, not nervously, but like he looked forward to the challenge of hunting for a new one.

I shivered.

Was I one of the people who'd lose their jobs? Would a buyer fire me? *Could* they fire me? I owned a significant amount of the company's shares. Simon would know what that meant. But he wasn't here.

"What about me?"

His mouth tightened. "I'm not sure I'm the best person to make a projection like that."

"Best guess," I said, "based on your observations and experience."

He cleared his throat. "Typically, the company founder stays on for a time to show goodwill. I've seen some cases where the founder is given a department or project to lead. It's possible you could keep your role as chief scientist, assuming the buyer doesn't already have someone in that role."

"But...?"

"But I've often observed that company founders leave the newly merged organization within six months. The founders sometimes don't care for the new company's management or for their diminished role and organizational power. Occasionally, new leadership wants to remove all traces of the prior company's culture."

"You're saying I'd be kicked out? In six months?"

"I'm saying it's possible. Though maybe you'd welcome a break? Less stress. Fewer reminders of what you've lost."

For a moment, I let myself imagine it. I wouldn't have to be a leader anymore. I could join Andrew and work on his educational YouTube channel full time. Or I could work in a place where no one remembered Simon and how much better he was at this than I was.

No. That was the coward's way out. I couldn't be responsible for the death of the company Simon built. I wouldn't.

"It won't come to that," I said with more confidence than I felt. "We'll get this test done on time. By March." The task list unfolded in my brain. And kept unfolding until it dropped onto West's blue-striped rug and flopped across the floor.

"Good." He rubbed his hands together, eyes gleaming. "We're counting on you, man. All the employees are."

"Then I'll get to work." I stood and walked out of his office, chin held high like I believed it.

But instead of turning right toward the lab, I turned left. Like I had all the self-assurance of Tessa Wright, I strode past Simon's office, the one with *her* name on the door now, and jogged down the stairs toward the game room.

We'd started the company long after the era of onsite laundry and nap pods. But Simon had a passion for vintage arcade games, and he'd installed part of his collection here. No one was playing *Space Invaders* this early, but on the other side of the console was a hutch that held a photo of Simon.

It wasn't the official headshot that was on the company website. It was a casual shot I'd taken with my phone the day we'd gotten the news that our second round of funding had come through. I'd told him to pose like a CEO of a multi-million-dollar company, but he couldn't stop laughing. The joy had shone in his half-closed eyes and on his glowing cheeks.

I plucked last week's wilted flowers out of the vase and tossed them into the trash. Then I scooped a token from the bucket next to his prized *Dragon's Lair* machine and set it in front of his photo.

"I promise, I won't let anything happen to your company," I said. "Whatever it takes, I'll do it, even if it kills me."

8

———

PROFIT FROM SICK PEOPLE

From Barry Wright's manifesto:
Vaccines are made of pathogens, which are basically diseases. Some of them will make you sick within days, and others lie waiting inside you for years. The pharmaceutical industry invented vaccines to make people sick so they can sell more drugs.

TESSA

When Oliver strolled into the lab at 9:30 a.m., I almost cracked a joke about his tardiness. He was so cautious that he might have turned his car around to get his umbrella and raincoat despite the morning sunshine. But I stopped when I clocked his expression. It was serious, like always, but the determined set of his jaw and the thoughtful, almost peaceful, softness in his eyes as he shrugged into his white coat halted my retort.

Carly had told me he went back East for Thanksgiving. He must have had a pleasant, relaxing weekend with his perfect family.

I hadn't had one of those since before my mother died,

though my long weekend was better than usual. For once, I had human company, even if Savannah spent most of it crying in my spare bedroom.

His peaceful determination didn't waver as he found me there. It was almost like he expected to see me in the space he'd made clear was his, not mine. Turning my back, I accepted the tablet Huong handed me and scanned the simulation results. I knew I was adding value here in the lab. Why did I care what snooty Oliver thought?

The scent of his aftershave gave me a second's warning before he spoke behind me. "Tessa, could I talk with you for a minute?"

I held in a sigh. I'd misinterpreted his expression. Clearly, he'd come back from the holiday weekend ready to pick another fight.

"These are great results. Thanks for walking me through it," I said to Huong. "Let's talk again tomorrow." I handed the tablet back to her. Squaring my shoulders, I nodded at Oliver and followed him to the only private space in the lab, a storage closet-slash-office in the corner. He held the door open, waited for me to enter, and shut us both inside.

There was a window at the far end, half-hidden by a stack of lab supply cartons. On the right side was a desk, but its surface held a dusty centrifuge. Even the chair held a box of pipettes. I tested one of the overloaded metal shelves by pressing a shoulder to it, and when it didn't give, I leaned against it and crossed my arms over my white coat.

He cleared some binders from a corner of the desk and perched a hip on it. He took off his glasses, wiped them with a cloth he pulled from his shirt pocket, and put them back on. He blinked. His eyes were the color of the blooms on the chicory that grew next to the railroad tracks where Dad and I used to camp.

"Look, Tessa, I'm sorry we got off on the wrong foot. I'm protective of this lab and this company. I only want it to succeed. Dr. Perrell tells me that you're the best person to help us get this test out the door." He swallowed. "I'd like to hit reset on all this. I'm glad you're here, and I want to work with you on accelerating the development of the test."

"Wait. What?" I glanced over my shoulder at the box on the shelf. "Does thermostable DNA ligase have psychoactive effects, or did I actually hear you say you want to work together?"

His mouth tightened at the corners. "I said that. Can we agree to cooperate?" He stuck out his hand like we'd shake on it.

I stared at it. "I have conditions."

He dropped his hand and rubbed it on his trousers. "Conditions?"

I stood straighter. "I promised Maya we'd get this test to clinical trials by early March. To make that date, we're going to have to take some risks. So, I need you to agree to do that."

He grimaced like he'd swallowed something bitter. But he nodded. "I will."

I knew from experience that saying something and following through were two different things. "Promise me. We're in this together. Equal partners."

He dipped his chin. "I promise."

"Okay, then. Over the weekend, I optimized your test simulation code so it runs forty percent faster. If we use it, we'll be able to slam through the computer simulations by the end of next week. Since people in this lab apparently only take instructions from you, I need you to tell them to use *only* the new simulation program. Okay?"

He winced like I'd asked him to cross I-280 during rush hour. "You tested the code?"

"Thoroughly. Huong checked it."

His chest expanded on a big breath, and he sighed. "Okay.

I'll do it. I'll also tell them your instructions are as valid as mine and they should follow them."

He'd said all the right words, but I wasn't sure I believed him. I'd test it the next chance I had. "Okay."

I didn't trust him. Despite those irresistibly sad chicory-flower eyes that held mine for a moment before he turned to open the door and those broad shoulders that looked strong enough to carry an entire company, I couldn't. After everything that went down with Harry, I knew better.

9

———

CENTRIFUGE

Centrifuge: *A machine used to separate the components of blood into layers based on density by spinning a sample at high speeds.*

OLIVER

A week after I'd agreed to work with Tessa, as I dropped solvent into a microtiter plate, I had an idea I didn't want to lose. I always had my best ideas while my hands were busy and my phone was in my pocket, inaccessible for a voice note. Once—okay, more than once—when I'd come up with a particularly complicated concept I wanted to capture word for word and Simon was in the lab, I'd asked him to grab my phone out of my back pocket to record a memo, but that was Simon, and he'd groped my ass in a work setting without a second thought. God, I missed him. Usually, one of the techs could stop for a second and write the idea for me on a sticky note.

I looked up from the surface of the biosafety cabinet and blinked to refocus through my prescription safety goggles. The next workstation over, where Sadie usually worked, was empty except for a Starbucks cup. Irritation washed through me.

Not only was eating and drinking in the cabinet forbidden, but it was disgusting. She wasn't working with volatile chemicals —she'd have used the fume hood for that—but our experiments worked on a cellular scale, and latte cells and cancer cells didn't mix. I set down the micropipette, peeled off my gloves, and scanned the lab.

"Where's Sadie?" I asked Yujun as he passed, tapping his tablet.

"They're having a meeting in Tessa's office," he said.

"Who's having a meeting in her office?" I glanced at the poster Tessa had hung, right under the posted lab rules. It tracked the days until March 1. Today, the number read 83, which might seem like a lot, though I knew it wasn't enough. Tessa must know it too. Was she laying people off? Was West in there?

"Some people. Aanya and Huong are in there. Need me to tell Sadie you need her?"

"No. I'll do it myself." I strode to the door, stabbed my coat onto its peg, and swapped out my goggles for my regular glasses. Ice prickled through my veins. I stomped down the hall to Tessa's office.

Ice? No, flames blazed through me. What right did Tessa have to take my people away from their duties? I'd followed through on my promise and told everyone to do as she said, but it was common decency to run her instructions past me first.

I didn't bother knocking on her office door. I simply opened it and charged in, ready for battle.

When it was Simon's office, there was a Centipede arcade machine in the corner and a miniature basketball hoop on the inside of the door. The walls had been painted in eye-watering colors, a bright persimmon on the back wall with saffron yellow on the sides. How many coats of primer had Tessa needed to turn them to their current warm gray? A fern had replaced the game cabinet, and a thick charcoal rug cushioned my feet.

She held up a hand to Sadie. "Yes, Oliver?" Her reddish eyebrows arched sky-high.

I glanced around the room. She'd gathered not only Sadie, Aanya, and Huong, but Ekaterina too. "What's going on here?" I snapped.

"We're brainstorming a new test."

The heat soared into my head, burning and noxious like an acetone-fueled fire. My brain might actually ignite right here in her office. "A new test? What the hell for?"

"For endometriosis," she said. "Did you know it affects more than six million people in the US alone? And that's only confirmed cases. Researchers think the numbers might be much higher. If we could create a biomarker test for it, we could—"

"I wasn't asking about the condition you want to test for. I mean, don't we have enough going on—"

"And are you also aware," she said as if I hadn't interrupted her, "that the condition affects at least one person in this very lab?"

"I, uh...no?" I thought back to the small amount of research I'd done on endometriosis. It was a condition in which cells similar to the lining of the uterus grew outside the uterus. The cells were invasive like cancer, but endometriosis only slightly increased the risk of developing epithelial ovarian cancer, so I hadn't researched it further. Abdominal pain, heavy menstrual bleeding, and fatigue were the key symptoms I recalled.

When I glanced at Sadie, she nodded almost imperceptibly. She took a couple of sick days each month and always returned to the lab pale and with low energy. I'd assumed she was depressed over her brother's death, but fuck, it was endometriosis.

I dipped my chin. As her boss, her health conditions weren't my business, but I was glad she'd trusted me enough to acknowledge it. Still…

"Don't you think we're busy enough trying to get our ovarian cancer test to trial on time?" I persisted. "I don't want to add to everyone's workload while we're already so busy. You should have lives outside of work too."

"Every one of these scientists and technicians has volunteered to work on the project in addition to her other duties," Tessa said. "It won't take away from the mission."

"You're sure?" I met each woman's gaze to check in. Every one of them nodded. "Okay, then. But please tell me or Tessa if you start to feel overwhelmed by the additional work, and we'll adjust your task load."

Sadie's smile was bright. "Thanks, Ollie. This test is going to help so many people. I'm honored to get to work on it."

My heart panged. Simon used to call me Ollie, and her smile was a twin to his, down to the crooked upper left incisor. It was almost like he was telling me to commit resources to this.

But it wasn't my dead partner who'd distracted my team. It was Tessa, a newcomer. And I didn't care that it was for a good cause.

"Could you all give us a moment?" I asked. "I need to talk to Tessa."

"That's enough brainstorming for today," she said. "Why don't you think on it, do some research, and we'll meet back in the lab at ten tomorrow?"

The others nodded and filed out, chattering about CA-125 and follistatin.

When Ekaterina shut the door, I turned back to Tessa. She was paler than usual, the freckles across her nose more conspicuous. Was she angry? Well, so was I. "Really? Like we don't have enough work, you've got to add a whole other *research project* to the mix?"

She pressed her hand to her stomach. In a much steadier voice than I'd used, she said, "I'm trying to use our resources effectively. All your checks and rechecks often leave team members idle."

"*My* checks and rechecks?" My voice rose into a register more common to a lab rat than a human. "This is *our* work. The risks of false negatives or false positives are too great for patients. And for our company." But she didn't care about that. Someone who cared about her company wouldn't have mistreated her employees the way she'd done.

"You can't avoid every risk," she said. "The risk of launching late is that someone who needs the test doesn't get diagnosed in time. She might suffer or even die because of it."

"But...but..." My brain spun its wheels, looking for purchase. Grandma Vee's cancer had gone undiagnosed too long, and she'd died for lack of an inexpensive test. Tessa was right.

She tilted her head. "Every member of that team volunteered to work on the project. They see the value of it. Perhaps because they're women, they understand how necessary a noninvasive test for endometriosis is. With a simple test, they'd qualify to receive treatment for a condition that's often ignored or stigmatized."

"Wait." My brain had stuck a couple of sentences ago. "Did you take every one of the female lab employees?"

"They volunteered. And, really, it's shameful that every female member of the lab fits in this office." She splayed her hand at the room, which was large as far as offices went, but it was still an office. "More gender diversity would benefit research across the board."

Goddammit. She was right—again. Like she could read the admission on my face, she shrugged. "We'll prioritize the work on the ovarian cancer test, of course. Regardless, I'm confident we can get both projects done on time. More products mean a better chance of this company's success. Now, if you wouldn't mind, I've got work to do. And I think you do too."

She'd dismissed me like I was irrelevant and not the founder of the company where she worked. I glared at her.

I wasn't irrelevant. I'd ensure we'd finish the cancer test on time like I'd promised.

But as I pivoted on my loafer and blazed out of her office, I wondered if my new resolution to finish on time hadn't been her intention all along.

10

FASHION ISN'T YOUR FRIEND

From Barry Wright's manifesto:
As an aside, the handbag industry has pressured women's clothing manufacturers to leave off pockets. I think the government might be in on it too. It takes a lot longer for a woman to grab a handgun out of a purse than out of a pocket.

TESSA

"Who the hell needs a pair of red leopard-print four-inch heels?" I plucked the offensive shoes from the pile I'd been sorting at Success in a Dress. It was Carly's favorite charity, and she'd somehow coerced us all into volunteering here one Saturday a month. And this week, I'd invited my friends Justine and Bridget to join us.

After the week I'd had, I needed extra support. Not only had Oliver been a dick about the endometriosis test, while my belly was on fire from the pain, no less, but I'd had a run-in with a former employee while I was grabbing dinner the other night. I'd gotten complacent and forgotten to use my usual pseudonym, Velma, for my takeout. The second I said my name to the bartender, the woman glared at me and called me a name that shocked even me and got herself kicked out of the restaurant.

I'd paid her tab because I'd deserved it.

I didn't deserve friends like these, but I was grateful for them.

Justine worked alongside Savannah, sorting through piles of donated professional clothing. Justine was an ace family lawyer, and I hoped they'd hit it off and she'd agree to represent Savannah in her divorce.

"Ooh, let me see those." Carly waggled her fingers at me. I picked them up by their stiletto heels and held them out to her. "They look like they've been worn only a couple of times—"

"Shocking," I muttered, already digging in the mound of shoes for a match to the more modest periwinkle suede sling-back in my hand.

"—so they've got plenty of wear left," she finished. "You sure you don't need these?" She dangled the shoes. "Now that you're working in an office..."

"A lab," I corrected her. "And there are rules. The first one being that closed-toe shoes are required."

Carly stuck out her lower lip. "Where's the fun in that?"

"I guess the fun part is that you don't drop a rack of test tubes and cut your feet," I said grudgingly.

"Ooh, do you get to wear a white coat?" Bridget asked. "I find those oddly sexy."

"Then you'd better stay out of the lab. We all have to wear them."

Carly wrinkled her nose. "Unless you get one custom-made, they're shapeless and baggy."

Was Oliver's coat tailored? Was that why I couldn't keep my eyes off the stretch of that ridiculous coat over his broad shoulders? I tightened my grip on the blue shoe in my hand. Blue like his eyes.

I dropped it on the table. I needed an industrial-strength cleanser to get Oliver Bond out of my brain. "What are you going to do with those shoes, Carly?" Nothing about the red leopard-prints reminded me of him. "Burn them?"

"Hell no! Bridget, do you have a red dress or suit over there?"

Bridget scanned the rack in front of her. "A skirt suit in size 14 and a sheath dress in size 2. Does anyone actually wear a 2?"

"The average American woman wears a size 16," Carly said, "but most models are size 0 or 2. Go figure." She held out her hand. "Give me that dress. It's less likely our clientele will want it, so I'll put it in our holiday display with the shoes. Lucie, do you have a chunky gold necklace?"

Lucie was at a desk sorting through trays of costume jewelry. "I've got ugly and butt-ugly." She held up one with thick gold chain links and another with a beetle pendant at the center. "I can't believe someone donated these. Scratch that. I can't believe someone bought them in the first place. Must've been shopping under the influence."

"Don't you remember?" Carly said. "Things like that were fashionable in the '90s. The chain one, please. It echoes the shape of the leopard spots, and I think beetles and leopards together might be too many animals."

"Ooh," Savannah said. I looked up from the shoes.

She'd been quieter than usual today. Actually, she'd been quiet for two weeks, ever since I'd dragged her out of her home on Thanksgiving. Lucie and Carly agreed that it had been the right thing to do, and we'd all been giving her space while she figured out her shit. The good thing was that she only burst into tears once or twice a day now. She might miss her copper pots, but she seemed to be finding solace in my kitchen.

"What is it?" Carly hurried over.

"This is my size. And it's so elegant." Savannah held up a black suit jacket.

"You have excellent taste," Carly said. "It's a classic Ann Taylor stretch wool that would pair perfectly with a pencil skirt or slacks. Try it on."

Savannah shrugged out of her zippered pink hoodie and slipped on the jacket.

Carly assessed her. "It's a little snug in the bust." She flipped open the side and scanned the inside. "But if we let out the seam allowance, it'll fit perfectly."

Savannah smoothed a hand down the front of the jacket. "I'm not one of your clients."

Fury and pity warred on Carly's face. I'd been teetering over the same line ever since she'd moved in with me, a mix of compassion for what her ex had put her through and a desire to prod her to get over the bastard and move on with her life.

"I think we could let you have it for a donation. Say, twenty dollars?" Carly flashed her a bright smile.

"That jacket will look great on you in court," Justine said. "Understated, professional. Perfect for sticking it to your ex."

Tiny sparkles erupted in my belly. I loved that my plan had come together. "I'll make the donation."

Savannah's expression dimmed for a second before it brightened. "It'll work for job interviews too."

"Job interviews?" I repeated. "What type of job interviews?" I hated to point it out, but my friend had no office skills to speak of. She'd somehow managed to brick her own phone last week while trying to download an update to her favorite game. I'd recovered it for her, only for her ex to turn off her line a couple days later. Now, she was on my plan. I hadn't shared a phone plan since, ugh—Harry.

"I could start out as a temp," she said, "and work my way up to an administrative assistant."

"Is that what you want?" I asked quietly. It was fine if she did, but Savannah was fifty-one. If she had career goals, she needed to start on them as soon as she could.

"I don't know what I want," she mumbled, shrugging out of the blazer.

Lucie stood, stretched, and meandered to the table in the center of the room, where Savannah had spread a feast of baked goods, hummus, and pita chips she'd magicked up in my kitchen. I'd been nervous about sharing my home after things went so off the rails with Harry, but living with Savannah was different, almost fun. Plus, I was eating better than I had since... since my mom died.

"God," Lucie said, "I can't stop eating these cranberry scones. They're amazing."

"Try some of the hummus," Savannah said. "It's good for lactation."

Lucie spoke through a mouthful of scone. "You did *not* make hummus for my milk production."

"I think about nutrition when I'm preparing food," Savannah said, her shoulders rising to her ears.

"Of course you do, honey." Carly rushed to hug her.

"I thought you were stress-baking," I said, "but you were designing a special menu for us. Hummus for Lucie and low-sugar fruit tarts for Carly."

Bridget brought me a cup of roasted nuts and seeds. "And Omega-3s for you."

I picked up a walnut, and as I crunched it between my teeth, the idea clicked into place. "Maybe Savannah should go back to school to become a nutritionist."

"School? At my age?" she scoffed. She walked to the table and brushed cookie crumbs into her palm, then tossed them in the trash. "No, thanks. I'd never be able to pay back the loans."

"We'll get your ex to pay for school," Justine said.

"Justine, I love how you think," Lucie said. "Savannah, you should totally do something with food. Remember that garbage seminar where we met? Maybe it wasn't garbage after all. Carly became a stylist to the stars. I finally finished my book. You even left that cheating asshole. We all launched into new, better phases of our lives." She shoved the last bite of scone into her mouth and chewed thoughtfully.

"What about Tessa?" Savannah said.

"What about me?" I spotted the mate to the blue suede pump and triumphantly set them together on the table. "Aha!"

"What about your second-act career?" Savannah asked.

"She's working at Discovery Diagnostics with Andrew's friend Oliver," Carly said.

"That's not a career change," Bridget said. "It's what you've been doing since you sold your business." I must have made a face at the reminder of the Red Rover fiasco, because she rushed to say, "You've been helping companies find direction."

"But..." The word was out of my mouth before I realized it. I never talked about my work. Emotions wrapped around my work like spiderwebs, too sticky to touch. My friends stared at me, and Savannah waited with her mouth open, so I kept going. "But this feels...different."

"Different how?" Lucie asked.

"The mission of the company is important. We're—they're helping the medical community diagnose and treat conditions. Conditions like...like mine." The words felt like broken glass as they made their way out of my chest.

"Endometriosis?" Lucie asked.

I'd never said the word to them. I was so used to keeping my secrets to myself. But my friends would never use them against me. Not like Harry had. "Yes. What Discovery is doing is amazing. They just need to do it faster."

"And you're helping them do that," Carly said. "Oliver says you're brilliant."

"Does he?" I arched an eyebrow. "He tells me I'm pushy and over prone to risk-taking."

"Hmm," Lucie said. "What else does Oliver say about Tessa, Carly?"

Grasping my hand, Carly dragged me closer to the food table. "You didn't hear it from me, but Andrew thinks Oliver has a crush on you. He has a thing for redheads." She shimmied her shoulders.

I shuddered. "No. No!" Oliver was, perhaps, the smartest man I'd ever met. And working in Silicon Valley, I'd met plenty of smart people. And, yes, he was hot in a Bruce Banner kind of way, especially when he slipped on his safety glasses and that dorky lab coat that should have hidden his toned physique. I shoved the image from my brain.

"Okay." Carly held up her palms. "So, it's not mutual."

"He's way too young for me," I said.

"You want to talk to *me* about an insurmountable age difference?" Carly smirked.

"Or me?" Lucie said. "There are definite advantages to being with a younger man. I have two words for you: refractory period."

Justine leaned forward on her elbows. "Tell me more. The gray-haired lawyers I date are too exhausted to get it up."

Carly fanned herself. "Oh. My. God."

"Stop," I said. "No one wants to hear about your amazing sex lives. Oliver and I *work* together." I was never going to fuck anyone I worked with again. Not ever. I'd learned from Harry how catastrophic that could be. "And, yes, I'm enjoying my work at Discovery Diagnostics. But I believe we were talking about *Savannah's* second-act career."

"Right," Lucie said.

We all looked at our friend. She clutched the black blazer to her chest, and it was all wrong. She belonged in her pastel track-suits in my kitchen, where I'd heard her humming country songs every morning since she'd moved in with me.

"What about cooking videos?" Carly said. She waved at the table of treats. "I haven't seen anyone make anything as beautiful as this spread."

"You don't cook," Lucie said. "Why would you watch cooking videos?"

Carly blushed. "I, um, I tried to make breakfast for Andrew once."

"The things we do for love," Lucie said. "I hope it didn't require the fire department."

"Regardless," Carly said, "Savannah, you should consider it."

"Oh, no, I couldn't." Her face was as pink as her track pants. "I'd look terrible on camera."

"Andrew could give you some tips," Carly said. "He's a pro with his nerdy YouTube channel. I could do your makeup and clothes. You should try it."

"You should," I said. "We can film it in my kitchen."

"Wait," Lucie said. "You're offering up the Fortress of Solitude?"

"Savannah lives with me now, so it's not so solitary anymore," I said.

"It's quite lovely," Savannah said. "Even if the cats do run the place."

"Then it's settled," Lucie said. "Next weekend, we're all going to Tessa's, and you'll have your on-camera debut. I promise if it sucks, we won't make you do any more."

"If it's okay with Tessa?" Savannah asked.

It was about time I let my friends see my place. They'd all invited me to theirs. Besides, I trusted them. They'd never expose me the way Harry had.

"Is it all right if Andrew comes too?" Carly asked.

"Yes." I forced out the word from my too-tight lungs. "But please don't mention it to Oliver. I need to keep my work and personal lives separate."

"Of course." She pursed her lips.

"I do," I insisted. Because bringing those two parts of my life together was like exposing phosphorous to oxygen. Explosive.

11

SENSITIVITY

Sensitivity: *A test's ability to correctly identify individuals with a disease.*

Specificity: *A test's ability to identify individuals without a disease.*

OLIVER

*A*nother Friday, another status report.

I leaned back in my office chair and stared out the window behind my computer monitor. It was a typical gray, freeze-your-ass-off December day in Silicon Valley. Light rain spritzed the window.

Still, if I couldn't be in my lab doing science, I'd rather be outside, cold and wet, than stuck here in my climate-controlled office writing reports. Simon and I had started the company with dreams of doing only what we loved—meteoric business growth and interviews on CNN for him; breakthrough discoveries for me—but that wasn't how it turned out. The growth had waned after Simon's death, and the science? Sure, we'd had some successes, but they'd slowed too.

I'd been tempted to make my report sound like we were

further along than we were—with 75 days left, according to Tessa's poster—but that wouldn't help anyone. Maybe it would keep Dr. Perrell off my ass temporarily, but when we fell further and further behind, everyone would find out. Better to signal now that we were lagging than to surprise everyone in March when we were supposed to deliver a test to clinical trials.

I clicked to send the email off to Tessa, who'd add her assessment and forward it to Dr. Perrell. She always copied me, which was decent of her, I had to confess. And although her notes were rarely flattering, they were fair. She always complimented the team for their hard work, and she'd learned enough of the science (I admitted grudgingly) to highlight key achievements that would set our product apart. Though when I'd pointed out last week she'd used *sensitivity* when she'd meant *specificity,* she'd gone off on me about my pedantry and my triple-validations until my skin felt raw.

I knew as the operations chief it was her job to ensure things at the lab proceeded smoothly and according to schedule. But what I did in research and development had an almost artistic element to it. Creativity didn't always follow a schedule. Simon understood that.

I picked up my phone to check the time. Almost five. I'd been hoping to start an assay this afternoon, but I'd spent too much time on my status report. I could ask Sadie to kick it off, then I could verify she'd done it correctly when I returned from my run.

Standing, I stretched my arms toward the ceiling, then I grabbed my gym bag from under my desk. Running in the icy rain would clear my head.

Inside the lab, I dropped my bag on the floor under the hooks, shrugged into my white coat, and glanced around the space. After five, it was around half full, so Sadie should've been easy to spot. But she wasn't at the bench she normally used or at the workstation where she ran simulations. I remembered seeing her earlier today. Where was she?

I strode through the lab, poking my head around corners, accidentally startling some people as they worked. Finally, I found her at the far end of the lab where we kept the spectrophotometer and where old cell counters went to die. Sadie leaned her hip against the bench, talking to Tessa.

My stomach clenched. What right did Tessa have to steal one of my employees' time, especially this close to the end of the day? I stepped closer, but they must not have heard me because they continued their conversation.

"Don't you want to advance in your career?" Tessa crossed an arm over her stomach and propped her other elbow on it, resting her chin on her freckled knuckles.

"Yes…" Sadie drew out the word. She twirled the end of her ponytail around her finger.

"You sound unsure." Tessa tilted her head.

"I owe so much to Ollie. Oliver, I mean. He gave me this opportunity when I was lost. I don't want to leave him. It would seem ungrateful."

Was Tessa poaching my employees? What the fuck? I held my breath so I could catch her response.

"I'm not saying you should leave. I'm saying you should take advantage of the company's tuition reimbursement program so you can go back to school. And consider cutting back your work hours while you take classes toward your doctorate."

"My doctorate?" Sadie repeated.

Shit. I'd wanted to encourage Sadie to go back to school. But with everything going on, I'd forgotten. My face heated. Unless I'd secretly hoped to keep her working full time while we got this test to market. I sent up a silent apology to Simon. I'd apologize to Sadie out loud later.

"You can't want to be a lab tech forever," Tessa said. "You

have such creative ideas. You'll be able to champion them your-self as a full scientist. Cutting back your hours would allow you to get your doctorate in seven or eight years instead of a dozen. It's a big difference to finish in your early thirties versus your late thirties."

"I hadn't thought of it like that," Sadie said.

Neither had I. I hadn't considered how long it might take her to finish while she worked full time. What if she had other goals, like a relationship or starting a family? Between a full-time job and school, she'd have no time for anything else.

"I know," Tessa said. "That's why I wanted to talk to you. To give you some perspective. And with your health condition, you've got to manage your energy. Taking on too much will exhaust you."

Fuck. I was a selfish asshole.

"You're right." Sadie looked at her sneakers. "How will I tell Ollie I want to cut back my hours when the semester starts?"

"Leave it to me," Tessa said. "I'll deal with him."

I cleared my throat, startling both women. Sadie's eyes widened, and her lips parted in horror. Tessa tipped up her chin. From our previous skirmishes, I knew that meant she was preparing for battle.

"No one has to deal with me," I said. "It makes sense to devote more time to your studies, Sadie. We can collaborate on a work schedule that will support your goals. Plus, I've got some contacts at Stanford. They might admit you as soon as January if we start right away."

The tension in Sadie's shoulders eased. "Thanks, Ollie. I won't let you down."

"I know you won't. And I won't let you down either." I'd promised Simon's memory I wouldn't. "But..."

"But?" Sadie asked. Tessa seemed to grow taller as she stepped toward me.

"But we're going to need all you can give the lab until then. We've got targets to meet."

Sadie grinned. "Got it, Ollie."

I shot a glance at Tessa. She tilted her head, those green eyes narrowed at me. She'd put on a lab coat, but her unbound hair cascaded in a red wave over her shoulder.

Glaring pointedly at it, I added, "Rule Three."

"My god, Dr. Bond," she said, winding her hair up into a ponytail. "Do you think this whatchamacallit"—she dipped her chin at the spectrophotometer—"is going to reach out and pull it?"

I had to shut my eyes for a moment. Why was her calling me by my title so hot? Especially while she touched her hair and talked about pulling it? Something molten bubbled in my belly. I gritted my teeth. Lab coats hid a lot, but I would *not* get an erection in my lab. "Safety first," I said, my voice sounding like gravel.

Sadie glanced between us. "Anything I can do right now, boss?"

I cleared my throat. "Can you start an assay for me before you go? The instructions are in my folder on the network drive."

"Sure. I'll get right on it."

"No need to stay after," I said. "I'll be back in time to check it."

She practically skipped off. I glanced up at the fluorescent lights. *I've done one thing right, Simon.*

But it wasn't all my doing. Tessa was the one who'd given us both a push. Who'd noticed what Sadie needed instead of what she wanted to see. Who'd set her on the path toward her professional goals. I met Tessa's gaze. "Thanks. That was kind of you." I almost choked on the word *kind.* It seemed so at odds with what she'd done to people at Red Rover. I'd set up a web alert on her name, and at least once a week, a disgruntled employee said something terrible about her. That was a lot of hate for something that had happened over a dozen years ago. It must have been truly traumatic.

The corner of her mouth lifted. "Don't tell anyone, okay? I've got a reputation to uphold." She pivoted on the heel of her black boot and strode away, red ponytail swinging.

It should've been illegal for anyone to look that good in a lab coat.

12

BIG SUGAR CONTROLS THE WORLD

From Barry Wright's manifesto:
In the 1960s, agents of the sugar industry paid scientists to publish a study that blamed saturated fat as the cause of heart disease, even though there was also a link between sugar and bad health. More and more sugar has been creeping into our diets, when we'd all be stronger if we ate some good old-fashioned meat and potatoes.

TESSA

"*T*hat was an adventure." Lucie kissed my cheek and handed me her coat.

"I like my privacy," I grumbled. "I'm starting to regret inviting you over."

"Navigating your security system wasn't that bad." Carly wiped her shoes on the mat and stepped over the threshold. I'd locked my girls in an upstairs bedroom, but thankfully, she hadn't brought her dog. My cats had never met a dog, but I suspected they wouldn't be fans of her excitable little fluffball. "How's she doing?"

"Honestly?" I grimaced. "Not great. She got a call from Jason this morning, then she deep-cleaned the kitchen. She was singing Jo Dee Messina on repeat the whole time." Before this morning, I couldn't have identified the country artist in a lineup, but I'd looked her up after the fifth warbling repetition of "A Lesson in Leavin'."

"Who?" Andrew stepped into the doorway, loaded down with a pair of duffel bags.

"Don't worry about it, honey." Carly brushed his arm. "We're talking about music from before your time. Why don't you go set up in the kitchen."

"Hey, Tessa. Cool security system." He nodded at me and carried the bags into the kitchen, where Savannah cooed at him.

"I thought this was going to be a trial run, not a Hollywood production." I held out my hand for Carly's coat, a buttery-soft buff cashmere.

"You know Andrew. He's...thorough." Her cheeks went pink.

"Ew. It's way too early for sexual innuendos." I stuck my face in the hall closet while I hung up the coats.

"Girl," Lucie said, "you're clearly not getting the right kind of sex if you think it's *ever* too early. Am I right?"

When I turned, Lucie nudged Carly with her elbow. I groaned. "Spare me the sexually satisfied commentary. I hope you both get cock-blocked at family Christmas gatherings."

"Ooh." Lucie's eyes flared. "Someone's jealous. How long's it been, Tessa?"

"Not that long," I lied. Even my favorite suction vibrator had failed me last night when a shaggy head of hair had popped into my brain. It had killed my libido since I obviously did *not* want my clit sucked by my frustrating coworker.

She twitched her lips to the side, then strode into the kitchen.

"Don't mind her," Carly said. "She's not getting enough sleep these days. Danny's helping with everything he can, but she's nursing, so the middle-of-the-night feedings are on her."

"Sounds like a nightmare," I said.

"But worth it," my childless friend said. "For her."

"I guess." I peered out the sidelight next to the door. "You didn't see Bridget out there, did you?"

"No." Carly frowned. "You think she got stuck in your security protocols?"

"She knows how to get in." She was one of the few who did since she'd ignored my pleas to be left alone after the Red Rover disaster.

"Then I'm sure she'll be here soon." Carly hitched up her enormous bag. "I'd better get started on Savannah's makeup."

Forty-five minutes later, Bridget hadn't arrived, and Savannah was unrecognizable.

"Is my hair supposed to be this crunchy?" Savannah asked. "I haven't worn this much Aqua Net since the '80s."

"You look fantastic." Carly held up a hand mirror. "I wanted to keep it consistent throughout the shoot. Don't you like it?"

"It's beautiful." Her blue eyes looked huge, shaded by mile-long false eyelashes, and her skin sparkled like one of those teenage vampires in the movies. She touched the side of her bob, then flapped her hand away like it had burned her. She puckered her lips like a fish.

"You like the lipstick?" Carly asked. "It's a new long-staying formula with a bit of gloss. The camera's going to love it."

Savannah's smile looked like her face was about to crack. "It looks great. It's just a little sticky."

"Can't she wash all that off?" I asked. "She should look like herself when she's cooking."

"She's working under lights," Carly argued. "The makeup will hide any flushing and sweating. But if you don't like it..."

"No, no, I love it," Savannah said. She shot me a glance that I understood to mean, *Stop causing trouble.*

I couldn't deny Savannah the peace she struggled to maintain in our friend group, so I stayed silent. Fortunately, a buzz in my pocket distracted me. It was the doorbell, and Bridget's face appeared on the screen. I tapped the button to open the gate.

"Ready, Savannah?" Andrew asked from behind the camera tripod.

"I guess. What do I do?"

"Be yourself," he said. "Start cooking and tell me what you're doing as you go. What are you making first?"

"Um. Okay. I'm going to start with an appetizer. Um, baked cheese crackers."

I slipped out of the kitchen and went to the door. I opened it as Bridget slammed the door of her Jaguar and stomped across the motor court in a pair of towering heels that raised her to average height.

I shut the door behind me. "What's wrong?"

"Fucking Cole fucking Campion is what's wrong." She stuck her fists on her navy sheath dress where it flared at her hips.

"Who?"

"Remember, I told you our CFO retired? Cole replaced him."

I winced. "I hoped they'd give you the finance department."

Her lips tightened. "Me too. But they made an outside hire. Young guy, in his thirties. When I took him to lunch, he seemed nice enough—at first. And smart enough that I thought he'd keep quiet for a while. Watch and learn."

"No?"

"He ripped my proposed budget to shreds. In front of the CEO."

"What a dick."

"Right? But"—she shimmied her head and shoulders—"I shook it off. My team and I will take another run at the budget.

We'll present one that's perfect next time. And I'll be prepared to defend it."

"You're a rock star." How many times had she told me the same thing? "Remember that. Eyes on the prize."

"I know. I'll be the company's first female CEO." Her delicate jaw hardened.

She'd busted her ass in college. She'd wanted to be a CEO even then. If anyone deserved it, Bridget did. I held her gaze. "You will."

Her eyes went glossy, and she blinked. "Dammit. I'm a hard-ass executive. Don't make me cry."

"Ew. Wouldn't dream of it."

She chuckled, then sniffed. "Something smells...not great."

I sniffed. It smelled like the time I'd lit a candle Carly had given me, and Anita wouldn't stop trying to smother the flame with her paw. "Burned hair?"

I led the way to the kitchen, where Carly was patting down the side of Savannah's head with a kitchen towel. Her blond hair frizzed up along one side.

"I'm so sorry," Carly said. "I never cook—"

"It's true," Andrew interjected as he loosened the camera from the tripod.

She glared at him. "I didn't realize how flammable the hairspray was. Are you okay?"

"I'm sure it's fine," Savannah said.

"Yeah, no," Lucie said through a bite of the apple she'd taken from the fruit bowl. "It's definitely not fine."

"Not helpful," Carly growled. "I'll run home for my hair cutting kit, and we'll trim it."

"Trim?" Savannah ran her hand along her hair and winced when her fingers met the crispy part.

"It'll look great. I promise. And if not, I know the best wig shop."

Savannah's mouth dropped open. "Wig?"

"Don't worry, it won't come to that," Carly said.

"This is why we have rules about pulling hair back in the lab." My friends' heads all turned toward me, and I froze when I realized the words had come out of my mouth. "I, um—sorry."

"I thought you hated those ridiculous rules," Bridget said.

"I...I..." But I couldn't say, *I do.* "They make sense, considering what's happened here."

Andrew smirked. "I'm totally telling Oliver."

"You do and you'll never play my collector's edition of *War of the Ring* again." I folded my arms.

He set down the tripod he'd been folding up. "You wouldn't."

"I'm dead serious," I said.

"This isn't about the silly lab rules," Lucie said. "I think you like this guy. Is something going on?"

"Absolutely not." I glared first at her, then at Andrew. "We're coworkers. We don't even like each other."

Andrew snorted but said nothing.

"Said every heroine in any Hallmark movie ever." Lucie always had something to say.

"This is real life," I said. "I've been there, done that, got tricked into selling my company by someone I cared about. Never. Again."

Lucie looked like she wanted to poke at my past again, but Savannah, always the peacemaker, said, "We believe you, hon."

Thankful for the reminder that today wasn't about me, I said, "Andrew, why don't you go get Carly's kit, and Carly can show Savannah some pixie cuts."

Savannah wailed, and everyone seemed to forget what Lucie had said about Oliver and me.

Everyone except me.

∽

The next day, Sunday, Savannah's sigh made me look up from my laptop. In my living room, she sat across the coffee table from me in one of the club chairs and tugged at her hair for the fiftieth time like that would make it grow out.

Carly had to trim a lot to remove the parts that had ignited when Savannah slid her tray of crackers into the oven. And then a lot more to shape it. It wasn't quite a pixie cut, but it was clearly the shortest hairstyle Savannah'd ever had.

"Stop," I said. "Your hair looks great."

"No, it doesn't. Carly did the best she could, but it looks weird with my body." She gestured down at herself, encompassing Kat, who was curled up on her lap.

"You're beautiful. I hate that you don't see it."

She pursed her lips. "Jason never thought so. Not after I had Colby and the weight never came off."

Something sharp caught in my chest, and I wanted to commit murder. "You're beautiful, and Jason's a tool."

"Thank you." Her lips wobbled. "You're the best. All of you are."

"Have you thought about what Bridget said yesterday?"

"You mean when she said video wasn't my calling? Yeah, I think that's obvious."

"The part about corporate catering."

She scratched behind Kat's ear, and I could hear the cat's purr from ten feet away. "I do like cooking for crowds. But I wouldn't know how to start."

"Start with something like a selection of muffins and breakfast pastries. You're great at baking. Then move up to lunch. Keep it simple. Salads and sandwiches are mostly what we eat at work anyway. Bridget said she'd hire you. And I will too. You can do all of it in my kitchen, and when you're ready to expand, I'll loan you whatever you need to get set up."

Tears pooled in her blue eyes. "You really think I can do it?"

"You can, and you're not alone. Bridget and I have contacts. Plus, we can help you draw up a budget. Andrew has a sister who can help you with marketing and social media. That's enough to start."

Her lips quivered when she smiled. "Y'all are the best."

"So are you. Are there any of those lemon cookies left over from yesterday?"

"I think so. I'll make some tea too."

"Where'd you find tea in my kitchen?"

"I went to the grocery store, silly. I shopped for a week's worth of healthy meals. All you had were those depressing freezer meals."

I liked how she always found her confidence when talking about food. I pressed further. "Depressing? I paid a lot of money to a specialist to tailor them to my body's nutritional needs. I like those freezer meals."

She scrunched her nose. "No. You like the convenience, but they taste like chemicals and sadness."

"Chemicals, maybe. But not sadness. Independence." I sat up on the couch.

"Whatever. With a little thought and preparation, I can make delicious food from fresh ingredients that can be served almost as quickly as those plastic-tray atrocities."

"You sound like an infomercial. Save it for marketing your catering business."

"You'll see that I can back up my claims better than Billy Mays. I'm making a delicious pot of chicken noodle soup for lunch." She smiled, smug. "I'll freeze some for the next time you're feeling bad, and it'll be as convenient as your freezer meals but better because it's made with love."

"That should be the name of your business."

She scrunched her nose. "Chicken Noodle Soup?"

"Made with Love."

"You're right! You know, I bet Colby could design a logo for me. I'll get it printed on an apron." She grinned. "I'll text him while I make tea." Carefully, she lifted Kat from her lap, then set her back on the chair. Her light-pink leggings were coated with black cat hair. "Be right back." When she walked back to the kitchen, Kat leaped off the chair and trotted behind her.

"Don't listen to Kat's lies," I called after her. "She can't have human cookies. Her treats are in the—"

"The canister on the counter. I know." She winked at me. "Why do you think she's following me?"

"Okay. I want two of those lemon cookies, please." Normally, I didn't care about desserts. We never had them around the house—the sugar conspiracy was one of Dad's favorites—and I'd never developed a taste for them. But Savannah's baked goods weren't saccharine like grocery-store cookies. They were light and crunchy with a hint of sweetness and tasted like the food angels would serve in heaven.

My laptop chimed, and I glanced at the screen. A security alert. My friends knew not to drop by unexpectedly. When people ignored the No Soliciting sign, my automated security system usually handled it. This one must be persistent if they'd triggered an alert. Tingles swept through me as I checked the camera.

My heart rocketed into my throat. "My god!" I jerked my hands off the keyboard like not touching the laptop could make it not true. Like I could hide from him.

"What's wrong?" Savannah walked in with a plate of cookies.

"Nothing," I lied. Revealing the secrets of my home to my friend was one thing. Exposing her to my past was something I wasn't ready to do. Maybe, if I ignored him long enough—

"Tessa!" came his tinny voice from my laptop's speaker. "Let me in."

Shit. I glanced back at the screen. His red hair had more white in it since last year. Its pink tint matched his ruddy, weathered skin.

"Who's that?" she asked.

"Goddamned election canvassers."

She propped her hands on her hips. "The election's been over for six weeks."

"Christmas carolers?"

"He knows your name. No one should be able to get past your security. I can barely figure out how to get back in after a grocery run."

I closed my eyes and sighed. Couldn't he have called first?

Of course not. He used only burner phones, and I never answered unknown callers.

"Gerty Theresa Wright," the tinny voice erupted from my laptop. "Let me in or I'll camp right here in your driveway."

My god. His truck. How had I forgotten? Wincing, I pressed the key that opened the hidden gate.

"Your actual name is Gerty?" my friend asked. "How did I not know this?"

"There's a lot you don't know about me," I admitted. "My parents named me after a Nobel Prize–winning biochemist." I closed my laptop and set it on the table, then wedged myself out from between Anita and Hedy. "Better hide, girls," I murmured. Anita raced up the stairs. Hedy, ever stubborn, tucked herself into a loaf shape.

"What should I do?" Savannah asked. "Call the police?"

"No. It's fine. Well, it's not fine. But I'll deal with it. I recommend you hide like Anita's doing. Otherwise, you can meet…" I trudged to the back door, the one that opened to the parking area, unbolted it, and flung it wide. "My father."

He leaned on the side of his ancient Ford F-150 with the tonneau cover. The truck was painted in a camouflage pattern, not the fancy design you got at one of those custom paint shops, but the sloppy kind you did yourself with slashes in a few shades of Rust-Oleum, bought with cash (obviously) at the local hardware store, the one without security cameras.

"You know they're monitoring your security system." His voice was as rusty as his truck, like he hadn't used it for a while.

"They're really not," I said. "Hi, Dad. To what do I owe the pleasure?"

"I always visit you on the solstice," he grumbled.

He didn't always. He hadn't for the past couple years. Still, something warmed in my chest at the thought of him driving all the way from his remote camp, wherever it was, to see me.

"Where are you staying these days?" I asked.

He ducked his head. "Does it matter? I'm not going back."

I didn't dare ask where he'd go next.

"Hi," Savannah chirped, stepping around me to extend her hand. "I'm Tessa's friend Savannah."

He blinked.

I let out a long exhale. "Savannah, this is my dad, Barry Wright."

She pumped his hand. "Lovely to meet you, Mr. Wright. Tessa's told me nothing about you."

"Good," he said, extricating his hand from her grip. "Probably better to forget you ever met me."

Closing my eyes to block out Savannah's wide eyes and open mouth, I breathed in for a count of four, then breathed out for a count of six. I let the hardness of the pavers under my slippers ground me. I opened my eyes. "You're not planning any activities while you're here, are you, Dad?"

"You know better than to ask that. Plausible deniability."

Pain stabbed through my abdomen, and I knew it wasn't from stray uterine tissue growing in my abdomen. "Dad, please don't—"

"Where can I park my truck?" He scanned the overcast sky. "I don't want it to get picked up by some drone."

"In the garage." I gestured toward it. "Or under that sycamore tree."

"Not enough leaves to cover. There's a live oak down the drive. I'll put it under there."

"I'll make us a snack," Savannah said, "while you're getting settled into your room."

I winced. "He won't be staying in the house."

She planted her hands on her hips. "Of course he will. You have, like, six guest rooms."

"She also has fluoridated water," Dad said.

At Savannah's puzzled expression, I shook my head. "He prefers to sleep in his truck."

He patted its camouflaged side. "I carry fifty gallons of rainwater with zero mind-controlling chemicals. I keep telling her to install a cistern, but here in the city, they'd probably pollute it with their chemtrails."

"Chemtrails?" Savannah asked.

"Don't ask," I said. "Dad, when you've parked, you should come inside for some of Savannah's cookies and tea. Don't worry, I've got bottled water."

"Bottled water?" he scoffed. "Worse than city water. Government controls that too."

"Fine, you can skip the tea." As he turned back to his truck, I said, "By the way, how long do you plan to stay?"

"Through next Sunday," he said. From the firm set of his jaw, I could tell he was holding something back, but I knew better than to ask.

13

BIOSENSOR

Biosensor: *A biological-based device that detects chemicals.*

OLIVER

"Thanks for doing this with me today," Andrew said, screwing the blue-and-green model of the earth onto the rotating arm of the model of the solar system. "I know work is nuts."

"Yeah." I tightened the latch on the camera tripod. We were working at my polished granite island. My place in Los Altos Hills wasn't the most convenient for my San Francisco–based friend, but with no significant other or pets wandering into the shot, it was better than his and Carly's townhouse. Neater, too, without all the knick-knacks and shit Carly put everywhere to make it "homey." I preferred to keep my kitchen streamlined and functional, like my lab. And my house was as lonely and echoey as the lab would be today, on the Sunday before Christmas.

I could've gone in today. But West had reminded me I needed to set an example of work-life balance for our employees. That meant not going in on Sundays. Still, I was itchy. With our deadline looming—tomorrow, there'd be 69 days on the damned poster—I couldn't afford to waste time. If I dropped in for a few minutes after we finished filming to check on my assay, it didn't really count as work. Right?

"All good?" Andrew asked.

I flicked on the camera and angled it so the model was in view. "Uh huh." What if something went wrong on the assay? Would I have time to start another? I ran the math in my head.

"Hey."

I looked up from the camera's screen.

Andrew's mouth was flat with exasperation. "What's with the one-word answers? Everything okay?"

"Oh. Um, yeah." I winced. This was my best friend. I could tell him what was going on. "No, not really. The results are good, but they're not great. I feel like the perfect biomarker is out there, barely out of reach, and if we had longer, I could discover it. I'm terrified that we're going to have to go with what we've got because of that fucking March first deadline, and it's not good enough. Plus, Tessa is always on my ass, pushing me to work faster and take risks. Last week she asked me to halve the sample size so we could finish the validation faster. That's insane, right?"

"Is it?" He flicked the switch to light up the sun at the center of the model.

"Of course it is. If we don't run enough samples, we could make incorrect assumptions and think our marker shows correlation when it doesn't. If we then take it to clinical trials and get a ton of false positives, it'll set us back months."

"Or..." He tipped his head. "It could put you ahead of schedule, and you'd get the test to market faster. You could catch someone's cancer before it's too late."

"That's what Tessa says. And yet *she's* the one distracting *my* staff with a separate project."

"Another project?"

"Yeah. She pulled all the women aside and got them working on a different test. For endometriosis."

"I've heard of endometriosis," he said, "but I don't think I understand what it is."

"It's a condition where uterine tissue develops outside the uterus. It can grow on the bowels or ovaries or elsewhere in the abdomen. And when that tissue is shed during the menstrual cycle, it causes pain and inflammation."

He grimaced. "Every month?"

"And sometimes at different points in the cycle, like at ovulation. Plus, it can cause pain with bowel movements or during intercourse."

"And Tessa's trying to diagnose it earlier so women can get treatment sooner?" He stopped fiddling with the solar model.

"She's trying to diagnose it, period. There's no test for it other than laparoscopic surgery. Often, people with the condition are sent to gastroenterologists or urologists or even psychiatrists for testing and treatment of other suspected conditions. There's a disappointing lack of awareness in the medical community."

"Women's health, am I right?" He rolled his eyes. "Carly's tried, like, three doctors to find one who knows anything about perimenopause."

"Exactly. Medical schools are getting better at teaching about women's health, but a lot of experienced practitioners lack training."

"So, it sounds like a good thing Tessa's doing," he said.

Tipping my head back, I glared at the ceiling the way I wished I could glare at Tessa. "Of course it is. But does she have to do it *now* while I'm trying to get *my* test done? The one that's going to save the company?"

"Maybe her test can save the company too."

"Maybe. Which makes it really hard to hate her."

"Do you?" he asked. "Hate her? Because you talk about her a fucking lot for someone you hate."

"She's the bane of my existence. She's Lex Luthor and Darth Vader and Hans Gruber rolled into one—" I barely stopped myself from saying *gorgeous*. "One supervillain."

But it was like he'd heard me. "She has really pretty eyes too."

They sparkled like sunlight on shallow water. And god, her hair. I'd imagined touching it dozens of times. How silky it would be. How it'd feel wrapped around my fist. Or tickling my face as she straddled me—

"Thought so." Andrew chuckled.

Realizing I'd said at least some of that shit out loud, I groaned. "Fuck off."

"Maybe you should stop fighting it and ask her out."

"Yeah, because dating someone I work with is a good idea." Even if I did get up the courage to ask, she'd never say yes. She was way too smart to risk damaging our delicate working relationship. And so was I...I hoped.

"You two are peers who both report to Dr. Perrell, so there's no conflict of interest. If you finally admitted you're attracted to each other, you wouldn't be repressing all these...feelings."

"It's not 'feelings,'" I insisted, not sure if I was trying to convince him or myself. "It's lust, pure and simple."

"Or obsession." He didn't even bother to lower his voice.

"We're done talking about this. I've got to check on my assay at the lab, so we need to get this over with. I'm going to hit the lights, and we're doing this in one take."

To his credit, he did manage it in one take. And keeping him in frame while he talked about the earth's orbit and the math behind the solstice distracted me from thoughts about Tessa for an hour or so.

Too bad the distraction didn't last longer.

14

WARGAMES

From Barry Wright's manifesto:
In the 1980s, the arcade game Polybius *was released in Portland, Oregon, in unmarked cabinets. Players reported illness, nightmares, and suicidal thoughts. One of my buddies said men in black monitored the games. Could the* Polybius *game have been a test of psychological warfare?*

TESSA

a tap on the doorframe of my office made me jump like one of the words on the screen, probably *Enzyme-Linked Immunosorbent Assay,* had electrocuted me.

West leaned in the doorway. "You look puzzled. Everything okay?"

"I'm fine," I said automatically. My dad's unexpected visit, Savannah's increasingly messy divorce, and my own stupidity regarding biomedical engineering were all safely put away in separate containers in my brain. They weren't glowing, ready to explode and contaminate my professionalism. Mostly.

He stepped into my office, hands in the pockets of his jeans.

Oliver always wore trousers, sometimes khakis on Fridays, and Dr. Perrell wore skirts with colorfully patterned blouses. I wore my standard uniform of black pants with shirts in neutral colors. But West, like most of the people his age who worked here, always wore jeans and a collared shirt, often with the sleeves rolled up. He didn't come all the way to my desk, but he came far enough inside that he could've closed the door behind him. Like he was offering a tête-à-tête. "You sure?"

"It's nothing to concern HR, if that's what you're asking."

"No." He took another step toward me. "I'm not asking as the head of human resources. I'm asking as your colleague. As someone who could be a friend. You've come into a tough situation with high expectations. Biotech is outside your comfort zone. And Oliver isn't making things easy for you."

I winced. There was nothing easy about the status report Oliver had sent me with its esoteric phrases I couldn't understand, much less summarize for Dr. Perrell. "Am I that transparent?"

He shrugged. "It's kind of my job to know when people are struggling."

"I'm not struggling." Certainly, he could hear the lie too.

"It's okay to admit you need help," he said. "You don't have to do everything alone."

"Don't I? They say Steve Jobs personally picked the shade of white used in Apple products." That was what I'd done wrong all those years ago. I'd let someone else do the due diligence on MuskOx Tech. I'd trusted Harry, and that had led to my biggest mistake.

A tiny crease formed between his eyebrows. "I'm not sure Steve Jobs is the example we want to emulate here."

Of course he'd say that. Human resources' role was to ensure everyone played nice and no one had grounds for a lawsuit. MuskOx's HR team had done a stellar job of that after the buyout. Anonymously, I'd set up a fund to help my former employees. When some of them had used it to bring wrongful termination lawsuits against the new owners, MuskOx Tech had batted each one aside like Hedy with a feather toy.

The memory left a bitter taste in my mouth. I swigged my coffee and shuddered. It was cold and almost as bitter.

"I'm good," I assured him. I'd dealt with the fallout of my mistake alone for the last fourteen years. I could do this alone too. "Just working through some science here. I don't suppose you know what an Enzyme-Linked Immunosorbent Assay—ELISA—is, do you?"

He raised his palms like a shield and chuckled. "Nope. My degree was in sport and performance psychology. You'll have to ask Oliver or one of the other scientists."

Hope flared inside me. I could ask Aanya. She was smart. Then the spark faded. If I went around Oliver, I risked word getting back to him. I'd look like a coward.

I was no coward.

"You're right." I rolled back my chair and stood. When there was something unpleasant to do, it was best to get it over with as quickly as possible. "Good talk." Careful not to brush against him, I stepped through the door. "Thanks."

The crinkle between his eyebrows was back. "Anytime."

I strode to the lab, where I put on the ridiculous coat and pulled back my hair with an elastic. Might as well go all in with the regulations if I was going to expose my ignorance and beg for help. My stomach soured.

Taking a deep breath, I walked to the bench where Oliver usually worked, next to the sign where I'd posted the number 69 today. It was spotless, as usual. But he wasn't there. I glanced at the closest computer workstation. No Oliver.

Sadie sat at the bench next to his, her earbuds in as she used a tiny pipette to drop a chemical into a tray with shallow wells, which I'd learned was called a microtiter plate. I waited for her to set down the pipette, then I tapped her shoulder.

She pulled out her earbud and smiled. "Hey, what's up?"

"Have you seen Oliver? I have a question to ask him."

"Not for a minute," she said.

"Okay," I said, "I'll check his office."

"Check the game room," she said.

"Game room?" I vaguely remembered the first-floor space near the cafeteria from the tour on my first day, but it seemed like the last place buttoned-up Oliver would hang out during work hours.

She nodded, then dipped her chin like, *Is there anything else?*

"Thanks." As I walked toward the exit and hung up my lab coat, a vague sense of disappointment tickled in my belly. Maybe Oliver was the sort of tech bro who played foosball and drank beer on a Monday afternoon. Just because he'd agreed to let Sadie cut back her hours to focus on her graduate degree didn't necessarily mean he was a good guy. Maybe he had an ulterior motive.

I descended the stairs to the first floor and walked past the cafeteria to the game room.

The room had windows on one end, and, yes, there was a foosball table, plus a ping-pong table and a big square table next to a bookshelf filled with tabletop games. The closer side had no windows and was lined with classic arcade machines. I recognized many of the games I'd played when Dad was at one of his mysterious meetings and I'd sneak out to the local gas station or an arcade if we were near a big city.

The game room was empty, except for Oliver. And he wasn't playing foosball or *Donkey Kong.* He bowed his head in front of an open display case in the closest corner to the doorway where I stood. His hands were in his pockets. There was a photo on the shelf of a blond guy laughing. Under its shroud of stubble, the blond man's chin was the same shape as Sadie's. Were his eyes the same shade of grayish blue? Was he a relative of hers?

Oliver reached toward the vase of flowers a shelf below the photo and pinched off the wilted head of a daisy. He twirled it between his fingers and murmured something too low for me to hear.

I had enough emotional intelligence to know I should tiptoe out. But the scene fascinated me. Ever since I'd met him, Oliver had given off a sad-boy vibe like the lead singers of the emo bands I'd been obsessed with in my teens. (My god, if he'd ever wear eyeliner, he'd look exactly like Gerard Way of My Chemical Romance.) I'd assumed it was a form of emotional manipulation like Harry's. But maybe it was real.

Unfortunately, I'd forgotten to hold the door, and it clunked shut, startling Oliver. He whirled to face me. He still held the browned flower in his hand, and I couldn't interpret the expression on his face. Was the flush on his cheeks from embarrassment or anger?

I held out my hands defensively. "Sorry, I had a question, and they said you were here."

He shook his head. "It's fine. I just...I come down here to think sometimes."

"Who's that?" I tipped my chin at the photo.

"Simon Grimstone."

So he and Sadie were related.

"He and I founded the company together," he said, "while we were still in college. We were best friends for, like, ever."

"Were?"

"He died two years ago. Two years, one month, and fourteen days ago. Car accident." He glanced at the photo. "We were like puzzle pieces. He completed me."

"Oh." I'd skipped over the company history to focus on the

science they were doing. That seemed to have been a mistake. "Were you romantic partners too?"

He whipped his head back to face me. "No, nothing like that. We were good friends. But he made up for my lack of business ability, and I had the deep scientific knowledge. He filled in all my gaps. I miss that. I miss him."

Shit. So he was a legit sad boy. My scalp prickled as a tiny crack opened in my stony heart. I reached up to rub my head and found I'd left the elastic in it from the lab. I tugged it out and shook out my hair, scrubbing my fingers at the prickly part that told me I'd misjudged Oliver.

When I looked back at him, he was staring at me. At my hair, actually, with his lips parted.

"What?" I asked. "Am I supposed to tie back my hair in here too? Are you afraid I might get it wrapped around the foosball rods?"

"No, I..." He licked his lips. Pouting lips I did *not* want to kiss. "No."

"Is there something between you and Sadie?" I asked. He wouldn't be the first tech bro to date a subordinate.

"No! God, she's like my little sister. She was so broken up when Simon died she flunked out of her graduate program, so I asked her to work here. We watch out for each other."

I stepped closer. In the photo, Simon's eyes looked red around the rims. "Does she come down here too?"

"Nah." He scuffed the toe of his sneaker on the floor. "She thinks it's creepy."

I chuckled. "She's not wrong."

He glanced back at the shrine. "I don't want anyone to forget him. He was such a force here. These are all his favorite games, and this room used to be full of people whenever he came down to play. He's what made this company great."

I thought of how Sadie's blue eyes shone with admiration whenever her boss spoke. "So are you, you know."

He shrugged. "Anyone can do what I do. Everyone in the lab does the same work."

"But you're their leader. They light up when you're here. Everyone wants to please you." There was a different energy in the lab when Oliver was there. Couldn't he see it?

"Sadie idolizes you," he said.

It was my turn to shrug. "You could use a few more female role models in the lab. Remember, there are only four women in a lab of twenty-five."

He winced. "I know. Our next five hires will be women or nonbinary people, I promise."

"Good." I folded my arms because suddenly, I wanted to reach for him. Dammit! Just because he'd committed to diversifying the lab didn't mean he wasn't a roadblock to my plans. It certainly didn't make touching my colleague a smart move.

"How did you know about Sadie's endometriosis?" he asked.

"I observe people," I said carefully. "And I observed that she seemed to be experiencing abdominal pain the day before she called in sick. Then, when she came back, she seemed pale and a bit unsteady."

"But how did you know it was endometriosis and not a stomach bug and anemia?"

"I...someone close to me has it. I've seen the signs before." My medical conditions were none of his business, but I could admit that much.

He nodded. "Now I get why you spun up the endometriosis project. You're right. We could use a more diverse perspective in the lab."

"Of course I'm right," I said. "You should admit that more often." I allowed the corner of my mouth to curl up and let him in on the joke.

He chuckled and tossed the spent flower in the trash. "Care to join me for a game of *Ms. Pac-Man?*"

"No, thanks. I prefer games of the tabletop variety." He'd probably only invited me to play to be polite. He was like that. Playing one of Simon's favorite arcade games was another step in his grieving process, and I wouldn't get in the way of that. "See you later," I said.

It wasn't until I sat down at my desk upstairs that I realized I'd forgotten to ask him about ELISA. Well, shit. I'd have to consult my good buddy Google. A search engine was safer than the temptation of Oliver and his sad eyes.

15
─────

ANTAGONISM

Antagonism: *In drug-drug interactions (DDI), antagonistic results occur when one drug reduces or eliminates the pharmacological effect of another drug.*

OLIVER

*P*eering at the results of the assay on Sanjay's screen, I let out a breath. For the first time all week, it didn't feel like the weight of the entire lab was stuffed inside my chest. "Great results, Sanjay."

"Thanks. I think we're going to make it. It'll be okay." He rubbed at the mark his goggles had left on the sides of his nose.

Everyone had worked hard over the last few weeks. And today, the first Monday after Christmas, when most people wanted to be enjoying time off between the holidays, the lab was buzzing with activity. Maybe it had something to do with the huge 62 on the wall. Or maybe it was because Sanjay had made a breakthrough. He'd found a relationship between not one but two hormones and ovarian cancer. His success caught on, and the next day, Aanya improved it. After that, it was like atoms crystallizing into a stable lattice. Here we were, gazing at our first truly successful test. For the first time in over a year, hope fluttered in my chest.

We only needed to replicate it a thousand more times to ensure it wasn't a fluke.

"I know what you're thinking," Sanjay said. "We'll run more tests. We'll know more by the time you get back from Vegas."

"I'm not going to Vegas," I said. "I'm going to cancel when I get back to my desk."

"Wait," Sadie said. "You're presenting your paper there. You have to go."

"No, I don't. This is more important." I'd personally monitor each of the assays to ensure nothing went wrong. It wouldn't be the first time I'd slept in the lab. It'd be like the early days of Discovery, when it was only Simon and me and a handful of employees, surviving on pizza and coffee and the euphoria of success.

"Wait. What's happening?" Tessa's voice made the hairs stand up on my arm under my lab coat. When had she come in?

"Oliver says he's not going to BMTC," Sadie said.

She stepped to the other side of him and flicked her ponytail off the shoulder of her lab coat like it was distracting her. "What's BMTC?"

I shrugged. "A biomedical conference. The big drugmakers go, and so do lots of hospital staff for the continuing medical education credits."

"Oliver goes every year," Sanjay said unhelpfully. "It's great exposure for Discovery."

"You're telling me," Tessa said, a warning in her voice, "you have the chance to speak at a conference where there are tons of potential customers for our test, to tell them about our work, to show how fucking *brilliant* you are, and you're *not going?*"

"You make it sound like a bad thing. I'm doing the right thing by staying here and focusing on the work." I pointed at the screen.

"That's Sanjay's work," she said. "Your work is promoting this company and our products."

"It's all *our* work. Besides, we won't have any products if we can't successfully test them," I growled. I didn't add that we wouldn't have a company either if this test failed. No one needed the added stress of knowing we could all be out of work in six months if we missed our deadline.

She faced Sanjay, who straightened under her scrutiny. "Are you going to do your work any faster if Oliver is here, breathing down your neck?"

"I wouldn't—" I began.

"No," he said. "I wouldn't." He met my stare defiantly.

Tessa tossed her ponytail. "Then you're going to—"

"Uh-oh," Sadie said. She'd gone to the window. "They're back."

"Who's back?" I asked.

"PETA," she said. "Wonder how they convinced a news crew to come this time."

I rolled my eyes. "I knew we should've put a sign at the front door declaring we don't have any lab animals on premises. I'll go talk to them."

"That's weird." Sadie leaned over the cluttered desk to stare through the window. "Is that a gun safe in that truck?"

My heart skipped a beat, then set off at a sprint. And so did I. I didn't bother to take off my lab coat as I fled the lab to bar the invaders from the building.

Footsteps followed me, but my daily running regimen kept me in the lead. Planting one hand on the frame of the security gate, I hurdled it, setting off the alarm. "Lock the doors," I shouted to the guard as I passed, "and call the police!" I rushed through the glass front door two seconds before it closed.

I stopped when I saw the protesters. They weren't the usual scraggly-bearded, beanie-and-Birkenstocks-wearing animal lovers. Most of them were men, and quite a few of them were gray-haired. I was thankful they'd left their rifles in their camouflage-painted pickup truck. I hoped no one had a concealed handgun.

A white man with graying red hair that looked pinkish held up a sign that read, BIG PHARMA = BIG LIES. "Wait," I said. "They're not PETA."

"No." Tessa brushed past me. "They're conspiracy theorists."

16

ALIEN ABDUCTIONS ARE REAL

From Barry Wright's manifesto:
*With the collusion of world governments, extraterrestrials abduct
humans and implant mind-control devices in their brains. How do I
know this? I've got friends who've described waking up outside with
no memory of how they got there, their heads aching. My buddy Burt
even remembers a flash of light and little green men looking down at
him. When the aliens are ready, they're gonna subdue Earth's
population with the press of a button.*

TESSA

*O*liver was ridiculously fast, but adrenaline and shame
kept me at his heels. I managed to slip out of the
building before the electromagnetic locks bolted with a buzz.

Now I understood why Dad had stayed a week past the
solstice. He'd brought a group of a dozen like-minded associates
to the Discovery Diagnostics parking lot. Some of them were his
age, grizzled and weathered from living rough, off the grid.
Others were baby-faced dudes, their eyes wide and shifty. There

were a few women in yoga pants who looked like they'd come in their minivans straight from the school drop-off line. When I met my father's gaze, his eyes narrowed in accusation.

"You didn't tell me you worked for big pharma," he said, loud enough for only me to hear. His lip curled as he scanned my lab coat, which I hadn't taken the time to shed.

"I don't," I said equally as quiet. "You'd be better off driving down the road to Gilead. Or better yet, going home. We do good work here."

He held my gaze for a moment, then lifted his bearded chin and shouted, "Companies like Discovery Diagnostics know the cure for cancer, but there's more profit in treatments. So they hide the cure and sell us snake oil."

"No! More! Snake! Oil!" one of the younger guys shouted. The rest of the group repeated the phrase as they waved their signs.

For half a second, Vaseline-lensed nostalgia washed through me. As a gangly thirteen-year-old, I'd been so excited when Dad finally said I was old enough to go with him to a protest. It had been at Diablo Canyon Power Plant, and we'd chanted, *No safe dose of radiation* and *Save our children's children.* In my cynical hindsight, he'd probably wanted me there so everyone would keep my generation's nuclear-free future in mind. But I hadn't thought of it then. I'd been thrilled that Dad finally wanted to do something with me aside from silently eating flapjacks in our camp chairs outside our trailer.

A broad body in a white coat stepped in front of me. He held up his hands. "Hi, folks. I'm Oliver, and I founded Discovery Diagnostics. What seems to be the trouble?"

"You're in charge, junior?" my father sneered.

Oliver propped his hands on his hips, further shielding me. "I am. Sir."

"Then you're the one I want to sign this statement." My

father held out a paper. I wondered briefly how he'd printed it. Had he trusted the network in my home, or had he gone to one of those sketchy internet cafés and used a VPN to bounce his IP address halfway across the world? Or did he have a typewriter in his truck?

Oliver took the paper and scanned it. "You're asking me to promise to release the cure for cancer we've got in our vault?" He chuckled. "We don't have a vault, and if I had a cure for cancer, I'd be a very wealthy man."

"That's exactly it!" A woman, her hair in a long braid down her back, pushed to the front. "It's more profitable to sell us your ineffective treatments. You're lining your pockets with our suffering!"

I tried to push around Oliver, but he flung out a hand. It landed on the front of my lab coat, and the strength in his fingers shocked me into stillness. His fingertips dug into my stomach muscles, grounding me in my body.

"I'm sorry you're suffering," he said gently. "And I'm doing everything I can to help. Discovery Diagnostics develops tests for cancer and other conditions that will help the medical community diagnose diseases earlier. Patients will be able to receive treatments sooner and have a better chance at survival."

He handed the paper back to my father, who snatched it from his grip. "Treatments," Dad scoffed. "Poisons, more like."

I met my father's gaze. I remembered it too. She laughed when clumps of her long blond hair fell out. She told ten-year-old-me it was a sign the treatments were working. But even a self-centered tween noticed when her clothes hung off her too-spare frame, when she came back winded from her slow shuffle to the mailbox at the end of the driveway. The chemo was poison, and in the end, it hadn't saved her. My nose prickled, and I blinked hard.

"Dad," I said, "go home."

Oliver's head whipped around, eyes wide. "What?"

No one in Dad's group blinked. He must have told them about his misguided, traitorous daughter who'd fallen prey to big, bad pharma. The one who needed saving from her ignorance.

"Can't." Dad's lips twisted. "I promised a show." He jerked his thumb at the guy with the camera on his shoulder a few steps away. A reporter with hair that didn't move in the breeze stood next to him.

"At my expense?" I said softly.

His green eyes went flinty. "You're on the wrong side, Tessa. I raised you better than this."

Had he? I was so young when Mom died. A blank paper for him to inscribe all his theories about the government, the healthcare industry, the cabals he saw everywhere. I believed that living off the land, in a community of like-minded people, away from the prying eyes of the government, was how we protected ourselves. *Trust no one* was our mantra. It served me and my anger toward the doctors who'd broken my trust by letting my mother die. And it served me later, when I'd learned enough through my independent homeschool studies to understand my father had it wrong and I couldn't trust him either.

I should be grateful he'd taught me that. I only wished I'd remembered it when I'd listened to Harry.

With one last, searching glare, he turned to his comrades. "Discover the truth. Down with Discovery!"

They chanted back, "Discover the truth. Down with Discovery!" They held up their hand-lettered signs and continued the chorus.

I grasped Oliver's wrist, which was still banded across my stomach. "Let's go back to work. I don't think they mean any harm."

"What about..." He nodded at the padlocked, heavy-duty metal storage box in my dad's truck.

"He never brings his guns to protests," I assured him. "He knows he could end up in jail for this. No need to add a weapons charge to it."

With perfect timing, two police cars pulled into the parking lot, their lights flashing. Some of the protesters groaned, but under his beard, my dad's jaw turned to steel.

"I'm sorry," Oliver said. "I didn't know it was your dad."

"It's fine," I said. "It's not the first time I've bailed him out. It won't be the last."

The protesters had spotted the police cars too, and their shouts increased in both volume and desperation.

Oliver leaned closer to whisper, "Go inside. I'll handle this." His breath stirred the shorter hairs near my face that had escaped my ponytail, and I shivered.

"We'll handle it together," I said, still holding his wrist. I wish I could say I immediately released it, but I needed the reassurance of his strong, steady pulse.

"Together," he echoed.

I dropped his hand then. It was too much to gaze into those innocent blue eyes of his, clear and open as the summer sky. Maybe he was as trustworthy as he seemed. He'd seen a secret I kept from my closest friends, yet he still offered to stand beside me.

So we talked to the police officers together. We stood side by side as some of the protesters clambered into their trucks and drove off Discovery Diagnostics' private property. People like my dad, for whom the cause was supremely personal, continued to shout their slogans until the officers took them into custody. Dad shouted through the police cruiser's window, his eyes wild and his expression savage, as they drove him away.

A chilly breeze tossed the hem of my lab coat as the news van's taillights receded down the street.

"You okay?" Oliver asked. We were the only ones left in the parking lot.

"This isn't the first time. Actually, it's the first time he's protested at my place of employment. But he's protested hundreds of times." I glanced back at the building, where a couple of people watched us through the windows. "He...he started after my mom died of cancer."

"I'm so sorry." He stepped forward and reached out a hand like he'd take mine.

I stepped back. "It was over thirty years ago. My memories of her are so faded I'm not sure what I actually remember and what Dad told me about her."

"You were so young," he said.

"So was she. Younger than I am now." I stared off into the trees that lined the back of the building. I'd made some poor choices that I regretted, choices that had narrowed my life for too long. But at least I'd had those years. Those choices.

He looked toward the distant line of live oaks. "My grandmother died of cancer too, though she was a lot older. Still, I miss her, and I wish we'd had more time together. It's why I do this." He waved at the building.

My lips twisted into a wry smile. "Same. I like to think I've finally made a choice she'd be proud of."

His hands twitched, but this time he didn't reach out. "She'd be proud of you regardless."

"Yeah, right."

I clocked the exact moment he remembered my worst choice. A steel door slammed shut behind his eyes, cooling the blue to slate.

"Come on," I said, "let's get back to work." And I forced my feet to propel my weary body back to the office.

~

"So," my dad said as he pulled his pickup into my motor court and shone the headlights on the front door, "same time next year?"

"Dad." I leaned back in the seat and closed my eyes. "You can't do this again."

"What?" His eyes crinkled as he chuckled. "I can't come see my daughter?"

I turned to face him. "No. You can't. Not if you're going to bring your conspiracy comrades to my *job.*"

"You can't be serious about working there. That Oliver is a liar, and he's convinced you with a fantasy that you can make a difference. You can't. Not with the government and the men in black and big pharma—"

"Stop." I waited until he closed his mouth, until he met my gaze. "I believe in this work. I believe in the company. I believe in *him.* And I believe I can help them change the world, one patient at a time."

He snorted. "I raised you to question everyone and everything."

"You did. And I do. Right now I'm questioning whether there's a place in my life for my father. And after today? I'm not so sure." My voice cracked, and my eyes burned at the backs with tears I refused to shed, even in the dark. "Next time you feel the urge to come visit, find a pay phone and call. I'll let you know if you're welcome."

He squinted. "It's worse than I thought. They've already poisoned your mind. Do you have any missing periods in your memory? Dreams of bright lights?"

"No, Dad. I haven't been abducted. I'm drawing a boundary. Please respect it." I tugged the door handle and shoved it open with my elbow. I jumped down and leaned into the cab. "Think about how your choices affect others. Goodbye."

I slammed the door and walked to my porch, then I watched him drive away. We shared a past. We shared skepticism and mistrust too. But I didn't have to like it.

17

ASSAY

Assay: A scientific procedure for analyzing the content or characteristics of a substance.

OLIVER

$\mathcal{I}$ was still riding the high of my successful talk, shaking the hand of one of my college professors who'd said he was impressed by my company's research, when the last person I expected to see at the BMTC conference stepped up behind him.

"Tessa?" Had something terrible happened at the lab, so terrible that she'd had to fly out to Vegas to tell me?

Patting the professor's shoulder, I told him we should catch up later, then I stepped to her side.

"What are you doing here?" She wore a black shirtdress and ankle boots, which shouldn't look out of place in January in Las Vegas but somehow did. In a roomful of pale, shuffling scientists, she glowed like the neon signs outside. Maybe it was the fiery shade of her hair. Maybe it was something else that lit her up. I glanced toward the ceiling to check if there was a spotlight shining on her.

"I got a last-minute meeting with Dr. Shah from Sanctuary Health Network," she said. "They want to buy our ovarian cancer test."

Relief turned to joy, then panic. "You mean the test we haven't fully vetted in the simulations, much less in clinical trials?"

"We'll get it done," she said serenely. "We have to."

She was right about that. If we didn't, Greenwich Biomedical, whose huge green banner hung outside the small ballroom I'd been presenting in, would come in and destroy everything Simon and I had built.

"Great job, by the way," she said. "You were so passionate when you talked about predictive thresholds." She had a little furrow between her eyebrows like it surprised her.

Maybe it did surprise her because someone who cared about her work, about her employees, wouldn't have done what she did at Red Rover. Though the more I got to know her, the more I couldn't square her past behavior with the present. A person who didn't care about the people who worked for her wouldn't have encouraged Sadie to cut back her hours and finish her doctorate. She wouldn't have spun up the endometriosis project as a development opportunity for our female scientists. And when those protesters showed up, she'd have stayed safely inside the building and pretended their leader wasn't her father.

It must have been scientific interest in discovering who my COO was beyond her flaming hair and her infamous past that made me blurt out, "Do you have plans for dinner?"

"I'm surprised," she said, leaning her elbow on the table as she lifted her wineglass, "that you started Discovery Diagnostics at all. Wouldn't it have been a safer move to work in R&D for one of the big pharmaceutical companies?"

"It would have," I agreed. During dinner in a quiet corner of the hotel restaurant, we'd post-gamed the conference, and she'd dictated a list of follow-ups into her phone. As she finished her second glass of cabernet, the conversation had turned more personal. "Simon made me feel like we could do anything together. Like it wasn't a risk at all. In hindsight, it was a huge risk to go out on our own. I guess he shielded me from the worst of it."

"Or," she said, swirling the ruby liquid in her glass, "you're better at risk-taking than you think."

I smoothed the imprint of my dinner plate from the tablecloth. "No. Since he's been gone, I've been paralyzed. Second-guessing everything, even my work in the lab, which he never touched."

"Grief can take different forms." She set down her glass, and even though I didn't look up, I could feel her lean forward. "My dad, for example. He was a pretty normal guy before my mom died. His grief turned to anger against the doctors and the pharmaceutical companies who couldn't save her."

"Yeah?" I looked up. This was the most personal thing I'd ever heard her say. "What was it like?"

"When my mom died?" She hesitated, then the fine lines across her forehead softened. "Terrible, of course. She got diagnosed at stage three, and the treatment plan was aggressive. They put her on chemo, and it was the worst. She was so sick and weak after. She'd have a few good days before her next treatment, and she…" Tessa blinked, and the rims of her eyes were red. "My god, I haven't thought about this in forever. On her good days, we'd do something outside. Roller skating. The beach. A park. I was eleven, and I didn't notice that our good-day activities got progressively lower-impact. She was getting sicker. In the end, there were no more good days at all." She traced the base of her wineglass with a long, pale finger.

I remembered how pale Grandma Vee got at the end and how she hardly moved from her favorite recliner. "Then what happened?"

"We'd moved to the city to be closer to the hospital for her treatments, but Dad always preferred the rural life. After her funeral, Dad sold the house and moved us to a cabin next to a forest preserve. I went to another new school. That was hard." She scrunched up her nose. "Dad joined some message boards. You know, conspiracy theories and such. He went to meetings. And after a while, he sold that place too and bought a camper so we never stayed in one place too long. Instead of sending me to high school, he homeschooled me. By which I mean, he left me to my own devices, and I educated myself."

"He pulled you out of school and didn't bother to teach you?" I clenched my fist. If I'd known that, I wouldn't have been so reasonable with him when he'd come to the office.

She waved away my anger. "If I'd been in regular school, I probably wouldn't have had the confidence to teach myself to code. I'd never have built my app. Though maybe I'd have learned more about people." She pressed her lips together.

I waited for her to finish that story, hoping to get another peek inside the enigma that was Tessa Wright, but she stayed silent, her fingers sliding over the smooth glass. Finally, she looked up. "Giving that talk today was a risk. How did it feel?"

I didn't miss how she'd changed the subject. But she'd opened up about her life more than she ever had to me, and I knew what a big step that was. So I went with it. "Terrifying at first, standing at the podium in front of all those smart people. But then I focused on the science. That's my comfort zone."

"Then that's what we'll focus on when we get back to the office. Keep that spark from today, that confidence, and do the science. I'll handle everything else. We'll be unstoppable." Her green eyes flared, and the spark she'd mentioned ignited in my chest.

"Unstoppable," I echoed, believing it. Believing that together, we could do anything. Especially if she could let down her shields like she had tonight.

"I've got an early meeting tomorrow with Dr. Deng from Quantum Oncology. Want to join us? I could use your expertise." She lifted a finger, and the waitress brought the folio. Without looking at it, Tessa handed her a black card.

Together. "Okay." I smiled. "If only to rein you in when you overpromise."

"I'm confident you can deliver." One corner of her mouth turned up, and *oh my god is she flirting with me*? My heart pounded.

"Are you?" My voice was a rumble.

"I am." Her tongue flicked out to wet her lower lip. I was going to need a minute before standing up.

"Thank you, Ms. Wright." The server set the folio back on the table. Tessa held my gaze for a long moment before she opened it.

Fuck. Tessa Wright was buying me dinner. Nothing she did was accidental, so this must mean something. Our company policy mandated that the most senior employee expense a business dinner. Who was more senior? We both had Chief in our titles. Was this a power play? Or a flirtation? My head swam.

I opened my mouth. Maybe it was a nudge from Simon, who was surely watching and yelling the way he used to do when we watched horror movies and the main character was too stupid to live. "I'll buy dinner tomorrow," were the words that came out.

She finished signing with a flourish. "Tomorrow night?" Her lips tilted. "Okay."

I adjusted myself under the table before I stood. "There's a mixer in the big ballroom. Are you going?"

She stood and tossed her napkin on the table. "A party with doctors and scientists? Sounds like a wild time."

I chuckled as I rose. "It *is* Vegas. Even scientists let their hair down." But mentioning hair was a mistake. I wanted to reach out a finger and touch a lock of hers. I cleared my throat. "I'm skipping it. Full day tomorrow."

She held up a finger. "Starting with our 7 a.m. breakfast with Dr. Deng. You promised."

"I did." Something warmed in my chest as we strolled side by side out of the restaurant toward the elevators on the other side of the lobby.

She stopped midway across the lobby. "I've got to stop at the desk to pick up my key. Goodnight."

A mob of guys my age sauntered past. One of them stumbled as he ogled Tessa. "I'll wait," I said.

"Okay." She gave an I-can-handle-myself shrug, then walked toward the front desk.

I lingered at a distance I hoped wasn't too stalkery. The lobby was filled with gamblers headed toward the casino, roving groups of partiers, and tourists. I waved at a few people I recognized from the conference.

My ears perked up when Tessa said, "No rooms?"

I stepped closer. The desk attendant said, "I'm sorry. We've been booked for months. We're hosting a conference. In fact, every hotel is full from here to Henderson."

"Oh." She shifted her feet. It was the first time I'd ever seen her unsure of herself. "Could you call over to someplace in Henderson for me?"

"Of course," the attendant said.

"Wait." The word surprised even me. "By the time you get out there, you'll practically have to turn right around to make it back for that breakfast. You'll hardly get any sleep. Stay with me."

When she speared me with those all-seeing green eyes of hers, my heart stuttered.

She stared at me for so long I almost took it back. But then she said, "Okay."

Was it possible to have a heart attack at thirty-three? Probably. Anything was possible in proximity to Tessa Wright.

18

THE WORLD ENDED IN 2012

From Barry Wright's manifesto:

An experiment gone wrong at the Large Hadron Collider at CERN in 2012 created a black hole that engulfed the earth and ended reality. No one noticed.

TESSA

*I*t didn't happen often, but I could admit when I'd been wrong. And this trip, the worst-thought-out, most impulsive thing I'd done in a while had gone off the rails in a spectacular explosion.

I used to be spontaneous. Back in my Red Rover days, after we accomplished a milestone, I used to take everyone out to one of those party places—the ones that felt like Chuck E. Cheese but for adults—or host smaller celebrations in the San Francisco penthouse. All I needed was a stack of pizzas, beer, and a playlist on the sound system. A last-minute trip for the executive team to Park City? Sure, Harry, and I'll pay for the whole thing.

I'd forgotten about Vegas, though. A hundred fifty thousand rooms filled up quickly when the weather was crap in most of the country and there was a convention in town. Too busy anticipating the look of shock on Oliver's face, I'd forgotten to call the hotel, and now I was paying for it.

Having to rely on someone else was the worst.

I stepped into Oliver's hotel room and blinked. This wasn't the suite of a company founder who made a very comfortable salary and had to be sitting on stock options worth millions. It was a small hotel room—with one bed.

It was a king-size bed, to be fair. But that was it. The bed, a desk with a more-stylish-than-comfortable task chair, a dresser, and an upholstered chair in the corner next to a lamp. For reading, I guessed, but who read in Vegas?

I peered around him for a second room, but the only other doors were obviously a closet and a bathroom.

I looked up at him. His Adam's apple bobbed. His jaw squared like he was clenching his teeth as he stared at that one bed. It was a very different expression from the one he'd worn at dinner. That one was soft, admiring, open. Dangerously so.

I liked this one better. I read it as resolve. We were finally going to get this annoying, confusing sexual tension out of the way. We'd do it here in the king-size bed. The sex would be okay. No one as repressed and risk averse as Oliver would be passionate. In the morning, we'd admit it was a mistake and move on. More than one night, especially with someone I worked with, was how disasters happened. I'd learned that with Harry.

After we had sex, Oliver would hate me even more than he had when I'd joined Discovery. And hate was a lot more productive than its opposite.

"Okay." I dropped my bag on the carpet. "Let's do this."

19

———

AEROBIC

Aerobic: *Refers to a process or condition requiring or occurring in the presence of free oxygen.*

OLIVER

*T*he door shut with a clunk. Tragically, the magic of Vegas hadn't conjured a second bed into my hotel room. Plus, it somehow seemed more compact than when I'd left it this morning. Tessa was much smaller than me, but her presence took up at least half of the room. And although I carefully avoided her gaze, I could feel it pressing into me.

"Okay, let's do this," she said.

I ripped my stare off the white pillows. "Do what?" I was *not* imagining what her hair would look like spread across them.

"Come on. I'm going to shower, then we're going to get past this."

"Get *past* this?" My voice came out as a prepubescent squeak. I cleared my throat. "Get past what? How?"

"Don't be dense. This." She waved between us like she could

see the invisible fingers of my obsession, the ones that wanted to touch her everywhere. "And by fucking, of course."

It was all wrong. The captivation I felt for her wasn't something to be flushed out of my body like a juice cleanse. It was something that, if she felt it too, I wanted to explore. Slowly. Cautiously. Then passionately. I sucked in a breath, but there wasn't enough oxygen in the room. Not with her here.

"'This'"—I pressed a hand to my thudding heart—"isn't something we can resolve by sleeping together."

She stared at my hand on my chest. "Sure it is. Isn't that why you insisted I share your *one* bed?"

"No. No! I was…I was being nice. We're colleagues. We haven't so much as kissed. Or held hands."

She tilted her head, sending that captivating hair cascading down the front of her black dress. The dress had buttons down the front, and I imagined unbuttoning the top one, the one that had teased me with a peek of the valley between her breasts all during dinner. "Which one is it, Oliver? We're colleagues and we shouldn't? Or you're a romantic, and this is moving too fast for you?"

"I…" No matter what I'd said, I wanted her. I wanted to drop to my knees, push up her skirt, and taste her. I wanted to make her stop asking questions and groan out my name. But not if this was only a one-sided attraction.

She smiled like she'd read the answer on my face. She stepped closer, not yet touching me, but so close her breath tickled my neck. My gaze dropped to her slightly parted, pink lips, and I swallowed.

She rose on her toes until all I had to do was tilt my face to press my lips to hers.

I hesitated. This was what I craved, right? A kiss? That's all this had to be. A sample. A test.

I tilted.

We touched.

My lips met hers with a zing of electricity.

It was awkward, as first kisses are. My lips were dry, and I wasn't sure if I should move them or not. Would the tug of my skin on hers be uncomfortable? I worried I'd been still too long, and I resolved to pull away in another second. Call it bad chemistry.

When she opened and licked the seam of my lips, heat flicked up my spine. I opened too and let her explore me. Her tongue slid against mine, and I imagined lying in the king-sized bed, the lamplight glowing on her naked skin. How many freckles did she have under her clothes? Could I count them all?

She set her cool fingers on my hot cheek, grounding me back in my body, back in our kiss. With gentle pressure, she tipped my face forward, deepening the kiss, and my arms went around her back, fitting her against my body, my hard against her soft. I was kissing Tessa Wright the way I'd dreamed of doing.

She shifted her hips, and I imagined sinking into her. The sounds she'd make. The sight of her bare breasts, the taste of her nipples. Would she rake her nails down my back? Grip my hips between her knees? Suddenly, it was too much.

This was our first kiss, and I needed to slow the fuck down. I opened my eyes, but my glasses had fogged, and I saw only a pink blur where her face should be. Her floral scent engulfed me, inflamed me. Tearing my lips from hers, I kissed feverishly across her jaw, willing my erection to stand down.

It didn't.

"Mmh. I'm ready to fuck you right out of my system," she said, tilting her head to the side to allow my lips to slip down the long column of her neck.

When her words filtered through my lustful haze, I pulled away from her to take a cleansing breath and force my brain back online. "Wh-what?"

She trailed the tip of her tongue along my neck, making me shiver. "You heard me. Let's take this to bed."

"No." The word ripped out of me. I didn't want a one-time thing. I wanted to know her from the inside out, to understand what made her the way she was. I needed days, weeks, goddamn *months* to explore her. I wanted my hemoglobin to carry her through my blood like oxygen. *Then* we'd fuck, and it'd be amazing. A true melding of minds and hearts. The steam on the inside of my glasses thinned until I could see more clearly. "No," I repeated.

She narrowed her eyes. "Is this one of those no-means-yes situations? I'm really not into that."

"No definitely means no." She stared at the bulge in my suit pants, so I added, "No matter what my body thinks. Look, I'll find a different hotel." My lust ebbed when I stepped away from her. I yanked open the closet door and pulled out my suitcase.

"Wait." Something soft landed on the back of my suit jacket. Her hand. "I'm sorry. I misread the signals. I thought you... Never mind."

I turned, capturing her hand in mine and pulling it to my chest. "I have feelings for you. And they're not the kind of feelings I want to fuck away."

She ripped her hand away. "I don't want feelings."

I stumbled back like she'd poked a scalpel between my ribs. We'd both misread the situation. "Give me five minutes to pack up, then I'll be out of your way." I set my suitcase on the dresser and opened a drawer.

"No, please." Her voice was as gentle as her hand had been a minute ago. I hated it. Hated the pity I heard. "It's late. I don't want you to be exhausted at our breakfast meeting tomorrow. We can act like adults and share the room. It's a big bed, and I'll stay on my side. Please put the suitcase away."

"Okay." My voice came out gruff. "I'll brush my teeth, then the shower's all yours."

I set my suitcase back in the closet and closed myself in the bathroom. I took off my glasses and leaned on the counter to stare at my reflection. My pupils were blown, and my hair was wild on one side where Tessa had dug her fingers into it. I combed it down with my fingers, then rubbed my eyes. When I'd gotten up this morning, I had *not* imagined ending my day with kissing Tessa. Not sleeping beside her. Would I get any rest at all, knowing she was right there and down to fuck?

I wished I were the kind of guy who could give her what she wanted—what we both wanted—and move on. But I'd already imprinted on her like one of Dr. Lorenz's goslings. After we slept together, when she was ready to return to a platonic relationship, I'd always be longing for more. Working alongside her would be torture.

In my brain, I knew I'd been right to turn her down. But I wished I could convince the rest of me.

I changed out of my suit and into the pajama pants and T-shirt I'd hung on the back of the door, hissing when the fabric rubbed against my sensitive, still-erect dick. I brushed my teeth and shoved the rest of my stuff into my toiletry bag. Holding my suit pieces in front of the bulging fly of my pajama pants, I yanked open the door and strode out.

Tessa sat on the chair, a toiletry bag and some folded clothing on her lap. She scanned my pajamas. "I see your love of roleplaying games extends to your sleepwear."

I glanced down at the D20s printed on my pajama pants and my T-shirt with the words, *This is how I roll.* I thanked my past self for tossing my nerdiest sleepwear into my bag. No one could be turned on by tabletop gaming. The tension in my shoulders eased, and even my erection flagged. I shrugged. "What can I say? I'm a geek, twenty-four seven."

Was that another smile that teased her lips? I'd seen more smiles from her this evening than in the two months we'd worked together.

When she disappeared into the bathroom, I hung my suit in the closet. I grabbed the extra pillows from the top shelf and took them back to the bed. It was big enough for two if I took precautions.

Leaving one pillow at the head on each side, I lined up the spares in a double layer down the middle. I pulled back the covers on the right side, the one farthest from the bathroom and closest to the door, and lay down. All I could see to my right was pillows. Good.

I left the lamp on so she could see when she came out and closed my eyes. The sound of the shower was soothing as long as I didn't picture her in it. Naked, soap suds trailing over her freckles.

Groaning, I pulled the pillow from under my head and smashed it over my face. I'd never get to sleep if I thought about her naked body. Or our kiss. Or kissing her in the shower. *God!*

I flipped, turning my back to the bathroom. I picked up my phone from the nightstand. I double-checked my alarm, then I switched to my messaging app. I'd text Andrew to keep my mind off my new, temporary roommate.

Hey

I waited a minute. Then I checked my email and responded to a question from Yujun. When I switched back to my messaging app, there was no response from Andrew. He was probably snuggled up with Carly. Maybe they were having sex.

Ugh! I scrubbed the image from my mind.

"You built a...pillow fort?" Tessa's voice behind me made me jump.

Without turning, I said, "It's safer."

She chuckled. "Safety *is* your thing."

"Of course it is." It had been even before Simon's accident. I set my phone face down on the nightstand and bunched up the pillow under my head.

Behind me, the mattress rustled, and there was a slight tug on the comforter.

"This pillow is too flimsy," she muttered.

"No, it's not," I lied.

"Look, I'm too old to sleep with my head at a weird angle. I'm going to take a pillow from the bottom of the bed. I promise not to kick you."

"Fine," I muttered.

More rustling. "Turn off the light?"

I reached up and flipped the switch. But the darkness only made it easier to imagine her slender curves on the other side of the pillows. What was she wearing? What position did she sleep in? I hugged the pillow tighter, willing it to inflate to support my neck.

It didn't. I sighed.

"Wishing we were fucking right now?" she asked.

Pretending to be halfway asleep, I grunted.

She sighed. "Me too, friend. Me too."

∽

I dreamed I was in a bed of roses, without thorns and spiky leaves, only the blooms. They were soft, pillowy, and so fragrant that when I woke, the scent of roses lingered in my nostrils.

So did a tickly bit of hair. I blew it off my nose.

Then I realized my face was buried in Tessa's hair, and it was what smelled like roses.

I forced myself to remain still as I assessed the situation. My heart rocketed when I realized I was pressed against her from chest to toes. One arm was flung across Tessa's middle. She wore something satiny that felt smooth against my skin. My other arm, numb and unresponsive, was shoved under her pillow. My knees were pressed up to the back of hers. And my dick? It was anything but asleep, nestled against her ass.

Fuck, fuck, fuck! Where had my pillow barrier gone?

I hoped she was sleeping through the tattoo my heart was banging against my ribs and hers.

I lifted my arm from her warm skin, then carefully scooted my hips backward. I extricated my legs next. Finally, I had enough space to plant my working hand on the mattress so I could drag my dead arm out from under Tessa's head. Cautiously, I rolled to my back, then to my other side. I levered up to sit on the edge of the bed as my hand prickled with returned circulation. The other one shook.

A glance at my phone told me it was about an hour before my alarm would go off. I'd forgotten to close the blackout curtains, so the lights from the neon signs on the Strip illuminated the pile of pillows that had migrated to the foot of the bed. Which one of us had tossed them there?

It didn't matter. It also didn't matter if we fucked or not. This woman would never be out of my system.

As quietly as possible, I grabbed my workout clothes and, still in my pajamas, rushed downstairs to the hotel gym, where I pounded out the adrenaline on the treadmill. I showered in the locker room, wishing I'd had the foresight to grab my suit. Instead, I had to return to the room for it, wearing my nerdy sleep T-shirt and carrying my balled up, sweaty workout tee.

I let myself back into the room, wincing at the loud mechanical whirr of the lock.

Tessa, already dressed in her black pantsuit, stood in front of the full-length mirror, fastening her earrings. "Morning."

"Good morning," I said cautiously.

"Better hurry. We're supposed to meet Dr. Deng in twenty, and it's a ten-minute walk."

I let out a long breath. Good. We weren't going to talk about last night. "I'll get dressed. Five minutes." I turned to the closet.

"Hey," she said. When I turned around, her reflection grinned at me. "Can you see the dent your dick left in my butt cheek?" She lifted the bottom of her jacket.

My face burned. "I'm really sorry. I don't know what—"

She chuckled. "I'm kidding. Don't worry about it. Get ready. I need you to wow an oncologist."

Despite the smoldering humiliation in my chest, I did my best to impress Dr. Deng. And fortunately, Tessa didn't show up to my second talk, so I could focus on what I was telling the audience. In fact, I didn't see her again that day. And when I returned to the room, her things were gone, even the long strand of red hair coiled in the sink.

20

___

WHAT IS REAL?

From Barry Wright's manifesto:
We live in an advanced virtual reality simulation. There is no objective reality.

TESSA

When I looked up from the scientific article I'd been distracting myself with, the sun speared through my office blinds right into my retinas. Shielding my eyes, I glanced at the mostly empty parking lot. I dropped my head into my hands. Dammit. I was being a coward.

I owed Dr. Perrell a write-up of the conversations I'd had at the conference, but because the breakfast with Dr. Deng had gotten technical, I needed Oliver to review what I'd written.

Sure, I could've emailed it to him. But that would've been even more cowardly. I'd wanted to hold my head up high as I handed him a printout to mark up. Show him that his no—multiple nos—hadn't hurt me. (So what if that was a lie?)

However, I'd procrastinated so long that he was certainly gone for the day.

I stood and stretched, my back creaking from sitting too long. Methodically, I packed my laptop and a couple of scientific journals for reading that night into my satchel. I slipped on my coat and walked down the silent hall to Oliver's office. It was empty, and the light was off. If he wasn't in the lab, I'd come back and drop it on his desk. That way, he'd know I'd been brave enough to try to see him.

The lights were still on in the lab. Someone was still working. Clutching my report, I scanned each cabinet, bench, and computer workstation, but no one was there. Had the last person left so recently that the lights hadn't yet automatically turned off?

"Hello?" I called.

A clunk and a muttered "Damn" answered me. I followed the sound to the supply closet. There was no mistaking the crisp lab coat that stretched across those broad shoulders.

"Hi." I gripped the report so tightly I knew I'd leave a sweaty handprint on it.

Oliver turned, holding a box of specimen stubs in front of his chest. "Hey. I didn't know you were in the office today. You missed the lab meeting this morning."

I rolled my shoulders back. "I was working on my report from the conference. I'd like you to review the section on our breakfast with Dr. Deng. I wasn't sure I captured the nuances of the scientific discussion correctly."

"Okay." He took the report from me. I winced at the smeared ink from my sweaty palm, but he didn't look at it. "Do you have a few minutes to talk?"

"I guess we should. Do you want to do it tomorrow when West can join us?"

"West?" He swayed backward. "Why do we need him?"

"If you're going to lodge a formal sexual harassment complaint, we should have someone from HR."

"Oh my god. No. I only want to talk. To you."

I willed my shoulders to retreat from under my ears. Although Oliver wasn't going to have me written up, he surely wanted to talk about something I definitely didn't want to hash through, like feelings.

He set the box on the floor. It was the only clear surface in the storage closet. "Look, I gave you some very mixed messages on Tuesday night, and I'm sorry," he said. "I—"

"Fuck you," I snapped. "I'm forty-three years old, not some fresh-out-of-college grad who gets confused by 'mixed messages.' I came on to you, you didn't want it, and I apologize for my mistake."

He shook his head. His too-long hair, hair I'd buried my fingers in when I kissed him, flopped across his forehead. "I did want you. I still do. But I want more than a one-night stand."

More wrung out my lungs like a dishrag. I struggled to catch my breath. "That's a terrible idea."

"Is it?" Behind his glasses, his blue eyes sharpened. "You're attracted to me. I'm captivated by you. We're both adults, mature enough to know what we want. I want to get to know you better. I want to know what's inside there." He pointed to my chest, where my rusty heart shuddered.

"What if…" I swallowed. "What if you don't like it?"

"What's not to like?" he asked, like it wasn't a rhetorical question, like he really wanted to know.

"Okay." I leaned against the doorframe. "You asked for it." I'd never told this story to anyone. So many people had witnessed it firsthand. I searched for where to begin.

"Back when I had my company—"

"Red Rover," he said.

"Yes. I met a guy, Harry. He was a hotshot entrepreneur who'd just sold his startup. It was a B-to-B business you've never heard of, but it was good money, and he was looking to roll it into his next opportunity. He gave me some advice I thought was valuable. He was British, a few years older than me, and very attractive. I liked him a lot. So I slept with him. And instead of leaving the next morning, he stayed and gave me more advice.

"I thought he liked me, too. Eventually, he invested in Red Rover, and I hired him as my COO. We were partners romantically and at work. He asked me to move in with him, and I did. I trusted him." My skin was so transparent I knew the burning humiliation showed on it. But I kept going.

"The company was on fire. I was on top of the world. Well, most of the time. I have a chronic condition." I closed my eyes. Shit, I'd gone this far, might as well reveal the rest. "Endometriosis." I hadn't had the diagnosis back in my Red Rover days, and Harry had dismissed it as me being dramatic about PMS until he'd been able to turn it to his benefit. I checked Oliver's face for a reaction.

His eyes widened, and I saw the pieces click into place.

"Before and during my period, the fatigue was almost debilitating. It was why I'd started the delivery business to begin with. So I, and other people, people with chronic conditions or disabilities, could get what we needed without an exhausting trip to the store. So we didn't have to cook if we weren't able. Turned out, it appealed to a lot of people. Our valuation went through the roof.

"Harry suggested selling while the company was at its peak. We'd all seen what happened when the dot-com bubble burst. So I..." I stared at the box on the floor. "When he came to me with a buyer, I was flat on my back with a worse-than-usual flare-up. He said we had to move fast or we'd miss the opportunity. He said I could take it easy and stop working so hard. And I...I was exhausted. I agreed."

I had to pause until I got my trembling lip under control. Finally, I looked up. His expression was neutral. At least he wasn't visibly judging me, not yet. "Harry assured me the buyer would take care of the employees, that nothing would change for them. I t-trusted him. I didn't do more than skim the contract before I signed away control. But he lied for his benefit and, he said, mine. It wasn't good for the employees. The buyer took away their benefits, their healthcare."

"You didn't know." It was nothing earth-shattering, but at least he'd finally said something.

I had to clear my throat. "I should have. I should've slowed things down and consulted an independent lawyer. I shouldn't have trusted him. Not with my company. And definitely not with my feelings." I felt my lip curl. Those feelings had made me weak. Vulnerable. Things I hadn't allowed myself to be for years. "He told me we should enjoy the payout together. Go to South Africa or Tuscany or fucking Antarctica. But I couldn't celebrate. Certainly not with him after I saw what we'd done."

"What'd you do instead?" he asked.

"I took the coward's way out. I quit. I moved into my own place, and I hid from the press, from everyone, waiting for people to forget. I set up a foundation to help the employees." I stared him in the eye. "It wasn't enough. I should've stayed and fought. But I didn't. That's what's wrong with me. That's what you won't like." I whispered the last part, and thank god I was leaning against the doorframe. It was the only thing keeping me upright.

He stepped closer and put a gentle hand on my sleeve. "You were young, and you got bad advice."

"I wasn't much younger than you are now." My words were tough, but I let his hand remain on me. It felt...nice.

"I had a better partner than you did. Better advisers. I was lucky." He stepped fully into my space.

His shoulder was so solid-looking and inviting. And after all that emotional vulnerability, I wanted to hide my face in it.

I'd told him how a workplace affair went terribly wrong. How it haunted me for a dozen years. I shouldn't let myself fall, not again.

He hadn't judged me for my massive mistake. He'd tried to rationalize what I'd done. And I was so tired of being alone, of never letting anyone in.

So I laid my cheek on his shoulder.

His other arm came around me, peeling me off the door-frame and offering me the kind of comfort I hadn't felt in a long time. I relaxed into his body and let my hands rest on his hips.

"I didn't know about all that," he said into my hair. "I thought…"

"You thought what everyone else did. That I didn't care."

"But you did care. You still do. The foundation. All your other charitable causes. And now you're doing something for people who are sick, to prevent their suffering." He stroked my back, and I melted into him.

I turned up my face to meet his gaze. "I'm no hero, you know. I'll always be trying to make up for what I didn't do back then."

"That's all any of us can do. We do our best today." He kissed my forehead, his lips lingering there until I felt my facial muscles relax.

"You're an apologist," I muttered.

"I'm a fucking supporter," he said, moving his lips to my temple. "Haven't you ever had one of those before?"

"Sure. My mom. My girlfriends, when I let them. But never a guy."

"Let me be that guy, Tessa."

I was tempted by the way he held me, protective and giving at the same time. He'd heard the worst of me and was unshaken. Maybe I could trust him to do the right thing, let myself go with him.

"Wait." I pulled back a fraction. "What are your thoughts on universal healthcare?"

"What's not to love about universal healthcare? I want everyone to have access to the tests and treatments we develop here. I don't mind working through some red tape to get it to them."

"My god, you're perfect," I murmured. I tipped up my face until only an inch of air separated our lips. "Kiss me."

His lips crashed onto mine, his regular caution gone. This was nothing like our exploratory kiss in the hotel. His evening stubble rasped across my skin while his tongue invaded me, silky-soft but insistent.

I took it all and gave it right back. I raked his scalp with my short fingernails, tugging at the roots of his hair as I took my turn and tasted him. One of his hands left my back for a moment, then I heard the click of the door a moment before he pressed me against it.

"There's no one else in the building," I murmured, smiling against his lips.

"The cleaning staff could come in. Better safe than sorry." He nipped my earlobe.

"God. Why is that so hot?" I slid my hand down the buttons of his lab coat and cupped the bulge at the front of his trousers.

Hissing, he grabbed my hand and pinned it to the supply closet door. His hand trembled like my pulse.

"Are we really doing this?" His breath gusted against my ear.

"Will you regret it if we do?"

He stared into my eyes so long I thought he'd say yes. He'd pull away, yank open the door, and run the way he had at the hotel in Vegas.

Instead, he dropped to his knees.

21

ANALYTE

Analyte: *The substance a test measures.*

OLIVER

*R*egret was the farthest thing from my mind as I touched the hem of her black skirt. Everything had taken a backseat to lust. From my knees, I gazed up at her face. "Can I push this up?"

"Here." She worked something behind her back, and a second later, her skirt shushed to the floor.

Her underwear were black too, high-waisted with tall openings at the legs that revealed the flare of her hips. I ran my hands over the soft skin there and curled my fingers over the waistband. "Can I?"

She rubbed her thighs together. "Please, Oliver."

I tugged them down and worked them off over her ankle boots. Then I looked up. Her pussy glistened, darkly pink and plump. My dick throbbed against my pants, painfully constrained in my squatting position. I rose to my knees to adjust it. Then I ran my hands up the insides of her thighs. Finally, I swiped a finger along her lips.

She groaned and thrust out her hips, which I took as enough encouragement to keep going. I smeared her wetness everywhere, then tasted it from my thumb. She was salty and sweet, and I couldn't wait another minute. I spread her with my thumbs and dove in, tongue first.

After a couple of exploratory swipes with my tongue, she gripped my hair. "Don't move. I-I mean, move your mouth *right there.*"

I'd always been an excellent student, so I followed her instructions, running the tip of my tongue along the inside of her right lip, then her left. I made figure eights, not going any deeper or leaving the spot that turned her on. Meanwhile, I reveled in her scent, in her softness, in the knowledge that I was the one making her thighs tremble.

She tugged at the roots of my hair, and I'd never been so glad I'd forgotten to get my hair cut (again) last week. The pain tingled down my spine, lighting up every nerve. The friction of my pants against my dick intensified, and pleasure coiled in my belly.

I hummed and brushed my nose against her clit. When she stiffened and made a choking sound, I glanced up to check that she was okay.

"Don't...stop," she groaned.

I went back to work, focusing again on her lips with an occasional swipe of my tongue on that sensitive nub. The third time I swiped, she shuddered and her fingernails scraped my scalp. The sound she made was a high-pitched, stuttering grunt that trailed off into a sigh as the tension left her body and she sagged against the door.

"God. Damn," she muttered, releasing her grip on my hair.

I licked her one last time, then kissed her still-stiff clit good-bye. I hoped I'd see it again soon.

But now I needed to attend to my needs before I came in my pants. I unzipped them and pushed down my boxer briefs. My chin was still wet from Tessa, so I swiped my hand over my face before I took myself in hand. The lubrication was exactly what I needed to finish the job. I groaned as I caught my release in my other hand.

"Wow," she said. "You were that close from eating me out?"

My cheeks burned. It felt cheap when she said it like that. "Yeah." I looked around for something to clean up with. I found a package of disposable microfiber cloths and wiped my hands and groin. My glasses were cloudy, and I breathed on them before I wiped them on the edge of the cloth.

Before I tugged up my shorts, I glanced at her. She hadn't moved from her resting spot against the door. Staring at my softening dick, she licked her lips. Maybe she hadn't meant that little jab. Maybe it wasn't so bad that I'd made her come in the lab supply closet. Maybe it was the teaser she needed to want more.

I refastened my pants, then grabbed another cloth. "Can I clean you up? These are pretty soft."

She held out her hand. "I'll do it."

With a few businesslike swipes, she wiped down her inner thighs. She pulled up her underwear and refastened her skirt. She tossed the cloth into the trash and put her hand on the knob. But she didn't turn it. She leaned back against the door and stared me in the eye.

"Out of our systems," she said, dipping her chin.

Everything warm and bubbly inside me chilled like I'd plunged into a liquid nitrogen bath. That's what this was? Her brilliant idea about one-and-done, like I could rid myself of my feelings as easily as I'd released my semen? Maybe that's what it had been for her, but our minutes here in the supply closet had only given me a hunger for more.

I knew better than to argue with her after what she'd said at the hotel. So I said what she wanted. "Right."

"Completely gone."

"Uh huh." She wanted the lie.

"Okay. We won't do this again. And there's no need to involve West."

I wanted something worthy of a conversation with West. If Tessa felt the way I did, I'd tell the whole company, the whole world, that she cared about me.

But she didn't. She made that clear when she turned the handle and stalked out.

22

DEN = ILLUMINATI HQ

From Barry Wright's manifesto:
*Under the Denver International Airport are miles of tunnels and lairs,
which serve as the headquarters of the Illuminati.*

TESSA

"That's great news." I grinned at Sadie. "We should start on it right away. Oliver," I called down the row to where he was talking with Yujun, past the sign that read, *38 days.*

Oliver looked up and flashed me the kind of smile that made my knees wobble. The kind that made me want to take back what I'd said Monday in the supply closet, about everything being out of our systems. The kind that made me want to push him back in there and try again. I had to tell him to stop looking at me like that because surely someone would notice that wolfish grin and wonder if something was going on.

Nothing was going on.

Or so I kept telling myself.

He sauntered closer to us. "What do you need, Tessa?"

The way he'd phrased it was pure evil. My cheeks burned. I sucked in cool air through my nostrils, but that only brought his evergreen scent into my nose, sharp and comforting as a fresh-cut Christmas tree. "Sadie and the team think they have a hypothesis for the endometriosis test." I nodded at her.

While Sadie told Oliver how the team had collaborated to develop a hypothesis based on the research they'd done and then successfully tested it in the computer model, I tried to breathe through my mouth without looking like a fool.

Fortunately, Oliver's expression turned serious as he nodded in response to Sadie's update. "That's fantastic. We'll queue it up for clinical trials after the cancer test."

"What? We shouldn't wait on this," I protested. "We should get it into trials as soon as possible."

"That's what I said." Oliver leaned against the desk. "Right after the cancer test trials."

"Haven't you ever heard of running jobs in parallel?" I said. "We should do them both at the same time."

He rubbed his forehead. "No, Tessa, we..." He looked up. "We shouldn't argue about this here. Come to my office?"

His question rose only slightly at the end, making it sound more like an order than a request. But he was right. We should present a united front to the team when we told them we'd be running the tests simultaneously since it would be extra work for them.

"Okay. Sadie, please draw up the plan for the trial and get the rest of the team to review it." I stared at Oliver's stony face, daring him to contradict my request. He said nothing as he whirled and marched toward the exit.

I followed him down the hall to his office. He ushered me in and shut the door.

I glanced at his desk. His very clean desk, where I could easily sprawl while he ate me out again...

No. It was gross to hook up in my colleague's office during *work hours.* Un-fucking-fortunately. I shook the image out of my brain. Despite his fuck-me expression earlier, Oliver wasn't the type. Neither, I reminded myself, was I.

He seated himself behind his desk, so I perched demurely on his guest chair and took the offensive. Professionally.

"Simultaneous trials are the way to go. So if one fails, we have another product to take to market." After I'd gotten Sadie's email that she had good news to share this morning, I'd spent most of the night planning how I'd state my case. Hell, I'd been planning it since the team and I came up with the idea for the test. Hope wasn't scientific, but it had served me well as I'd started Red Rover. I'd decided the best way to get what I wanted was to appeal to Oliver's risk aversion.

He shook his head, and a lock of hair flopped onto the left lens of his glasses. He didn't bother to brush it away. "Simultaneous trials will put an undue amount of strain on the lab's resources. We must consider our employees when we make these decisions. Our priority is the cancer test since that's what our marketing department has been preparing for."

His arguments were all solid. But waiting months for the cancer test to be done meant thousands of women with endometriosis would suffer because of our delay. "It's a risk we can manage. We'll offer the team an additional week of vacation after this push. Cater dinner and provide transportation for anyone who has to work late. Nothing great is produced without risk."

"Nothing great, huh?"

"I read it on a motivational poster," I mumbled.

"But do you believe it?" He finally flicked the errant lock of hair out of his eyes, and he hit me with a calculating stare, one I remembered from game night at Carly's. Was Oliver Bond about to take a risk *at work?*

I lifted my chin. "Sure, I do. I invested all my college savings into Red Rover and took out a loan to pay my tuition."

He nodded. "Then I'd like to offer an exchange of risks. I'll agree to take both tests to clinical trials—"

"Simultaneously?" I interrupted him.

"Yes, assuming they're both ready. In exchange, I want you to give me a chance."

"A chance?" I thought I knew what he was asking, but I wanted him to say it.

"Give *us* a chance."

"You want sex in exchange for crashing the schedule." It wouldn't be the first time a man had offered to fast-track something for my business in exchange for sexual favors. But Oliver didn't seem slimy like that.

"No. No!" He leaned forward over his desk. "Give me a chance to woo you."

"*Woo* me? Are you secretly ninety inside that hot body?"

"I'm being serious. I want a shot." He swallowed, and I watched the bob of his throat. I wanted to lick it. "Sex is off the table."

"Off the table?" I repeated. "Then what's the point?"

"The point is for us to explore *emotional* intimacy. Like when you told me about Harry."

I'd told him about Harry right before he'd gone down on me. This was the most bizarre power exchange I'd ever negotiated. "So what will giving you this shot you want entail?"

He thought for a moment. "Dinner. We both have to eat."

"I avoid restaurants. People still recognize me sometimes." I flicked my red hair, which I'd refused to change despite the negative attention it brought me. "Some of them aren't too nice. You don't want that kind of attention. Not when this product launch is so critical."

"We'll have dinner at my place," he said. "Low-key."

"Like a Netflix-and-chill situation?"

The corner of his mouth lifted. "Sure. But no sex."

"I still don't get it. Is this some kind of bizarre millennial dating ritual?"

"I'm pretty sure you're a millennial too." He crossed his arms.

"I'm right on the dividing line with Gen X. I play both sides. But I still don't get it."

"I want to get to know you. Let you get to know me. Figure out if there's a spark."

"I think we both know there's a spark after the supply closet."

"Something sustainable," he amended.

"Like, you want the whole damn forest fire."

"I do."

Unfortunately, I knew how forest fires went. Harry had torched my personal and professional lives and left nothing alive, not even a seedling. My heart was scorched and barren, unable to support the spark Oliver wanted. He'd see.

"Fine. Dinner is your shot. Regardless of how it goes, we run both trials as soon as they're ready. No delays."

"Agreed." He stuck out his hand.

His hand was dry and warm when I shook it. His long fingers brushed the inside of my wrist. A shiver traveled from my hand all the way to my blackened heart, which gave a throb.

Nope, that wasn't a spark. That was me being touch-starved. When I got home, I'd ask Savannah to give me a hug. I'd snuggle with my cats. Then I'd be fortified for the next time he caressed my skin in a not-at-all sexual way.

"Deal," I said.

23
———

FLOW CYTOMETRY

Flow cytometry: A technique in which lasers are used to analyze the physical and chemical properties of cells.

OLIVER

A couple nights after we made our deal, I felt like crowing when I welcomed Tessa Wright into my kitchen. She was willing to give me a chance. She wouldn't admit it, but our hookup in the supply closet had to mean something to her, or she'd never have come, not even to advance her project. After she told me the real story of Red Rover, I knew she had integrity.

Integrity was sexy.

"This is, um, nice," she said. She nodded at the big windows that would have given us a view of the live oaks that surrounded the house if it weren't dark outside. My house wasn't the biggest or most luxurious in Los Altos Hills, but its wooded property reminded me of growing up in the Northeast. "You don't have a gate. You never have trouble with trespassers?"

"Sometimes there's a stray hiker or two who wander off the trail. More often, it's foxes or bobcats. An occasional coyote."

"Hm." She tore her eyes away from the windows. "Smells good."

"Thanks. Everything's ready. You can wash up in the bathroom around the corner there while I plate it up. Is sauvignon blanc okay?"

"Sure. Only one glass, though, since I'm driving."

"Of course." No matter how much I wanted her to stay, I'd be telling her goodnight before midnight. I'd vowed to slow things down and build our relationship on a rock-solid foundation.

That didn't mean I didn't watch her glorious ass and her swaying red mane as she turned and walked down the hall. But when she closed the door, I took a deep breath to reset my brain and got back to work.

Between the two of us, Simon had always been the foodie. Still, I knew my way around a kitchen. When I asked her about food sensitivities, Tessa said she avoided dairy and red meat, so I roasted fingerling potatoes and broccoli and grilled some chicken breasts, which I topped with mango salsa.

She was back in a couple of minutes, and I set our plates on the granite island, figuring it would be more intimate than the dining room.

She stared at the plate. "You made this?"

I glanced at the dirty pans in the sink. "Yeah? Do you not like it?"

"No. It looks delicious. I've never met someone who enjoys cooking. Besides my friend Savannah, who's...yeah."

"Why don't you like cooking?" I asked.

She picked up her fork and stabbed a potato. "I guess it reminds me of home. How things used to be before my mom died."

I stilled, like if I didn't move, she'd forget I was there and keep talking.

"When I'm in the kitchen, I think of her. How our lives could've been." She wrinkled her nose. "Tell you what I'll never do again: cook over a campfire. I did way too much of that as a teenager after she...after." She bit into the potato and chewed, then she hummed. "Great potatoes."

"I got them at the farmer's market last weekend."

"Savannah loves the farmer's market! You two should meet. You'd love each other." She took a bite of chicken.

I sipped my water. "I'd love to meet your friends. And your father, under better circumstances."

"Oh, he's gone back to"—she waved her hand in a circle—"wherever."

"Wherever? You don't know where he lives?"

"He prefers it that way. Off the grid. No one, not even me, knows where he lives. He doesn't want to be monitored." She shrugged. "It's actually kind of impressive that he visits me. There are dozens of security cameras on my street."

I hadn't so much as picked up my fork. This was more interesting than food. "Because of his protesting...work?" Was that how he saw it?

"Mostly because of the conspiracies. You know, like 5G wireless is used to spy on people or the government will round up people like him who know the truth, etcetera."

"Ah. And you don't believe those things? No judgment." I believed most of the same things my parents did, especially when I was as young as she'd been when she lost her mother.

"Which one? That vaccines have chips in them and doctors are making us sick? I mean, I understand why he believes the conspiracies. It was horrible watching my mother die, and it's comforting to blame someone rather than the inherent unfairness of life. But no, I did research and found enough evidence that I didn't believe the same things. You know, this chicken is really good. You should try it."

"Talking with you is much more interesting." I leaned an elbow on the counter.

She looked down, letting her hair conceal her pink cheeks. "You're creeping me out. Eat."

I did, and we talked about mundane things, like work and my house, while we finished dinner and then cleaned up the kitchen. I refilled my glass of club soda and carried her half-full wineglass to the couch. She nestled into the corner, and I sat a cozy distance away on the adjacent cushion.

She sipped her wine. "Thanks for having me over. Dinner was delicious."

My heart skipped. "You're not leaving yet, are you?"

"Shouldn't I?" She fluttered her eyelashes. "Before we do something we have to tell West about?"

I leaned back against the cushion. "I'd like to tell West about us."

"*Us?*" She flicked her hand between the two of us. "This was just dinner, according to our deal."

"Our deal was that you'd give me a chance. Which means an emotional connection." I swallowed. "*I* feel an emotional connection."

"What if I don't?" She squared her jaw.

I lifted the shoulder that wasn't sunk into the couch. "It doesn't change how I feel. And how I feel could affect how we work together."

"Not yet."

"Not...yet?"

"Don't say anything yet. Please. I... When Harry and I were together, everyone knew. I tried to be discreet, but—and I only figured this out later—he knew if everyone was aware we were sleeping together, that'd give him more power. And I guess it did. Anyway, I…" She swallowed. "I don't want to be like Harry."

From the strain in her voice, the pained expression on her face, I knew how hard it was for her to say his name. So, as gently as possible, I said, "Not that I'd ever want to hurt you, but it's safer to tell West. In case things don't work out, you'd be protected. But I'll wait until you're ready."

"Thank you. Safety is a big thing for you." It wasn't a question.

"My dad's in insurance." I shrugged, like it explained everything. "He's all about managing risk. Nonslip rugs. Fire ladders in the upstairs bedrooms. Every time it snowed when I was a teenager, he'd take me to a parking lot to practice handling spinouts. I guess I internalized it.

"Which is why it shocked everyone when Simon and I started the company. It was the riskiest thing I could've done. But Simon was so confident, so persuasive, he convinced me it was a risk worth taking."

"He was right," she said. "You built something great."

"We did. But when he…" I almost stopped there, to let her intuit the end of that sentence. But she'd been open about her dad, so I could be vulnerable too. "I knew his partying was out of control. I talked to him about it, but it pissed him off. So I stopped saying anything. I wish I hadn't. I wish I'd nagged him nonstop. Then maybe he wouldn't have gone to that last rave. Maybe he wouldn't have gotten so drunk he stepped off the curb into traffic."

"My god." She set her hand on my arm. "I'm so sorry."

"Me too." My arm warmed under her touch.

"And that's why you don't drink?" She dipped her chin at my sparkling water.

"Yes."

She narrowed her eyes. "You're not responsible for his actions, any more than I'm responsible for my dad's."

"I know. Intellectually, I know."

Her smile was tight. "He'd be proud of you for the work you're doing."

"I know that too. Still, I miss him."

She rubbed my arm, and I put my hand over hers. I stared deep into her eyes. They were the color of a salt pond, deep and clear. I could see straight through them to the kindness she tried to conceal underneath her scientific exterior. I could love this woman.

Like she read the thought on my face, she slipped her hand from under mine and stood. "I should go."

I rose too. We were close enough that I could've counted the freckles scattered across her nose and cheeks. For a second, I considered closing the distance to kiss her again. To give her what her wide pupils said she wanted.

She wanted what was easy. Something we didn't have to make public, a fling she could walk away from. But I was starting to think I'd never walk away from Tessa Wright.

So I stepped back, away from the temptation of the freckles I wanted to count everywhere. "Can we do this again?"

One side of her mouth turned up. "Okay, I'll let you cook for me again."

If that was what she could give, I'd take it.

24

MESSAGES IN THE CORN

From Barry Wright's manifesto:
Crop circles are messages from extraterrestrials.

TESSA

When I pushed the cart into Oliver's lab on a Friday in late February, I could feel the difference in the vibe. Even a couple days ago, people had bent over microscopes, furrowing their brows, pausing only to scribble a note on their lab tablets. The space had felt tense. Of course it had. Everyone knew the stakes. But today, people leaned against the tables, their goggles pushed up on their heads or folded neatly into pockets, smiling and patting each other on the back. Someone had ripped down the poster, which read, *9 days*. We didn't need it anymore. There was joy even in my jaded, dusty heart.

"Tessa!" Sadie scurried to my side, her lab coat flapping open in a way Oliver wouldn't have approved. "It's the lab techs' job to bring in and put away the supplies."

"Not these supplies." I untucked the flaps of the beaker carton to reveal my prize.

"Champagne?" she squealed.

"We all earned it by getting both tests into clinical trials nine days early." I pulled a sleeve of clear plastic cups from the box. "Let's get this party started."

As the team popped the corks and poured the bubbly, I held back a smile. How long would it take Oliver to realize what was going on and try to spoil the fun? It served him right after the sexual frustration he'd put me through over the past three weeks. Dinners at his place with his sleeves rolled up to reveal his sexy forearms, watching the action movies we discovered we both loved while I cuddled up to his side on his sofa, his arm around me and his warm, solid body full of promise.

And not a single kiss.

I imagined his face when he found us drinking in his lab, puzzled with that little line between his eyebrows. Then his lips would turn down, and his forehead would furrow. That adorable long piece of hair would flop down over it and then he'd growl my name in the tone that made me shiver.

Shiver? I stood straighter. I was a grown woman. I didn't *shiver*. Not for any man—or woman—and certainly not for Oliver, who was my goddamn coworker. Because I knew how it would turn out. Humiliation, heartbreak, and all the work I'd done here wasted.

Though, would it really be wasted? We'd sent the ovarian cancer test to clinical trials this morning. Maybe someone else's mother could get a diagnosis before it was too late. She'd recover and go back to her job as a teacher or an architect or an ambassador. Some other daughter, some other husband, wouldn't lose their mother and wife and be irreparably broken.

More selfishly, I was proud that we were on track to send the endometriosis test to clinical trials next week. If it did well in the trial, as I was certain it would, I'd have made a difference to all the people out there who could get diagnosed and treated. Who could get relief. And I didn't need credit or recognition for that. I'd know in my heart what I'd contributed to people like me.

But right now, I wanted to be called out for bringing a case of champagne into the lab, where food and drink were forbidden. For starting a dance party. I'd take the blame for it even though it wasn't my speaker that was blasting out hip-hop. I blinked away from Yujun, who was doing the Running Man.

Where the fuck was Oliver?

I tapped Aanya's shoulder and leaned in close to whisper, "Where's Oliver?"

She shrugged. "Haven't seen him all afternoon. But he should be here! Want me to find him?"

"No. Stay and enjoy yourself." I handed her my untouched cup of champagne. "I'll find him."

In the hall outside the lab, the beat of the music thudded through the floor. Fortunately, Dr. Perrell's office was at the far end, where I hoped she wouldn't hear it. With her twins' weddings looming, she'd been more joyless than usual.

I jogged downstairs toward the game room and winced when I heard the tinny electronic music of *Pac-Man.* Oliver should've been celebrating with the team, not communing with Simon's spirit. Simon had nothing to do with this victory. This was Oliver's win, and mine, and the team's.

As I approached the game room, I checked the burning feeling in my stomach. Although my period wasn't due for a few weeks, it didn't feel like that. It felt emotional. It couldn't be jealousy, could it? I couldn't possibly be jealous of a dead man.

As soon as I turned the corner and saw West's back hunched over the console, not Oliver's, the heaviness lifted. Goddammit, I *was* jealous of a dead man.

I'd have to process that later. "Hey, West," I called.

Immediately, he turned. "Tessa! Did you want to play? I suck at this, so my game should be over in—" The unmistakable pulsing, falling tones of Pac-Man's death interrupted him. "I guess it's your turn now." He plucked a token out of the bucket and held it out to me.

"Actually, I'm looking for..." Nope.

I would not admit I was looking for Oliver. I'd made him promise not to say anything about us to West, and I wasn't about to blow our cover. I'd never let West know that although we were professionals in the lab, there was a Tessa-shaped indentation on Oliver's couch. Or that we talked for a few minutes every night before bed. Or that he texted me a silly photo or meme each morning. This morning he'd sent me a picture of an adorable orange kitten glaring at the camera. He didn't even know I had cats, but he said that one reminded him of me. My phone and that photo weighed in the pocket of my black blazer like incriminating evidence of my feelings.

"Oliver?" he prompted. His expression was neutral, not the knowing smirk I dreaded.

"Yes." Heat spread from my cheeks, down my neck, and into my chest. My blazer was suddenly suffocatingly hot. Was this shame or one of the perimenopausal hot flashes Savannah and Carly were always talking about?

"Haven't seen him. Have you checked his office?"

"No. I'll try there. Thanks."

"Oh, and Tessa?"

I'd already turned to leave, but I stopped, steeled myself, and turned back.

"I'm glad you're settling in at Discovery. You seem happy here."

"I am. I'm excited to come to the office every day. We do good work."

"That's excellent news," he said. "You should love your work. You deserve happiness."

"I...deserve it?" I echoed. How did he not know what I'd done? How I'd betrayed my employees the last time I'd fallen for someone? It wasn't exactly public knowledge that I'd been sleeping with my number-two at Red Rover, but practically everyone we worked with knew or suspected. It was why I'd turned down every partnership and board position any man had offered me since. I couldn't shake the fear that it came with expectations. Or that people would assume it did.

"Of course you do." He shrugged. "Everyone should seek out what makes them happy."

He'd said it so matter-of-factly, like it was one of my friend Lucie's truths. But as I climbed the stairs toward Oliver's office, I wondered. Did Oliver make me happy? Was that the feeling in my stomach when my phone buzzed every morning? Was that why I'd let Carly paint my nails in a light pink instead of the black polish I always chose? Was I...happy?

When I was in my twenties, I was excited. Striving. Energetic. I supposed I was happy. I'd never paused to examine my feelings.

In my thirties, I was broken. Sad. Repentant. I definitely wasn't happy. If I was being honest, I was lonely.

Now, in my forties, I was trying to let go of the past and live in the moment. It was why I'd gone to that terrible seminar. I thought if I could find my power, I could make something of my life again. And even though the seminar was garbage, I'd met Carly, Lucie, and Savannah. They'd inspired me with their strength and hope. Maybe that seminar wasn't the magic bullet I'd wanted, but it had set me on the road to a brighter future.

Still, happiness wasn't anything I'd ever imagined for myself. I didn't deserve it after the mistakes I'd made in my youth.

I paused in front of Oliver's door. Could I have been wrong about that too?

I didn't have the answer when I knocked.

"Yeah?" It was only one word, but after four months of working together, I could picture his expression when he said it. His voice was brusque, like he'd been thinking deeply about something but was too polite to ignore an interruption. He'd be running his hands through his hair until whatever product he used was gone, and it flopped over the rims of his glasses.

I turned the handle and walked in. The overhead light flicked on. He'd been sitting so still at his desk that the automatic light sensor assumed it was vacant.

When he tore his gaze from the screen, he didn't smile. He pinched his lower lip between his thumb and his fist, and the line between his eyebrows had deepened into a ravine.

"My god, what's wrong?" I stepped into the office and shut the door. Had someone died?

"Now that we've gone to clinical trials, we're going to have data coming back in a few weeks. I can't decide how to analyze it." He frowned at his screen. "Should we use LDA or logistic regression?"

My shoulders dropped away from my neck. Classic Oliver. My college statistics course was a long time ago, and I'd had to deep-dive into statistical methods for this job. "Well, the benefit of linear discriminant analysis is that it's simple and efficient. But logistic regression could be more appropriate, assuming our data doesn't follow a normal distribution."

"I know," he said. "So how do I decide what's best?"

His uncertainty wasn't because he was unintelligent or young or even indecisive. He proved in the lab every day how brilliant he was. And despite being ten years younger than me, he'd grown this company from a couple of college kids at a lab table to a billion-dollar company. That required emotional maturity. No, it was because Oliver cared so much about his company and everyone who worked here that he didn't want to take even the tiniest risk of letting them down.

I got it, I really did. But I also understood that success requires risk. Though in this case, there wasn't much. Either model would work to evaluate the test results. Maybe one would be slightly more predictive than the other, but we wouldn't know until the product was out in the market and we had a larger data set. I circled his desk until I stood behind him. Then I reached over his shoulder and turned off his monitor. I set my hands lightly on his shoulders. "Is this okay?"

"Yeah."

As I kneaded his muscles, the tension in his shoulders eased. When they'd softened from apocalypse-tense to everyday-tense, I said, "Got a coin?"

"A what?" His voice was low, almost dreamy.

"A quarter. You know, we used to use them in vending machines and arcade games before everything went cashless."

"Maybe?" He opened his top drawer and fished in the corner. He pulled out a quarter and blew lint from it before holding it up. "This is what you charge for a shoulder massage?"

"No. This is how you make a decision between two equally good—or bad—options. Flip it. Heads, LDA. Tails, logistic regression."

His shoulders tensed, and I lost every bit of progress I'd made in softening the muscles. He leaned forward to peer back at me. "We can't flip a coin! This is a decision I have to make as the lead scientist."

"You are making the decision," I reminded him. "You're just using a tool to help." I tapped the coin sticking out of his white-knuckled fist. "Aren't the models equally good?"

"Yes, but—"

"Then it doesn't matter. Go on." I nudged his fist.

He opened his hand until the quarter lay flat on his palm. Then he picked it up. "Heads, LDA, tails, logistic regression?"

"That's it."

He flipped the coin, caught it deftly in his right hand, and plopped it onto the back of his left. When he pulled back his right hand, he said, "Tails. Logistic regression."

"Does that feel right to you?" I asked. "Can you accept it?"

"Yes. It's a valid model."

"Then logistic regression it is. Done." I pushed back the hair that flopped over his glasses. "You should go down to the lab and celebrate. Someone brought in champagne."

He snorted. "*You* brought in champagne."

"I'll neither confirm nor deny it," I said, starting to step back.

He grasped my wrist, stopping me. "Thank you."

"For the champagne? Like I said, I—"

"No." He was up out of his chair faster than I'd have thought possible, still holding my wrist and crowding into me. My hand landed over his pounding heart. "Thank you for being my...my partner in all this. For helping me. For grounding me when I get too deep in my head."

"That's what I was hired to do," I reminded him. But I knew I'd done more than what was in my job description. And here I was, edging over the line of what was appropriate for my job as I tipped up my face to stare at his lips. He'd bitten them while he'd been mulling his options, and they were pink and plump.

"That's not what this is," he growled. "This is more." He angled his face down until his lips hovered a breath above mine.

He was right. We were more than coworkers. More than friends. And we were about to cross the border into the land of Even More. It shimmered in the air for a moment in the narrow space between our lips.

Then I leaned across the divide and kissed him.

I'd kissed him before, in Vegas and again in the supply

closet, when it had been a desperate attempt to smother the sexual tension that glowed like a Bunsen burner's flame whenever I was near him. But this was different. Gentle. Exploratory. Like we were mapping a new territory. His lips pressed against mine, firm but soft at the same time, moving like he was speaking lazily against my mouth. What was this kiss saying? *I want you. I need you. But let's take it slow.*

It wasn't enough for me. It was one thing to observe and another to act as a catalyst. I slid my hand up the side of his neck and tunneled my fingers into his hair. Then I pressed with my fingertips, pulling him closer into me.

He let out a quiet gasp, and I licked across his lips. His hands landed on my lower back and slipped lower to my ass, gathering me against him until I felt the press of his erection against my stomach.

Now we were getting somewhere.

I widened my stance, and as if he'd read my mind, he moved his thigh between my legs. I clenched his leg with mine until I had pressure right where I needed it.

Flinging my head back, I groaned at the pleasure that sizzled up my spine. He kissed along my neck, up to the tip of my chin, then across to my ear. His breath roared against it, making me shiver everywhere. I ground harder against his leg.

"You like that, huh?" He slid his hand inside my blazer and palmed my left breast over my shirt. As I pressed against his thigh, he scissored his fingers against my nipple, plucking it to a needy peak. It wasn't enough, not with two layers of fabric separating his fingers from my skin, and I let out a frustrated grunt.

"Fuck, Tessa," he whispered in my ear, "you think you can get there like this?"

"No," I whined. "Too...many...clothes."

"I think you're wrong." His words shocked me—I was *never* wrong, and certainly not about my own damned body—but what shocked me more was when he bit down on my earlobe. Simultaneously, he pinched my nipple hard enough that the sting radiated down my body and set off an earthquake between my legs. I let out a choking gasp.

"Let go, Tessa," he rumbled as he kissed the spot under my earlobe.

And I did. My breath stuttered as my control detonated. Everything narrowed to that spot where I met his thigh until elation exploded through my body. He held me up, murmuring words I didn't have the brain cells to understand into my skin. I sank into it, letting the climax ripple through me like raindrops into a pond.

When the waves stilled, I was in his arms, pressed against him from my thighs to my chest. He cradled my head against his shoulder, twining his fingers into my hair while his lips rested on my temple. I got the sense he'd been purring soft words the whole time, but I caught the phrase, *good girl.*

I was no one's good girl. I was a woman, ten years older than the man who'd rocked my world with his thigh and a goddamn kiss. But damn me if my blackened heart didn't give a silly flutter at his words.

I was sticky between my legs, so I dismounted his thigh, hoping my release hadn't soaked into his trousers. I brushed against his hard-on, and he hissed. I'd show him I wasn't a good girl. I set my hands on his belt and started to tug it free.

His hand landed on mine. "What are you doing?"

"Returning the favor." I tried to shake off his hand, but he kept it there, stilling me.

"This isn't that. Besides, we're not having sex in my office."

"Don't worry. I'll just blow you." I tugged the end of his belt out of the loops.

"A blowjob is still sex." He stepped back, out of reach.

"A handjob, then," I said.

"No."

I had to respect the line he'd drawn. But I didn't have to like it. "You got me off in your office."

"That's different."

"How?"

He ran his hand through his hair. His glasses had started to fog where they met his cheeks. "It just is."

"Fine. Good luck with that." I tipped my chin toward the bulge in his flat-front pants.

"I'll survive," he said through gritted teeth.

"Then let's go join the celebration in the lab. We'll see if there's any bubbly left." I tossed my head, hoping I didn't have sex hair.

"You go," he said. "I'll join you in a minute."

But it was more than discomfort about his erection that deepened the line between his eyebrows. He bit his lip and wouldn't meet my gaze. Oh, no.

"Are you worried about our bargain?" I asked. "I know you said no sex, but—"

"No. I'm fine."

"Then what's wrong?"

"Nothing." Finally, he glanced up at me and smiled, and I wished he hadn't. It was soft and...and...*sweet,* and it set off fluttery feelings in my midsection, which was still sensitive from the orgasm. "I'm good. Are you good?"

I had been, a minute ago. "Look, this doesn't have to change anything."

"Doesn't it?" Those blue eyes speared right through me, like they could see the oxytocin sloshing around in my brain.

"No. Just...just don't fall in love with me, okay?"

"I won't," he said.

I wasn't sure I believed him.

25

BIOINFORMATICS

Bioinformatics: *The use of computer science tools to analyze biological datasets.*

OLIVER

Hey, are you coming in today?

TESSA

No, working at home

Are you okay?

Not feeling great

I'm sorry. Anything I can do?

I already emailed Sadie, but please be sure she
sends me this week's endo trial results

Sure. But I meant, is there anything I can do to make you feel better? I make a mean chicken soup

I bet. No thank you

This isn't because of Friday night, is it?

Are you asking if I'm not coming into the office today because I'm sulking? You may have left me with the female equivalent of blue balls after that kiss at your place, but I am an adult, and I don't sulk

Kind of sounds like you're sulking…

If you must know, I'm having some pain with my period

...

...

...

I'm so sorry. Are you sure I can't come over? I'll bring you a heating pad

Thanks, but a heating pad won't cut it.
Painkillers are awesome. But not safe to drive.
Savannah is taking care of me

I'm glad you're letting someone take care of you.

Jealous you're missing this?

(The attached selfie shows Tessa with her hair piled in a bun on top of her head, wearing an old, frayed T-shirt with animal hair on it. She is wearing no makeup, and her pupils are dilated.)

I'm positively green

I don't know whether or not to take you seriously

I'm very serious. Can I come over?

I don't think that's a good idea

Okay, how about later this week?

I'm sure I'll be back in the office by Wednesday or Thursday. My symptoms usually subside in a few days

...

...

Okay. I'll wait. I hope you feel better soon.

~

I couldn't wait.

When she didn't show up in the office *three days later,* on Thursday, my anxiety went into overdrive. In her texts, she said she was fine, but I needed to see it myself.

I hoped it justified the lie I'd told. I'd asked the most junior person on West's team for Tessa's address, and her eyes had practically turned into heart shapes when I'd said I wanted to send my colleague flowers because she'd been sick.

It was the *sending* part I'd lied about.

But something wasn't right about the address I'd been given.

Clutching a bouquet of red and white roses wrapped in crinkly plastic, I stood in front of a small apartment building on the outskirts of San Jose. The two-story building was a nondescript, weathered gray, and the small lawn hadn't seen a mower in weeks. A cracked pot at the entrance held the remains of a plant that had given up a while ago. A sprawling, bushy tree screened half of the building from the road, and dense evergreens surrounded it at the rear. The back of my neck prickled. Anyone could've been hiding back there. A stalker. A murderous gang. An arsonist, though that might have done the owner a favor.

Tessa had owned a billion-dollar company. She couldn't live here. That human resources person had to have been bullshitting me. It served me right for showing up without an invitation.

I picked my way up the cracked sidewalk to the entrance, where a rusty bicycle leaned up against the front wall. There was a cobwebbed video doorbell, the old kind that was as big as my farsighted dad's mobile phone. This one had a small video screen mounted above it. Taking a deep breath, I pressed the button.

After a second, the video screen flared to life. A burly, bald white man squinted at the screen. "No soliciting!" he growled.

"I—I'm not selling anything," I said. "Does Tessa Wright live here?"

"Who?" He leaned closer until I could see the dark hair sprouting from his ear.

"Tessa. Wright." I enunciated each syllable.

"Never heard of 'em. Go away." The video glitched in the middle like it was a bad connection.

"Wait!" I said. "Are you sure?" Was *I* sure? Not at all, but this was the only address I had.

"Don't come back." The video screen went black.

What the actual fuck? I took a step back and stared up at the building. There were no signs of life in the upper windows, not even a twitching curtain.

If this were a roleplaying game, and I'd encountered a troll or a gatekeeping lackey, I'd have options. I could climb the building and try to open a window, I could scurry around the back to try to find another door, or I could take another swing at the gatekeeper.

I wasn't against a climb, but I figured a second go was the easiest way. I brushed the hair out of my face, took off my sunglasses, and forced a smile. I rang the bell again.

"No soliciting!" It was the scowling guy again.

It was odd that he'd said it in exactly the same way with the same squinty-eyed expression. "Are you an AI?" I wondered aloud.

"AI? Never heard of 'em. Go away, or I'll call the police." The words were slightly different, but the glitch in the middle was the same.

I shoved my glasses back on. She was an evil genius.

And I was going to get into her goddamned lair.

Not bothering to tell her robot doorman goodbye, I circled the building to the tree line. It was so dense that no light penetrated the barrier of palm-sized, waxy leaves. Taking a fortifying breath, I flicked on the flashlight on my phone and pushed in.

The trees were spaced far enough apart for me to pass, but the dense canopy blocked the sunlight. Leaves brushed against my arms and my face. It wasn't unpleasant—they were leathery with a spicy scent—but it was deep enough that I started to fear I'd chosen wrong, and there was nothing on the other side but more trees, or possibly an ogre. Until I bumped into a chain-link fence.

The black vinyl coating explained why I hadn't seen it. It was practically invisible in the gloom. But a fence meant there was something behind it to protect.

If it was Tessa, I also wanted to protect her.

"Moment of truth," I mumbled, pacing the fence. "This is where I go from being a concerned friend to being a stalker." She'd said it wasn't a good idea for me to come over. But she hadn't said no.

I could turn around, shove back through the trees to my car, and call her like a normal fucking human. Knowing Tessa, she wouldn't tell me if she was hurting. She'd minimize her pain like she'd done over text. It had to be severe if she'd missed four days of work.

My heart spasmed. Over the fence, through a few more trees, and maybe battle a flame-breathing dragon, and I'd be able to look Tessa in the eye. If she said she didn't want me there, I'd turn around and leave, no matter how my stupid heart ached.

So I climbed.

My loafers weren't the best shoes for scaling a fence, and they'd be scratched up by the end of this quest. Still, I stuck them into the holes of the fence, and with the bouquet tucked under my arm, hauled myself up the ten-foot barrier, thankful for the lack of razor wire at the top.

As I swung my leg over, my trousers snagged on the metal, and I winced at the ripping sound. God, I hoped Tessa was on the other side of this adventure.

I dropped down, kicking up a cloud of dirt. Then I pushed past one more row of trees to emerge, blinking, into the sunlight. My loafers scraped against a driveway. A motor court, actually. I squinted across the expanse of concrete. On the other side of the pavers was a house. It wasn't quite a mansion, but it was about the same size as my much less secluded home. Unlike the apartment building out front, it was well maintained, with sparkling white stucco. Gerbera daisies in magenta, saffron, and pink grew among deep-green bushes and trailing succulents in the surrounding flowerbeds.

The front door opened, and Tessa stepped into the doorway. Her skin was paler than usual, and she shielded her eyes from the sunlight. She leaned against the doorframe. "I see you were undeterred by my security system."

"*That's* a security system?" Brushing leaves off the sleeves of my dress shirt, I crossed the driveway. "I expected at least a hedge of thorns and some attack dogs."

"The cats vetoed the dogs. And it looks like something got you." She pointed at my pants.

I looked down. Dammit, there was a rip right at the inseam. It only slightly dimmed the joy of my victory. "Any determined person can get through that."

"Not without setting off the silent alarm."

I swallowed. Did climbing a fence count as breaking and entering?

She gave me a weak smirk. "Lucky for you, I took pity and called off the police."

My shoulders loosened. "I appreciate it. I wanted to check on you. And give you these." I held out the bouquet.

She took them from me. "I thought I told you not to fall in love with me."

"I didn't," I lied. "These are get-well flowers."

"Yellow roses are cheerier. They mean friendship. These roses are red and white, for everlasting love. I'd have thought your Ivy-League upbringing would've taught you that." She buried her nose in the bouquet and looked up at me through her eyelashes. Without mascara, they were auburn like her hair.

I hummed noncommittally. I'd known exactly what I was doing at the florist, yet I hadn't been able to stop myself. She stared for a moment as that big brain of hers worked. Finally, she said, "Come on. I'll introduce you to the girls."

I rubbed at the ebbing ache in my chest. She was well enough to stand and walk. And she wasn't sending me away.

We entered the house into a tiled entry. She led me to the left, and we passed a small table with a round tray that held pots of tall, blooming orchids.

The kitchen wasn't as well laid out for cooking as mine, but it was spacious with a large island in the center. Savannah, whom I'd met a couple of times at Carly and Andrew's, leaned a hip against it, her arms folded as she stared down an orange tabby who sat on the light-colored stone top, cleaning his ear with one white paw.

When she saw me, Savannah grinned. "Oliver! So nice of you to come check on Tessa." She held out her arms.

"Hi, Savannah." I walked into her embrace. She gave the best hugs, and she smelled like butter and vanilla. "Am I interrupting your visit?"

"No," Tessa said. "Savannah lives here."

"Temporarily," Savannah said.

"As long as you need to. Forever if you like."

Savannah's nose twitched. She sniffed, then flicked her fingers at the cat. "Shoo, Hedy."

Tessa scooped the cat off the counter and hugged it to her chest. "Are you two fighting again?"

"Cats don't belong on counters." Savannah tossed her short blond hair. "I don't want to pick cat hair out of my dinner."

"She lives here too." Tessa kissed the cat's striped forehead. "She's curious. She's not used to food being made here."

"Oh." Savannah's smile faded. "I hate that I'm disrupting—"

"Don't be ridiculous," Tessa said. "She'll get used to it. You're not disrupting anything. And this house is plenty big for the five of us."

Five? How many people lived here?

Like she could hear my brain exploding, Tessa turned to face me. "Oliver, meet Hedy Lamarr."

The cat's yellow eyes narrowed as I reached out a hand for her to sniff.

"Don't worry," Tessa said. "She's suspicious of everyone."

The cat wrinkled her nose, showing one sharp incisor, but, still bold from my adventure, I held my palm there, below her chin. When the cat didn't bite me, I scratched her neck.

"Huh," Tessa said.

The cat tipped up her chin so I could scratch the white spot on her throat. "Good girl," I murmured.

Tessa shuddered, then set the cat on the floor. It twined around her legs, leaving a coating of white hairs on her black leggings.

"She loves you, Oliver," Savannah crowed. "When I got here, it took her almost a whole day before she sat in my lap." The cat trotted to her and rubbed her face against Savannah's ankle. Despite their earlier argument, she bent and scratched Hedy from her shoulders to her tail. Then, her tail held high, the cat turned and stalked out of the room.

Savannah glanced at the clock on the stove. "It's almost time for your medicine."

"Thank god," Tessa said. "Gimme."

Savannah reached into a cabinet and pulled out a prescription bottle. She opened it, tapped out a tablet, and put it in Tessa's palm. Tessa swallowed it dry.

"Why don't you go lie down?" her friend asked. "You're so pale."

She was right. Tessa's freckles seemed darker against her white face. A guilty chill washed through my stomach. "I'm sorry I made you get up. Why don't we go to bed?" I choked.

"I mean, I'll take you to bed." Fuck, that still wasn't right.

My face was on fire. "I mean, you should lie down."

She huffed a tiny laugh. "Yeah, I probably should."

"Want me to put those in a vase?" I nodded at the roses Tessa had set on the counter.

"I'll do it," Savannah said. "Do I need to put these out of the cats' reach?"

"No, roses are nontoxic." she said.

Savannah caught my gaze. "Make sure she rests, okay?"

Tessa rolled her eyes. "I don't need *two* mothers. I'm perfectly capable of taking care of myself."

"Sure you are," Savannah said, "but we're here, and we want to take care of you. Go and lie down. Since we have a guest, I'll make a roast chicken. It'll be a few hours before dinner is ready. You two have plenty of time to...rest." She pressed her lips together like she was holding back a smile.

I didn't need to rest, but Tessa clearly did. There were purple half-moons under her eyes. As much as I wanted to stay so I could ensure she was okay, I didn't want to prevent her from sleeping. "I'll help you to your room, then I'll go."

"My god, I'm forty-three, not eighty-three." But she took my arm.

Tessa led me toward the adjacent living room. The space looked comfortable, with a dark gray slipcovered sofa and a soft blanket in light gray flung to the side. Her laptop sat open on the coffee table. Another cat, this one with short blue-gray fur, gazed at us from the other end of the couch. "This is Anita Borg."

How much did I love that Tessa had named her cats after women inventors and programmers? More than I should. I loved everything about this woman, except for how she pushed me away.

I let Anita sniff my hand, and she rubbed her cheek against it. "Two for two," I joked.

"Oh, Anita's a slut." Tessa sniffed.

"She likes all the guys you bring over here?" The words felt like broken glass in my throat.

"Apparently. She's one for one." After dropping that bomb, Tessa dropped my arm and sailed into the short hallway. I shut my mouth and followed.

Tessa's bedroom was on the main level. The curtains were drawn except for a narrow opening in the center. I squinted to make out details in the gloom. Her bed had a charcoal uphol-stered headboard, and her bedspread was a deep purple. There was a small desk in the corner. A single leather armchair with a matching ottoman anchored the other side. The wood floors extended in here, and a rug with a Turkish geometric design covered the space between the bed and the bathroom. Another one softened the floor under the chair and the desk.

Tessa let me take it all in, then she quirked her lips. "You staying?"

"Let me help you with the pillows." I grabbed one of the fluffy charcoal pillows. But as it turned out, it wasn't a pillow. It was a black cat that went boneless when I picked it up. I bobbled the unexpected weight for a moment before I got my hands under the ball of fluff and cradled it to my chest.

"I see you've met Kat Johnson."

The cat purred against my ribs as I rubbed a finger behind her ear. "You matched your pillows to your cat?"

She picked up a pillow that definitely didn't have eyes or claws and tossed it onto the bench at the foot of the bed. "It's her favorite hiding place. Kind of like that scene in *E.T.*"

I hummed and scratched Kat under the chin.

"Ugh, you've never seen it, have you?" She gazed up at the tray ceiling.

"*E.T.* came out ten years before I was born, so...no? Why? Should I see it?"

"It's what got me into tabletop games. It defined my generation, but it's no big deal." She pulled back the covers and climbed into bed.

"We could watch it together sometime."

"Eh, it was very much of its time. I'm sure it wouldn't hold up now." She yawned.

Time for me to go. I set Kat on the bed, and she nestled against Tessa's ankles. "Need anything else? Water? Your laptop?"

"No." She tugged the covers up to her chin. "Thanks for the flowers."

I crossed back to the bed. "You're welcome. But it'll take more than your bullshit security system and a few comments about our age difference to get rid of me."

"Will it?" She blinked up at me.

I leaned over and kissed her forehead. "Bet."

"What does that even mean?" she murmured.

"It means I'll be here when you wake up—if you want."

"Yeah." She yawned. "Promise?"

My heart swelled. "I promise."

I whispered the last part because she was already asleep. After one last glance at her peaceful face, I walked to the door and quietly shut it behind me.

In the kitchen, Savannah hummed as she seasoned a chicken.

"She's asleep," I said.

"Yeah, her meds take her out," she said. "She usually sleeps for a couple hours after."

"She has a lot of pain?"

"It's unpredictable. Some months, it's mild. I'd say typical period pain. Other times, it's agony. And it can flare up around ovulation too." She winced. "Sorry. That's probably TMI."

"I care about her. I want to know about her pain and her condition, including her periods."

Savannah stared at me for a second. Then she put her arms around me and pulled me into a surprisingly strong hug. "I like you."

"Thanks?" I relaxed into the hug.

With one last squeeze, she released me. "I mean, I like you for Tessa. She deserves a man who loves everything about her."

"I do." I'd needed that. The hug and her words. "I love everything about her. But she doesn't feel the same."

"Doesn't she?" Savannah's blond eyebrows tucked up under her hair.

"She told me not to fall for her," I mumbled.

"Was that for her sake or yours?"

"Does it matter?"

"I think it does. Use that smart brain of yours." She picked up the pepper again and shook it over the chicken.

Why would Tessa tell me not to fall in love with her if not to protect me and my fragile heart? Unless she was protecting her own heart.

She'd told me about that dickhead, Harry, and how he'd ruined her company. She hadn't mentioned how she'd felt about him. Had she loved him before he'd broken her trust?

"I'd never betray her," I said.

"I think that's true. But does Tessa? She's got some, like, baggage around romantic relationships. I know I'm the dumb one of our friend group, but I know about that guy who screwed her over at Red Rover. And I met her dad. She's got trust issues for sure. Did you know our friend group had never been to her house until a couple months ago? Except for me." She puffed out her chest. "And now you."

"You think I have a chance?"

"You're here, aren't you? Inside her fortress. She's taken us both in. Like that little jerk." She pointed at my feet, where Hedy

Lamarr rubbed her face on my pants, leaving a smudge of orange and white hair.

"Have you seen *E.T.?*"

She blinked. "Of course. Reese's Pieces were my favorite candy for years after."

I let that nonsensical statement slide. "Could we watch it together, and you can give me the, um, context?"

"You want me to be your Gen X whisperer?" She grinned. "Okay. Help me get the chicken in the oven. We'll do the low and slow version."

I washed my hands and got to work. I chopped vegetables and staged them for roasting while she put the chicken in the oven. Then I showed her how to use Tessa's television, and we found the movie.

By the time it ended, I understood a little more about the woman I'd fallen for. And I needed a tissue.

26

WILD TYPE

Wild type: *The most commonly occurring form of a gene or allele in a natural population.*

OLIVER

When the chicken was done, Savannah convinced me she should be the one to tap on Tessa's door to see if she was interested in joining us for dinner. I'd hardly had time to wipe down the countertops when Savannah's slipper scuffed on the tile, followed by the slap of Tessa's bare feet.

Her hair stuck up on one side, and she had a pillow crease across that cheek. She wasn't as pale as she'd been that afternoon, and her cheeks reddened when she saw me.

"You're still here." She combed her fingers through her hair and winced when they snagged on a tangle.

I wrung the dishcloth to keep myself from going to her and touching her feral mane. "I promised I would be."

She hummed and glanced at the third place setting on her table.

"Do you want me to go?" I thought we'd grown closer over

the last few weeks, that my plan to woo her was working. Had I misread the signals again?

"No," Savannah answered for her. "Of course not."

"Do you want me to leave, Tessa?" I repeated.

Her gaze flicked to me, then to the table. After a moment, she said, "Stay."

It was something people said to dogs, but I didn't mind. After I'd burst into her home uninvited, after I'd seen her struggle with her pain, all I wanted was to remain a little longer to see that she was okay. Fine, and also watch her eat food I'd helped prepare. Some long-dormant hunter-gatherer part of my DNA had switched on.

When I pulled out her chair, she rolled her eyes. "Are you going to toss your cloak over a mud puddle? Write me a sonnet?"

"Come on now." Savannah set a plate of food in front of her. "It's only a chair."

"I thought shit like that died out with the boomers," Tessa grumbled. "Our guest is a millennial. Like your kids."

I pulled out Savannah's chair, and she patted my hand before she sat. "How old do you think I am? My kids are Gen Z. And aren't you the one always telling me age is just a number?"

I was listening so hard for Tessa's response that when I reached for the remaining two plates in the oven, I missed and touched the hot metal rack. I stifled a yelp.

"One hundred percent," Tessa said. "When we're talking about you."

Eyes watering, I stuck my thumb in my mouth to cool the burn, then more carefully grabbed the plates and carried them to the table.

"You two are both millennials," Savannah said. "The generation started in 1981."

Tessa glanced at me as I set her plate in front of her. "Officially, I'm an elder millennial," she said, "but I identify as Gen X. I'm a hardened skeptic."

"Well, I'm fully Gen X. And speaking of birthdays," Savannah said, "I've decided I want a party for mine. I never used to make a big deal about my birthdays, but now"—she breathed in deep, then let it out—"I want a big deal."

"Good for you," Tessa said. "You deserve a party."

"When is it?" I asked.

"In two weeks. I know that's not a lot of time to plan." Savannah turned to Tessa. "I was hoping we could have a party here." Savannah said. "Your place is perfect for entertaining."

"Except for the hidden entrance," I mumbled.

She waved her hand. "It adds to the charm. We can leave the gate open."

"There's a gate?" If I'd known that, I could've saved my pants.

Tessa's eyes were wide and wild like a cornered animal's. "A party *here?*"

"Only our closest friends," Savannah said. "No one you'd regret knowing where you live. The girls and their partners. My three kids, if that's okay. I'll cook. But you don't have to decide now. You can think about it."

Looking slightly sick, Tessa poked at her chicken with her fork.

"We could go to a restaurant instead," Savannah said.

Tessa scrubbed a hand over her face. "No. We'll have it here. Invite your kids. But *not* Jason."

"Of course not." Savannah bristled. Then she said more gently, "Eat. You need the protein."

After that, Savannah changed the subject, asking me about work, and soon Tessa joined in, seeming more like my prickly, brilliant colleague. Someone I'd kissed and whom I'd chased to her house when she didn't show up for work. Fuck, what was wrong with me? I wished I could be normal around her. Be her coworker and keep some boundaries. But whenever I caught sight of that long, auburn hair I wanted to tangle my fingers in, her freckled skin I wanted to caress, every rational thought left me.

"You're staring," she whispered, leaning toward me when Savannah got up to get more water.

I blinked away from her soft-looking lips. "Sorry, I...are you feeling okay?"

"Yeah. The nap helped."

"It's time for another pill." Savannah plunked the bottle in front of her.

"I think I'll be okay," Tessa said. "In fact, I'll do the dishes."

When we protested, Tessa said, "You cooked. I'll clean."

"Savannah did most of the work," I said, "so I'll help you."

"Fine," Savannah said. "My bestie and I'll watch." She snagged the black cat, Kat, off the counter and pulled her into her lap, scratching behind her ears.

As I put away the leftovers, my new best friend, Hedy, rubbed her striped face on my ankle until I gave her a bite of chicken. (After Tessa said it was okay.)

When the kitchen was spotless again, Savannah stretched and gave a big fake-sounding yawn. "I want to read for a bit in bed. G'night, y'all."

"You're leaving?" Tessa's eyes went wide.

"I don't think y'all need a chaperone. In fact, Oliver, why don't you walk Tessa to her room. Make sure she doesn't fall?" And she winked at me before walking out.

Savannah had to be the least subtle person I'd ever met. Yet I liked her. A lot. I crooked my elbow. "You ready, Tessa?"

"It's only seven-thirty," she grumbled. "I'm not tired yet."

"Okay," I said. "Want to watch TV or play a game?"

She considered for a moment, those jade-green eyes

assessing me. "No. I have a better form of entertainment in mind." She took my arm. "Let's go."

My mind spun as we strolled to her room. Did she mean the type of entertainment I thought she did? I'd made the rules before, but now I'd broken them all by invading her castle like a rogue. I opened the door for her, and she passed me, close enough for a waft of her clean scent. My mind blanked.

She asked, "You staying?"

My gaze was drawn to the bed like it was a black hole. "If you want."

"I'm not tired." Her tone seemed to be a warning.

I barreled right through the caution tape. "Me neither."

"Good." Her lips quirked up at the sides. "Give me a minute." She went into the attached bathroom.

I used the bathroom in the hall. There was some toothpaste in the drawer, but I didn't presume to use the toothbrush that was still in its package. Instead, I used my finger, then I rinsed my fingers and ran them through my hair to get it out of my eyes. I needed a haircut.

Back in her bedroom, I straightened the covers, then pulled them back on her side. No, she'd asked me to stay. I folded back the sheets on the other side too. Like in Vegas, the bed was big enough for both of us.

The bathroom door opened, and she emerged wearing a soft-looking bathrobe in dark gray. I swallowed.

She tipped her head to the side. "You're still wearing clothes. Were you serious about wanting to play a board game?"

"Um...not really?" I could think of a lot of things I wanted to do with her, and none of them involved dice.

"Are you one of those guys who's icked out by period sex?"

"God, no." As if to prove the point, my dick pressed against my zipper.

She set her fingers on the tie of her robe. "Then why are you still dressed?"

I looked down at myself, surprised my clothes hadn't spontaneously combusted. I shucked off my trousers, wincing when I rediscovered the rip in the seam. They tangled at my ankles.

Shit, I'd forgotten to take off my shoes.

I sat awkwardly on the bed to wrestle them off. When my legs were free, I unbuttoned my shirt. My fingers shook, so it took longer than it should've. I left my boxers on, but they didn't hide my erection at all.

I stepped closer to her and traced one lapel of her robe. "Can I?"

She nodded.

I untied the belt, then pushed the robe off her shoulders. She was naked underneath, and I took a minute to enjoy the glorious view of her freckled skin. They covered her body, denser on her arms and lower legs, lighter over her breasts and stomach. My breath quickened as I ran my hand down the smooth skin of her arm, like I'd been dying to do for months.

Her touch feather-light, she caressed from my shoulder to the top of my right pec. "You're hairier than I thought you'd be."

I furrowed my brows. "Is that a bad thing?"

"No." She swirled a finger into the hair over my breastbone. "It's an observation. I like it."

"I love your body." Her breasts were on the smaller side, a perfect fit for my palms. I traced a line from her shoulder to her nipple, then circled the areola with my fingertip. "Good?"

"Mmm." She closed her eyes.

"Does your endometriosis give you pain with sex?"

"Someone's done his research."

Her breath hitched when I gave her nipple a gentle pinch. "It's an important question."

"Not usually. Only if it's particularly rough."

"And you'll let me know if you feel any pain?"

She pressed her breast into my hand. "Yes. Promise."

I lowered my mouth to her breast and licked the reddened tip. Then I closed my lips around it and sucked. Her warm skin tasted earthy with a barely-there tang of something fresh and herbal. I opened my mouth wider to take in more of her. She clasped my head and held it to her, so I kept going, licking and sucking one breast while my fingers plucked at the other nipple. She responded with a moan, her chest heaving.

I trailed my other hand to her hip and spoke against her skin. "What can I touch down here?"

"Any...anything. I'm wearing a m-menstrual disc. We can even do p-penetration. If you want."

God, did I want. I wanted everything. With one last draw on her nipple, I pulled away. "Lie down."

"Bossy." She pulled a thin, dark blanket from the bottom drawer of her bedside table and spread it over the sheets.

"Is that a sex blanket?" I'd never seen one in real life.

"Things could get messy." Her russet eyebrow lifted, daring me.

"I like messy when it comes to sex. And I love being prepared."

"Of course you do." She sat on the edge of the bed and reclined onto the blanket.

Her body was perfect. Her cheeks and chest were flushed, and her nipples were red. And, damn, her freckles. I could spend hours counting them, if she'd let me.

She grabbed two pillows from the other side of the bed and set them next to her hip.

"What're those for?" I asked.

She flashed me a sultry smile. "What, we're not building a barrier tonight?"

I scratched my chin. "Well, if you'd rather I stay on my side and not eat you out, then—"

"Wait." She rubbed her thighs together. "I want the eating out. I was joking."

"Thank god." I grabbed the pillows from her joke of a fort and nudged them under her hips, spreading her legs wide. "Comfortable?"

"Yes, though if you ask me for a set of stirrups—"

Her cheeky comment turned into a gasp when I licked her swollen labia. I explored her with my tongue, remapping all the places I'd learned in the supply closet. But this time there was no fear of anyone walking in, no burning sense of guilt about having sex at work. So I got comfortable on my knees and reveled in her soft skin, her sweet taste, and the tangy scent of her arousal. I licked, nibbled, and caressed until her thighs trembled and she slid her fingers down her stomach.

I batted them away. "This one's mine," I growled as I tapped the nub with my thumb.

She stiffened. "I'm so close," she rasped.

I wanted to stay here forever, edging her, worshiping her. But I couldn't resist giving her what she wanted. "Don't worry, baby," I said. "I've got you." Then I couldn't talk anymore because my mouth was on her clit. I sucked the way I'd done with her nipples.

She groaned, then her hips quaked under me. Finally, a yell ripped from her throat as she tensed. I eased up on the suction but didn't stop licking and fingering her until her body went limp and she tapped weakly against my forehead. I kissed the inside of her thigh, then scooted up the bed and grinned. "Tired yet?"

"Don't be smug. Also, why are you still not naked?" Her hand landed lightly on my erection where it tented my boxers.

My vision went gray around the edges. "I didn't want to presume."

She clenched the head, and the room faded until there was only her hand on my dick, electrifying every cell in my body. Even my hair follicles were sensitized. I was going to explode. I pressed my hips into her hand. She wasn't touching my skin yet, and I was dying. "Lube? And a condom?"

"Top drawer."

I opened the drawer of her bedside table and found the bottle, plus a handful of condoms and a selection of vibrators.

"My god, you look like a kid in a candy store," she said.

"Your bedroom is the most amazing place. Can I use one of these on you?"

"Later. Right now, I want you."

My heart was going to fly right out of my body, and I couldn't keep the grin off my face.

"Stop being smug and fuck me," she growled.

I noted a finger vibe I'd use later, then I set the lube and a condom on the bed.

When I shucked off my boxers, she licked her lips. "On second thought, why don't I suck you off?"

My fingers froze on the condom wrapper. "That sounds amazing, but I'm right on the edge. I want to come inside you." Like a caveman, I wanted her to feel me inside her, to leave an imprint there as if that were possible. Sex does funny things to people's otherwise rational brains. I had enough presence of mind to add, "If that's okay."

"You won't be grossed out?"

"Why would I be grossed out? I love your body. It's doing what it's meant to do."

Her lips wobbled for a second, then her expression neutralized. "Fine. Let's do this."

Before she could change her mind, I rolled on the condom and squirted lube into my palm. I slicked up the condom quickly, then I touched a slippery finger to her outer lips. She hissed.

"Still good?" I asked, smearing the liquid over her.

"Yeah. I wasn't sure I'd be ready again so soon, but I guess"— her breath stuttered—"I guess I am."

I slipped a finger inside her, and she groaned. "More."

I swiped up the rest of the lube from my palm and pushed two fingers inside her. She ground against my hand, gasping when my palm touched her clit. "Now, Oliver," she said.

My fingers made juicy sounds against her skin, and she was open and ready. I was ready, probably too ready. Silently, I started counting down from one hundred as I slipped my fingers from her body. Grasping the base of the condom, I nudged her opening with my head. Then I thrust in.

Her muscles fluttered around me, and it was all I could do to keep counting. I stilled, adjusting to the pressure as my balls tightened. I couldn't go off like a teenager. I had to prove to this woman I had some control. I took a centering breath and gazed down at her.

She watched me with an unfamiliar expression. Was it uncertainty that made her bite her lip?

Bracing on my hands, I leaned forward and kissed her, trying to reassure her—maybe myself too—that we were good, that neither of us had anything to fear. Not from each other, and not from this new intimacy. For once, I wasn't thinking about work. All that mattered was the amazing woman beneath me with her glorious body and her beautiful face.

When I pulled back to admire her, her expression went hazy. "Do that again," she murmured.

I leaned down to kiss her, pouring every bit of reassurance I could into it. The fact that we were coworkers, our age gap, our wildly different perspectives on risk, none of it mattered. Our bodies knew it. We only had to convince our brains. Her body tightened around me, and I pulled back again.

"Are you close?" I asked. "Just from kissing?"

"*Just* from kissing?" She gripped my ass, her short nails digging into my skin and making me grunt. "Five minutes ago, I came so hard I saw stars. Your dick is inside me, and you're kissing me like it's your job. How do you do that?"

"What can I say? I'm a natural. And I like to be thorough." I wished it was my job to kiss her. It was effortless, unlike my real job. So I did it again, and this time when she constricted around me, I pulled out then snapped my hips forward, tapping her clit with my stomach. Nonsense words poured out of my mouth, praising her body and telling her how good it felt.

"God, yes," she said against my mouth.

I thrust into her again. She wrapped her legs around me, pulling me closer until our hips met. I ground against her. It was all I could do to hold off until I felt the compression of her orgasm as she let out a hoarse cry. Finally, I let myself thrust wildly into her until my release surged through me, pleasure flooding all the way to my toes.

When my rational brain came back online, my shoulders stiffened. She'd said sex could be painful when it was too vigorous, and I'd lost control. "Did I hurt you? Was that too much?"

She grasped the back of my head and pulled me down for another kiss, this one softer, more constrained. "It was perfect. But no pet names."

"Pet names?" I glanced around for one of the cats.

"You called me baby. The first time, when you went down on me, and again just now."

"Did I?" I vaguely remembered it, but I'd said a lot of stuff.

"Did you forget? You're not even the one who's been taking prescription painkillers."

Was she arguing with me while I was still inside her? "What's wrong with baby?"

"It's soft and gentle. I'm neither."

No, but my feelings for her were both. "What can I call you?"

"Tessa." She moved her head in a way that would have been a toss if she weren't lying down. "Not Theresa, and *never* Tess."

I kissed her neck. "So princess is out?"

"Absolutely."

"Dear?"

"I'm not *that* old."

"Ginger Spice?"

"My god, I wanted to be her so bad in 1997. But no." Her expression went steely. "Absolutely no pet names. What did I say about falling in love with me?"

I had to clear the lump from my throat to let the lie through. "I'm not in love with you." *Not completely.* But I was teetering on the edge. Gently, I pulled out of her.

There was a smear of blood on the condom, and a small amount trickled onto the creamy skin of her upper thigh. "Hang on, I'll be right back with a tissue."

When she saw the condom, she winced, and her cheeks flushed. "Sorry. It's gross."

I clambered off the bed, but I didn't go into the bathroom. "Blood isn't gross. We work with it all the time in the lab. Your period is a normal human function. I had a great time. I'm still having a great time." At least I was, until she'd reminded me she'd never make the mistake of falling for me.

In the bathroom, I tossed the condom in the trash, wiped myself clean, and washed my hands. I met my disappointed gaze in the mirror and narrowed my eyes. *You just slept with the world's most amazing woman. Focus on that, not on the fact that she doesn't want you for anything more than your dick.* Taking a deep breath, I grabbed a few tissues and returned to the bedroom.

She was sitting up, scrubbing at her thighs with a tissue. "Thank goodness for the blanket, right?" Her voice was too high, and she didn't meet my gaze.

"Hey." I stilled her hand and took the wadded-up tissue from her. Then I wiped the stain from her leg more gently than she'd been doing. "I love this blanket. I think I might get one for myself."

She snorted. "Sure you will."

"I'll get two. One for my couch and another for the bed. We can make love everywhere."

"You mean have sex. Don't romanticize this."

Ouch. I knew she was on defense after letting herself be vulnerable, but it still hurt. I glanced at the pile of clothes by the side of the bed.

"Want me to go, or can I stay over?"

"The security system is a pain to navigate at night. You can stay. If you want." Her shrug was anything but casual.

"Thanks. I'd like that." I lifted her hand and caressed it. Her cheeks went redder, obscuring the freckles.

I returned to the bathroom to toss the trash and wash my hands. She went in after me, so I folded the blanket onto her side and lay down to wait.

She returned and settled beside me, then flicked off the lamp. I slipped my arm over her waist. "Is this okay?"

"Sure." In the darkness, I couldn't see her expression, but that one word seemed to come from behind a brick wall.

"Did someone make you feel bad about your period?" I asked.

She snorted again. "Nearly everyone. My dad, my ex, society at large. Women are expected to have children, but no one wants the mess that comes with it. Mine are so heavy I don't usually hook up when I'm having my period."

Hook up? Hurtful. But I stroked from her ribs to her hip. "Your body is amazing, inside and out."

The pillow rustled when she turned her head, but it was too dark to see her expression. "You really believe that, don't you?"

"One hundred percent."

"Stop being perfect," she said, "and go to sleep."

27

A SATANIC RITUAL WITH FROSTING

From Barry Wright's manifesto:
Birthday parties are a tool of satanic cults. People sing a ritualized song to a person in a room lit only by candles. What else could they be doing but calling up evil spirits?

TESSA

"Are we sure about this?" My voice was squeakier than I intended as I surveyed my kitchen. Savannah's buffet of appetizers stretched across the island.

"Is it crooked?" Oliver looked back over his shoulder. He held one end of a gold-foil Happy Birthday banner and was taping it to the window frame in the breakfast nook.

"It *is* crooked. But I meant, all this." I waved at the snacks, gold-tinsel boas, sparkly sunglasses, party hats piled on the coffee table, and the cake on the dining table with *Happy Birthday, Savannah* piped in icing on the top. (Although Savannah had insisted on preparing her birthday meal, I'd ordered the cake from a nearby bakery. No one should have to bake their own birthday cake.)

More than all the festivities in my formerly quiet home, by *this* I meant Oliver's presence here, where soon my friends would show up and see us together. I was pretty sure they knew we'd been sleeping together for two weeks, though Oliver left early each morning to shower and change at his place before we went to work separately. I couldn't have asked Savannah to keep that juicy bit of news from Carly and Lucie.

Playing it off as casual sex with a younger man, my coworker, was one thing. Having him here as my date or cohost or, I didn't know, more than casual sex was over the line. Lucie, at least, would make a huge deal about it.

Savannah had been chill so far. Last weekend, Oliver had worn those obscene gray sweatpants I couldn't stop salivating over. She'd treated him like part of the household by greeting him when he poured us coffee and asking him if he'd be joining us for dinner. I'd even caught her asking him about the steps he'd taken to start his business and what he'd done to keep it successful. A frown had flitted over his forehead at that, but he'd shot a glance at me and talked about surrounding himself with smart people.

Leaving the banner dangling, he descended the stepladder and rubbed my shoulders. "Is a party too much? I can start texting people to cancel. I'll stand out on the street and wave them away."

"You would, wouldn't you?" I uncrossed my arms and wrapped them around his waist. Then I kissed him. "It'll be fine. It's only Savannah's kids and our closest friends."

"This spread looks like it'll feed everyone you've ever met." He nuzzled my ear.

"I didn't want anyone to go hungry," Savannah said, setting a steaming casserole on the island. "If we have leftovers, we can send them home with the guests."

When the door flew open, I startled.

"Happy birthday!" Carly fluttered in with Andrew, who held a magnum of wine. "Savannah, you look gorgeous." Savannah's cheeks went pink to match her ruffly dress, which she wore with Carly's present to her, a pair of gold sneakers.

"Thank you." Savannah engulfed her in a hug.

When Savannah turned to hug Andrew, Carly approached me. "You look pretty too." She leaned toward me as if to kiss my cheek but wobbled back.

"It's okay," I said. "You can hug me." I felt better in my body since that night Oliver slept over for the first time, when instead of being revolted by my menstrual blood, he'd reminded me it was natural. His frequent touches—a caress on my cheek before he left each morning, a brush of my hand when he gave me his printed reports at the office, a casual kiss on the back of my neck as I sat on my couch and worked on my laptop in the evenings— must have desensitized me.

She wrapped me in a hug, not as tight as one of Savannah's, and whispered in my ear, "You're glowing. Happiness looks good on you."

"Who said I was happy?" I grumbled. But she was right. A month in, the results of the clinical trials were promising. The team smiled and laughed at work, and so did I. Living with Savannah was more fun than I'd imagined, plus she'd been feeding me an anti-inflammatory diet that was supposed to improve my symptoms. Each time Oliver walked into my house, my heart gave a silly skip. When he held me at night, all seemed right in my world.

Oliver stepped away from Andrew and rested his hand on my lower back. "More guests incoming."

I didn't jump this time when Lucie and Danny strode in. Danny carried a crate full of bottles. "Happy birthday! I brought our bartender," Lucie said, her brown eyes blazing. "You've got to try his new cocktail, Of Mice and Gin. It's amazing. I've pumped, and he's driving, so we're all going to get birthday-sloshed—except Danny. And teetotaling Oliver."

"Thanks, Danny," I said. "You can set up over there." I gestured at the small bar tucked away in one corner of the living room. The prior owner had been into entertaining, and I'd half-heartedly filled it with a few wineglasses and my favorite Irish whiskey.

Slowly, the room filled with guests. When Justine walked in with Bridget, she made a beeline for Savannah. Since she'd started working on her divorce case, they'd gotten friendly, and I suspected they'd grow closer once the case was done and Justine could ease off on her professional distance.

Bridget stayed with me for a few minutes to talk about our work. I updated her about the progress we'd made at Discovery —nothing confidential, of course—and she told me about her latest tiff with the CFO, Cole Campion. And as usual, she complained about her sexist boss, the CEO.

"You should leave," I said. "Another company will recognize your awesomeness. A smaller company would be glad to have someone of your caliber in the CEO role. You deserve it."

A smile played on her lips, and she leaned closer. "In the plane last week, he was on the phone with his financial adviser. He was trying to be subtle, but I'd bet my retirement fund he was talking about exit strategies. I suspect when Bill retired, he got jealous."

"No! Really? I thought they were going to have to carry him out of the CEO's office feet-first."

"Apparently, his wife wants to spend more time with him. Can you imagine? With that jerk?"

"Nuh-uh. Only nice guys from here on out." Like magnets, my eyes fixed on Oliver, who was chatting with one of Savannah's sons. He had a little frown line of concentration between his eyebrows, but when he caught me looking, he smiled.

"Mmm," Bridget said. "I see how it is. He makes you happy." It wasn't a question.

"He does...for now."

"For now? What's that bullshit?"

"I don't know. He's wonderful and all: smart, kind, and amazing in bed. But it's too good to be true. He'll turn out to be a liar, like Harry." Even as I said it, I knew Oliver would never mislead me the way Harry had done.

"Or he won't."

"Maybe." I couldn't let myself hope that Oliver and I would stay together forever. I knew literally no one who'd done it. Savannah had been with her college sweetheart for thirty years, and now Justine was helping her through a divorce. Believing in love wasn't logical. Or safe.

Danny and Lucie appeared beside us. Danny balanced a tray of drinks in one hand. Deftly, he pulled one from the tray and handed it to me. "Celebratory cocktail?"

"What's in it?" I asked.

"It's basically a blackberry bramble. Muddled blackberries with lemonade and gin, plus sparkling water for fizz. It's sweet and refreshing."

Lucie grabbed two glasses from the tray and handed one to Bridget. She raised her glass. "To Tessa. May she host many more parties, and may she continue to have excellent sex."

"Lucie." Danny frowned at his girlfriend.

"Fine. Only as much excellent sex as she wants."

She drank, and after lifting my glass to her, I did too. I was having fantastic sex, the clinical trials were showing strong results, and I was happy for the first time in years. After a childhood where my security could vanish the second Dad decided we'd stayed someplace too long, I knew how precarious happiness was. This time, I hoped if I was smart about it and anticipated the problems, I could keep it all.

Like Lucie and Danny. On the surface, they seemed dissimilar. She was ten years older with a college degree and professional success, while he was a young, handsome bartender who'd lived downstairs from her. They'd taken a risk when they'd accidentally gotten pregnant and in the end, it had worked out for them. They now ran a bar together, and they seemed incandescently happy, both together and apart. A perfect example of a couple who had succeeded against all odds.

Could I have that too?

"See?" Lucie leaned into Danny. To his credit, he kept the tray steady and didn't spill a drop. "Told you she was getting the good D on the regs."

"It's true." I stared at the pink drink. Was there truth serum in there? Who was I, to talk about my sex life in public when I'd vowed never again?

Danny kissed the top of her head. "I'm going to pass out these drinks. Tessa, do you have more glasses?"

"The ones I borrowed from Oliver are in the left cabinet in the island." I'd considered renting glassware and plates, but Oliver had enough for me to borrow. He liked having guests at his place. I scanned the room, where all our friends lounged on my couches and stood in my kitchen. Maybe I did too.

Danny walked off, and Lucie said, "Come on. Let's grab Carly, then we can take a pic together to commemorate the time you let us into your stronghold."

I already knew Carly was talking with Oliver and Andrew. The awareness of him was new. When he entered a room, especially at work, my gaze went straight to him, and my stomach gave a not-unpleasant skip. Hormones were impressive chemicals. Maybe if I had a biology degree like Oliver, I'd better understand what was happening and react more rationally. But what would be the fun in that?

When we joined their group, he seemed to have a similar

awareness of me. Without looking away from Carly, who was talking, he slipped his arm around my waist and pulled me to his side. My stomach flipped again, and I inhaled his Christmas-tree scent. Pheromones: another interesting organic chemical. I put my hand on his back and rubbed between his shoulder blades. His back vibrated, and if not for the noise of conversation, I think I would've heard him purr.

Carly was laughing about something that had happened at one of Andrew's mother's famous brunches. They were notoriously high in drama since all four of her children were less tractable than she'd have liked. Andrew's stubborn independence particularly irked her, especially after he'd gotten engaged to her frenemy.

"...Andrew was about to go nuclear. I mean, she called me 'vintage,' can you believe it? Then Audrey tried to backpedal and said I was aging like fine wine."

Andrew mimed digging a hole with a shovel.

"I told her it was better than aging like milk. Brunch ended pretty quickly after that."

Under my hand, Oliver's chest rumbled with laughter, and although I'd missed most of the story, I smiled too. It was good to see him having fun with our friends. I could picture a future where he and I and my friends and their partners did things together. I was starting not to mind the crowd of people in my home.

Lucie said, "Props to Audrey. You've got to respect someone so committed to running the show."

"I'm not so sure," Andrew said. "She has eyes everywhere. I thought it'd be over when I left home, but she knows everything I do." He rolled his eyes.

"It's because you're a public figure now, sweetie." Carly laid her hand on his arm. "She watches your math videos. We can't even be frenemies anymore." Carly leaned toward Lucie and me.

"After she got over the initial shock of Andrew leaving a high-paying job to star in dorky math videos, she became his biggest supporter. Not a week goes by when some school doesn't call him because Audrey suggested it."

"That's sweet and also cringe," Lucie said. "What are your parents like, Oliver?"

"Cold and stuffy," he said. "Don't get me wrong—they're proud of me, but there's a reason I live on the opposite side of the country."

"God, I wish I'd thought to move two thousand miles away from my cold, stuffy parents," Lucie said. "But that's perfect. Plus, you'll never have to meet Tessa's parents either."

My skin went cold with premonition as Carly reached for my hand. Her mother had died a long time ago too.

"Actually, I already met her dad," he said.

My cheeks went hot as my friends stared at me. "Wait, I thought your dad was dead," Lucie said.

"No, he's only eccentric," Oliver continued cluelessly. "He organized a protest at the lab."

"What?" Lucie ground her jaw. She hated dishonesty. And even though I'd never said my dad was dead, I'd let my friends believe it. It was easier than explaining my fucked-up childhood. I didn't want their pity.

"They don't know?" Oliver asked, his eyes wide behind his glasses. His hair flopped over them in a way that seemed adorable that morning but now I found irritating. Ice-cold anger crawled through my veins.

"Come with me." I turned and jogged up the stairs. A second later, his footsteps echoed behind me. I stormed to the farthest guest room, the one where I'd closed up the girls, and stood in the middle of it, arms crossed. Anita leaped off the bed and rubbed against my leg.

Oliver stopped in the doorway. "Look, I'm sor—"

"Close the door."

He stepped fully into the room and shut the door with a soft click. "I'm sorry. I didn't know you hadn't told them about your dad. *Why* didn't you tell them?"

"Because it's not something I'm proud of, and it's none of their business."

"But they're your friends."

"Exactly. *My* friends. Which means you have no right to decide what they know about and what they don't."

"But..." He tilted his head. "Don't you trust them?"

"I do. Now I don't trust you." Like she was telling me how unreasonable I was being, Anita meowed. I bent and picked her up. But instead of flopping onto my shoulder the way she usually did, she leaned over my forearm and watched Oliver, flicking her tail.

He paled. "I'm so sorry. What can I do?"

"I don't know." I stared down at Anita's soft blue-gray fur. What he'd done wasn't so terrible. I'd have eventually told my friends, maybe on a night when I'd had an extra glass of wine. When Savannah was beside me. *She* hadn't told anyone, so I could trust her.

Unlike Oliver.

When he stepped closer, Anita shifted her weight toward him. He held out his hands, and she leaped into them. She turned and glared at me as if to remind me, *We like him.*

We did. Which made it hard to despise him, even after he'd broken my trust.

"I'll do anything," he pleaded. "I won't speak for a week. I'll wear a hair shirt."

I couldn't help but smile. "Sounds itchy."

"I'll write that sonnet about you. It'll be awful."

I chuckled. "God, no. Look, be careful what you say about

me. It takes me a while to trust people. The fact that you're here is an anomaly."

"I understand. And I'm honored."

"Okay." I took a deep breath. He'd said all the right things, and even though it felt like I was wearing that hair shirt under my skin, I needed to let it go. He'd meant well. And I liked him. "Let's go downstairs before they get into the good liquor."

"Tell me where it is, and I'll pour you a glass." Gently, he set the cat down on the bed, then rubbed the tense muscle between my shoulder and my neck.

"Yes, please," I said.

He leaned forward to rumble in my ear, "After everyone goes home, I'll give you a back rub."

"Sounds fantastic."

He held my hand as we walked back downstairs to the party. He stayed by my side, laying his hand on my lower back or brushing the inside of my wrist or leaning his shoulder against mine whenever he could, like his touch could reassure me he'd never betray my trust again. And I let him because it felt good. He knew all the ways to set my heart thumping in anticipation of what we'd do alone when everyone went home. But from now on, my skin would be a barrier. I wouldn't trust him with any more of my secrets.

28

GLOBAL WARMING? NO,
IT'S THE CHEMTRAILS

From Barry Wright's manifesto:
*Those "condensation trails" left by aircraft are actually streams of
chemicals the government is using to control the weather.*

TESSA

When I woke up, I knew exactly what kind of day it would be: a pain day.

Stabs radiated through my abdomen as I lay on my side. The weight of Oliver's hand seemed to focus the throb of it. Gently, I lifted his palm and set it behind me. I tucked up my knees, curling around the ache.

Behind me, he shifted his body closer and touched my shoulder. "What's wrong?"

"Hurts."

He sat up. "I'll get your medicine."

I breathed slowly in and out as deeply as the pain allowed, trying to imagine a tiny amount of the pain leaving my body on each exhale. It was total bullshit. The only thing that would dull the cramp was naproxen.

He was back in a minute with a glass of water and the prescription bottle. Although he'd pulled on his sexy sweatpants, I couldn't focus on anything but the knives cutting me open.

"Can you sit up?" he asked.

I moaned and instantly hated myself. He shouldn't see me like this. Since he'd spilled my secret at Savannah's birthday party almost two weeks ago, I'd blocked him from everything but my bed. Now I wished I'd kicked him out last night. I'd known my period was coming, and the cramps that came with it, but I'd been too wrung out from orgasms to move, much less tell him to go away.

I grasped his hand and let him pull me up to sitting and leaned against the headboard. I breathed through another wave of pain, then brushed the tangled hair out of my eyes. He shook a tablet from the bottle into my palm, then handed me the glass of water. I gulped it down and closed my eyes, willing it to dissolve quickly into my bloodstream.

"Do you need to go to the bathroom?" he asked.

I groaned, anticipating the pain that would shoot through me with every step. "Yes."

"I'll carry you." He bent, already scooping his arms under my knees and back.

"Absolutely not." My voice was stronger now. "Give me your hand."

I let him pull me up to standing and leaned on him until we made it to the bathroom door. "I've got it from here."

"You sure? I don't want you to fall." The adorable little line creased between his eyebrows.

"I'm a forty-three-year-old woman who's been successfully walking since I was one. I'm not going to fall."

"Okay." But he didn't release my elbow.

I extricated my naked body from his grasp and shut the door.

By the time I'd used the toilet and brushed my teeth, I realized that standing upright pulled muscles that only wanted to curl in like a pill bug. I accepted that I wouldn't be going to work today or—I glanced in the mirror at my snarled hair and pale face—going on camera in meetings.

I tugged on a pair of loose joggers and a Berkeley hoodie from my closet, along with a pair of thick socks, then I padded down the hall. Oliver sat at my kitchen table reading something on his phone, a cup of coffee in his other hand. He wore the green Dartmouth T-shirt that lived at my house now.

"I thought you'd be on your way to work," I said, pulling a mug off the rack.

He jumped up. "Let me do that. Lie down on the couch."

"I can pour my own coffee." My voice came out testy.

"Of course you can." He set a soothing palm on my back. "But I want to do it. Go rest."

"I'm not an invalid." I grabbed my laptop bag from the hook by the door. "I've been dealing with this since you were in diapers."

He only hummed and popped two slices of bread into the toaster.

I shuffled to the couch and powered on my laptop.

He set a steaming mug of coffee on the table. "You don't have to work today. You can take it easy."

"Of course I have to work today. How else is the budget going to get done?"

"It can wait. Or I can do it. I've got my laptop. I'll work in your study so I don't bother you."

"So you can hover over me? No, thanks. Go to work."

He perched on the other side of the couch. "Are you sure? What if you need something?"

"Then I'll get it for myself like the grown-up I am." When his smile faded, I said, "If I truly need help, Savannah's here. Go to work. They need you."

He worked his jaw. "Fine. I'll text you to check in."

"Okay. But I might take a nap, so don't worry if I don't text back right away."

He swallowed like he'd tasted something bitter. Worrying was his superpower. "Okay."

He lingered for a few more minutes, bringing me toast and a banana, then a pillow and a blanket from my bed. Finally, he leaned over and kissed my forehead.

"I'm having an endometriosis flare-up, not dying," I grumbled.

Grinning, he rested his knee on the edge of the couch, tipped up my chin, and kissed my lips. He was gentle at first, but I grabbed the collar of his sweatshirt and pulled him closer. I might be ten years older than he was, wearing a faded college hoodie fraying at the cuffs, and high on some pretty serious pain meds, but I was still sexy.

He went with it, bruising my lips, then licking inside with the bitter taste of coffee on his tongue. With a nip at my lower lip, he pulled away. "Better?"

"Yeah, I think so." My head was swimming too much to remember which chemicals were produced by kissing, but they must have had some palliative effect on pain too.

"Good. I'll bring you a scrip for more of those tonight."

I crossed my arms. "You're not that kind of doctor."

"No, I'm the sexy kind." He gave me one last, lingering kiss and walked out.

I stared at his ass until he shut the door. *Isn't that the truth.*

Being alone didn't feel as good as I thought it would. The room seemed empty without him, and I almost, *almost* wished he were here to refill my coffee when it was empty. Instead, as

the naproxen dulled my pain, I set my laptop on the floor,
burrowed under the blanket, and slept.

I woke when my phone rattled against the coffee table.

OLIVER

How are you feeling?

I assessed my body.

Tired. But better

Great. Need anything?

"Good, you're up." Savannah walked in with a glass of water
and the pill bottle. "Want a sandwich?"

My stomach felt sour from the long nap. "No, I'm okay."

"You need to eat something with your medicine. How about
a cookie?"

"Mmm. Is there any coffee left?"

"I'll make a fresh pot." She returned to the kitchen, and I
picked up my phone.

No, Savannah's taking care of me

My phone buzzed with another text.

CARLY

Savannah says you're having a rough day.
Anything I can do?

Of course she'd told on me. Irritation prickled in my fingers.

No, I'm okay. She's hovering tho

LUCIE

Want us to come over tonight, or would it be
more helpful to leave you alone?

I'll let you know later

I didn't hate the idea of them coming over for some comfort snacks. But that meant I couldn't spend the night with Oliver.

What?

I wanted to spend the night with Oliver *instead of* my best friends?

Goddammit.

I hadn't protected myself from him at all. He'd weaseled his way inside my defenses with his amazing dick. And those lips. Not to mention his fingers.

I was in trouble.

To distract myself from those troubling emotions, I picked up my laptop, set it on my knees, and opened my email.

New messages cascaded into my inbox like usual. Questions from Dr. Perrell. A message from the CFO I'd have to come back to later. An update from West about the key positions we were recruiting for.

But there were also several messages from Sadie. And Aanya and Huong and Ekaterina.

Hey, how are you doing?

Sending good vibes your way!

Heard you had a flare-up. Feel better soon!

What.

The.

Hell.

How had they found out?

Only one person could have told them.

It was one thing for Savannah to tell our best friends I was in pain. It was another thing for Oliver to talk about my condition *at work.*

I closed my eyes, willing the rage to recede. But it flowed hot in my veins.

"Savannah," I called. "I'm going to need some chocolate. Lots of chocolate."

$\sim$

*L*ater that afternoon, Oliver came home.

Not *home.* My home, not his. Not at all. I smoothed my hair away from my face and straightened my shoulders.

Instead of hello, I said, "Why did you tell everyone I was sick?"

He frowned. "They asked where you were."

"They asked *you* where I was? Do they know about us?"

"No." He put up his hands defensively. "Of course not. They asked in general. I said you'd called in sick."

"Why'd you have to say anything at all?" I wanted to stand up, pace around and look strong. But my stomach was full of knives, and it was all I could do to sit upright.

"Be-because they asked. Because they care. Because I care."

"You shouldn't have said anything. It's my news to tell. Or not."

"I'm sorry," he said. "They wanted to know. I thought it might make you feel better to know they care about you."

"It didn't." Maybe it was true, or maybe it wasn't. Regardless, I didn't want Oliver to share my personal medical situation with anyone. That was much more important.

"I'm sorry," he repeated. He perched on the coffee table and took my hand. "What can I do to make it up to you?" He ran a finger up my palm to my wrist.

I snatched my hand back and folded my arms across my chest. "Not that."

"Really?" He rested a finger above my knee.

"Really." But even to myself, I sounded uncertain.

His voice went deep. "Because if you're feeling up to it, I could slip off those sweatpants and do what I did the other night when you screamed my name."

"What was that?" I pretended not to know exactly what he was talking about.

He dipped his chin. "I think you know."

I looked away. "Shit."

He scooted closer until our knees touched. "I really am sorry I crossed the line." He leaned forward and kissed me sweetly on the lips. Then he put his lips to my ear. "Let me take you to bed. I'll make you come, then I'll bring you dinner. Or we can do it in the reverse order."

"Savannah made fresh cookies, and I've been eating them all afternoon. I can do without dinner."

"Then I've got time to make you come twice. Let's go." He stood and held out his hand to me.

I took his hand and let him lead me to bed. But as I hit my climax, and as he curled his body around mine, I reminded myself it was only about sex. I couldn't trust him with my heart.

29

ANTIGEN

Antigen: *A substance that induces an immune response in the body.*

OLIVER

"Wait. You missed our exit." Tessa turned her head to watch it roll by outside the window.

"No, I didn't," I said, trying not to sound smug.

"I'm pretty sure you did. The office is back there."

"We're not going to the office."

"We're not?" She cocked her head at me, a few of her freckles disappearing into her scrunched-up nose.

"The trials are going great. The results are strong. The team can handle it for a couple of days."

Smirking, she rubbed her ear. "Wait. You must be a body-snatcher. Because the real Oliver wouldn't trust something to the team. Not two weeks before we're scheduled to wrap up the trial."

Keeping both hands on the wheel, I shrugged. It felt performative, but if I focused on Tessa, I could keep my mind off work. Mostly. "It's only going to get busier after this when we produce the final analysis and the regulatory approval submission. This is our last free weekend for a while, and work has been brutal. You deserve some relaxation."

"So do you." She reached across the console and squeezed my knee. The warmth of her touch radiated up my leg. Taking a short trip to spend time together and reconnect was a brilliant idea. True, we'd spent almost every night together for six weeks, but seeing her at work every day and having to pretend we weren't together was hard on me. It had to be hard on her too. I could feel a brittle barrier forming between us like a snail's shell.

Her hand slid up my leg, and the warmth turned into a tingle. The one place I didn't feel that brittleness was in bed. I couldn't get enough of her. And despite the fact that her best friends always asked before they hugged her, she couldn't keep her hands off me either.

"Whoa," I yelped as her fingers grazed my groin. "No feeling me up while I'm driving."

"Spoilsport." She moved her hand back to her side of the car.

"Distracted driving kills more people than plane and train crashes combined. Besides, there'll be plenty of time for that at the spa."

"We're going to a spa? Like a day spa?"

"No, we're staying through the weekend. I want you fully relaxed by Sunday."

"But what about the girls? And I didn't pack anything. This isn't one of those nudist spas, is it?"

For once, I was the one reassuring her. "Savannah is taking care of the cats. Also, she packed you a bag. Though you can be as naked as you want in our room."

"I guess you've thought of everything. As usual." She leaned back in her seat. "Mind if I connect to your car audio? We need some tunes for a road trip."

Tessa's taste in music was a combination of '90s emo rock,

old-school hip hop, and more modern angry empowerment anthems, but I didn't mind. My car had an entry for Tessa's phone like we were a real couple. We were on our way to a relaxing getaway together. Maybe, if everything went well this weekend, she'd agree to an out-in-the-open relationship beyond her close circle of friends.

The spa was exactly like the photos on the website. The lobby was decorated in soothing beige and plum with white roses and purple lupine in vases. It smelled like sea sage even though we were a few miles from the beach. Sunlight filtered through a set of skylights, and something soothing and nonbiological, like wind or waves, played through hidden speakers.

"This is..." When Tessa's voice trailed off, I held my breath. Did she hate it? Would she have preferred something in the city, wherever she normally went? Should I have gotten her a gift card instead? "...lovely."

I breathed again and let go of her suitcase handle so I could tangle my fingers with hers. "Glad you like it. Let's check in."

After I gave our names to the woman at the desk, she said, "Ms. Wright, we understand you might be interested in some of our low-touch services. We offer a sauna, both traditional and infrared, light therapy, and ionic foot detox. We even have a float tank. We can also tailor our regular massage and body wrap services to fit with our clients' sensitivities."

Tessa blinked for a few seconds. I'd never known anything to stun Tessa into silence, but this did it. Then she whirled and kissed me hard on the lips. Finally, she turned back to the receptionist. "Let's see what you've got."

I took a step away to give her space and, grinning, stuck my hands in my pockets. This was going even better than I'd planned.

When the door opened and closed softly, I glanced at the newcomer. A blond guy, about my height and good-looking in a

Jude Law kind of way, sauntered into the room. His gaze traveled over me but fixed on Tessa's red hair. He tilted his head. "Tess?"

She froze like a sparrow listening to the scream of a hawk. Slowly, she turned to face him. "Harry." Her voice was flat. "What are you doing here?"

This was Harry? I scrutinized him from the gray hair at his temples to the lines around his eyes. I cursed the signs of aging that only made him look more distinguished. His clothes were that effortless kind of casual that communicated wealth and confidence.

"This is my favorite spa. I live down the road in Santa Cruz, but I'm sure you knew that." He stepped forward. "What are you doing here, love?"

It sounded like a question he knew the answer to.

"I'm here with my...with my boyfriend." Her voice wavered. "What are the odds?" Gently, she nudged me out of the way and took a step toward him.

I hadn't realized I'd stepped in front of her. I wished I could do it again when he grasped her elbows and kissed her on both cheeks.

"Boyfriend?" He scanned me more closely. "I suppose he *is* a boy." He stuck out his hand. "Harry Boseman."

I gripped it as hard as I could. "Oliver Bond. *Dr.* Oliver Bond."

His handshake was just as brutal. "A doctor? Well, well, well. I didn't realize they were passing out advanced degrees in kindergarten these days."

I took a deep breath to say...I didn't know what. I hated to disturb the peace of the spa, but this dickwad was pissing me off.

Releasing my hand, he said, "We should catch up after your treatments. The restaurant is lovely. They serve the most refreshing cucumber martini."

"I don't think so," Tessa said. "I'm here with Oliver, and three's a crowd."

Something big and bright expanded in my chest. It must have spread onto my face because Harry scowled at me. A second later, his expression turned bland.

He gave Tessa another two-cheek kiss, but this time, he lingered at her ear. Just loud enough for me to hear, he murmured, "Call me, love. We'll catch up."

"Goodbye, Harry," she said firmly. Then, turning back to the receptionist, she said, "Do you have anything for couples?"

I stood up straighter. My weeks of planning had paid off. She loved it. And given enough time, she might love me too. Not bothering to give Harry the victorious smirk he deserved, I took in a lungful of the sage-scented air and rested my hand on her back as the receptionist resumed her review of the spa menu with Tessa.

~

*D*uring the couples' massage she chose, she instructed the masseuse how and where to touch her. Once she sighed in pleasure, I relaxed too and melted into the table they'd set up in our room. I must have fallen asleep because the next thing I knew, Tessa touched the back of my hand.

"Hey," she whispered.

I opened my eyes to find her sitting on her table, a towel wrapped around her. I felt the corners of my mouth curve up. She was so beautiful with her hair piled up on top of her head, secured with a clip. Russet tendrils escaped at her temples, and a few silver threads glittered in the candlelight. Her freckled skin shone in the dim light.

"Hey," I murmured. "You okay?"

"I'm great. I feel so lazy."

"Lazy is good. You deserve it." I hated to bring it up, but his presence crowded into our private room. "Earlier...meeting Harry. Are you okay?"

A line formed between her eyebrows. "It was unexpected. But it's fine. I run into him from time to time. Silicon Valley is small. Something I'm reminded of every time I run into one of my many former employees who still hates me for what happened."

I regretted mentioning that douchebag and stirring up memories that made her smooth forehead wrinkle. My stomach tensed. If things went badly with the ovarian cancer test and we had to sell Discovery to Greenwich, she might despise me too.

Should I tell her about the possibility of a sale? I'd want to know. I craved information to soothe my worries. But Tessa was different. She rolled with new challenges. Besides, the clinical trials were going great. We wouldn't have to sell. It wasn't worth stressing her out. Not when she was this relaxed.

"Good," I said. "Now, what can I do to help you feel even lazier?"

She traced a finger up her forearm. "I'm going to shower off the massage oil."

I propped myself up on my elbow, careful not to move too suddenly since I was hard under my towel. "Okay. I can call the front desk and have them take away the tables."

"Or...you could join me? Massages make me horny."

I sat up so quickly the towel flopped to the floor. My erection bobbed in front of me. "Thank god. I thought it was only me."

Grinning, she slid off the table and dropped her towel. "Race you to the shower. Loser gives head first."

I lingered to blow out the candles. It wasn't safe to leave them unattended.

When I made it to the bathroom, she had the water started

in the shower that was large enough for six. "You didn't even try." She pouted.

"Getting on my knees for you is what I want to do." I slipped my arms around her, resting my palms on her butt, which was the only part of her not slick with massage oil. I squeezed the lower curve of her ass. "Now get in the shower so I can have my wicked way with you."

When she rose on her toes to kiss me, her stomach pressed against my dick and sent a surge of pleasure through me. "Let's see who's more wicked," she murmured against my lips.

I followed her into the shower, where warm water enveloped me from all sides from six body sprays on the walls and a rain head from above. I poured the sage-scented body wash into my palm, lathered it up, and stepped behind her.

"Mmm," she hummed, leaning against me. My cockhead slipped against the oil on her back. "That's what I'm talking about."

"Is it?" I stepped back and started at her nape, soaping up her skin and smoothing off the oil.

"I expected you to start lower." She tried to scoot back, but I held her in position, rubbing the suds over her shoulders, her arms, and her hands. Her wrists went loose and floppy. "But this is pretty good too."

I kissed the clean skin of her shoulder. "Exactly." Then I started again on her back, stroking down toward her waist. Her butt was free of the oil, but I washed it anyway, teasing a finger into the valley between her cheeks. She hummed and widened her stance. Was she into ass play? I didn't have much experience with it, but I liked the idea of exploring it with her, later.

I smoothed down the backs of her legs and kneeled. "Hold the grab bar and lift your foot."

"Are you serious?" Her breathing was quick and shallow. "My foot?"

"There's oil on your feet, and I don't want you to slip. Hold on." I waited until she grasped the handle, then I lifted one foot at a time to scrub the soles of her feet. "Turn."

She did, which put her tempting pussy right at my eye level. "I'm ready to collect my winnings now," she said. "I'll even hold onto the grab bar."

"I'm not finished." I poured more body wash into my hands and started at her toes, then worked my way up her shins, over her knees, to her thighs, where I paused. "Hmm, I don't think this is massage oil." I scooped some of the shiny liquid from the inside of her thigh onto my finger and popped it into my mouth. "Definitely not almond oil."

"My god." Her cheeks were red. "If I'd known you were going to—"

I brushed my knuckle over her clit, and she froze. "I think you need to learn some patience, sw—" I choked back the pet name. But with my finger on her nub, she must not have noticed.

"Antici…" She smoothed her hand down my cheek. "…pation. Am I right?"

"What?"

"Don't tell me you've never seen *The Rocky Horror Picture Show.*"

"Okay." I squirted more body wash into my palm. "I won't tell you."

"Sometimes I wonder if you're actually a millennial."

"Is that really what you want to be thinking about right now?" I rubbed soapy circles on her hipbones, then smoothed my hands across her stomach.

"I guess…" Her breath hitched when my hand brushed the underside of her breast. "Not."

The masseuse hadn't touched her breasts, but I did, rising to rub circles over them as her nipples hardened under my palms. Moaning, she pressed into my hands. She'd never come when

I'd touched only her breasts, and I'd always wondered if she could. Another time. Reluctantly, I moved away to her chest and neck.

"Want me to do your face?" I asked, pointing to the spots of oil where the masseuse had massaged her forehead and temples.

"Okay." She closed her eyes.

I rubbed two soapy fingers over her forehead, down the sides of her face to her cheeks, then across her freckled nose. I finished with a brush across her chin. I rinsed my hands and went back over her face with my wet fingers, wiping the suds away. When I stopped touching her, she wobbled.

"Are you okay?" I asked, gripping her elbow.

"I'm really relaxed." Her voice was low and sultry.

"Here." I turned off the body sprays and guided her to sit on the edge of the bench. I kneeled on the tile, out of range of the drenching showerhead. Steam billowed around us. "Comfortable?"

"Yeah."

"Hold onto the handles."

As soon as she grabbed them, I pressed her knees apart and ran my hands up the insides of her thighs. She groaned when I grazed her lips with my thumbs. "Fucking finally."

"What did you say before? Antici..." I teased her with my fingertips. "...pation?"

A string of curse words fell from her gorgeous lips. I spread her, then dived in to taste her, sucking, licking, and probing. Her breath stuttered out of her. She was close from the *anticipation.* Primal pride surged in my chest. I gripped the backs of her thighs, holding her in place, and fluttered my tongue around her vaginal opening.

She clutched the back of my head, pulling me to her. "Oliver. I need..."

"I know, baby," I rumbled. I licked up to her clitoris and tapped it with the tip of my tongue.

She pulled my hair. "More."

I gave it to her, gently sucking on her clit the way she liked until her shout echoed through the shower. Then I licked her down from her orgasm until she released my hair and melted against the tile wall.

I stood on shaky legs. I was close too, my dick leaking and aching from the pressure.

She gazed at it, licked her lips, then looked up at me. "Want to fuck me?"

"God, yes," I groaned. "Let me wash off, then we can go to bed."

"In here?" she said. She flicked her gaze around the shower like she was envisioning the best spot for it. "You can sit on the bench, and I'll sit on your lap."

"Condoms are in my suitcase," I said. "I'll wash off, then—"

"I get tested at every physical, and I'm clear of STIs. I've got an IUD." She bit her lip.

"I'm tested too," I said. "Are you sure?"

"I know what I want. Now sit."

A thrill ran up my spine, and my dick went even harder. I sat on the bench, and she rose on her knees to straddle my lap. I slid forward to give her knees space as she grasped my dick, then guided it inside her. We were both so slick from arousal that it was an easy glide until her ass rested on my thighs. She tightened around me, and my vision went gray at the edges. "I'm not going to last long."

"Good, because neither are my knees."

"Hold onto my shoulders." I gripped the handles and rocked my hips up. She flung one arm behind my neck and dropped her other hand to where we were connected. Her fingers caressed the base of my dick for a moment before settling on her clit. Her muscles fluttered around me.

Electricity raced up my spine, and I rocked into her once, twice more before my release shuddered through me. A second later, her hand stilled, and she groaned as her orgasm milked the last drops from me.

I leaned my head back against the tile, gazing at the sexiest, most brilliant person I'd ever met. Today had been perfect, between the massage and the shower. She was so relaxed, and she'd let me into her trust. We could have so many more perfect days together if she'd keep her walls down. Hope bloomed in my belly.

I gazed up at her pleasure-drunk smile. "I love you." I kissed her lips, then her cheek, then her jaw. "I love you." I buried my face in her shoulder. "I love you."

She hummed and kissed my hair. But she didn't say it back.

30

RESET

From Barry Wright's manifesto:
We call it the Great Reset. An international governing power—not a government but one of those conglomerates like the UN—will create a global disruption, such as a war or pandemic. After that, the power will take away individual ownership and autonomy, looking like they're doing us a favor the whole time. And they'll end up with total control over the population.

TESSA

Outside the window, the sky was ink-blue, the way it never was in San Francisco or Silicon Valley. Stars glittered over the rolling hills that surrounded the resort and were obscured at the horizon by the distant mountains. The only sound was Oliver's deep breathing as he slept. The arm that had pinned me to him was still flung over my side of the bed.

I wished there was a balcony where I could slip outside and hear the yips of the coyotes or a great horned owl or even an obnoxious mockingbird, but Oliver never would have chosen a room with a balcony. It wasn't safe. He even slept on the side of

the bed closest to the door, thinking he could protect me from
anything that came in.

What I needed protection from was already in the room. It
was him and the *baby* that had slipped past his lips, the
dangerous feelings that kept me from correcting him.

He knew, but he didn't understand how I used to sleep
outdoors next to a campfire all the time with nothing but my
sleeping bag and Dad's shotgun protecting me from any critters
that might slither or stalk past. He didn't know what it felt like to
face threats far more terrifying later: tech bro culture, a back-
stabbing partner, disgruntled employees who threatened
retribution. I pulled the fluffy robe up to my neck.

He thought together, we'd be safe. It was why he'd whispered, "I love you," into my skin like the Litany Against Fear
from *Dune.* He thought his love could offer me safety, but I knew
love was anything but safe.

I'd learned that from my dad.

Seeing Harry yesterday was a shocking but timely reminder.
I'd loved him too, desperately, naïvely. I'd trusted him to look
out for our—my—best interests, to advise me, to comfort me,
and to love me back. He hadn't. He'd used me for profit, and
after he got his payout, he walked away.

And now, like a fool, I'd tangled myself up with Oliver,
someone I worked with, someone who needed something from
me, someone who didn't understand my need to protect myself
and my secrets. He'd told Carly and Lucie about my dad like it
was no big deal. But exposing that shameful truth was a very big
deal to me.

And what else would he reveal about me, and to whom? I
liked living my secluded, private life. All it would take was one
leak for the media circus to blow up again. For some nosy
reporter to find my home and write me up as that eccentric
woman who used to be famous. No one would work with me

again, not even my favorite charities. I'd have destroyed the glass-brittle legacy I'd worked so hard to reconstruct.

I was older and wiser than I'd been with Harry. I couldn't let myself fall for it again. I'd fight to keep my independence, and I wouldn't get hurt.

Oliver shifted in the bed, tucked one of my pillows against his chest, and buried his face in it. My icy heart melted a little. He was so goddamned adorable, like a kitten. Maybe he actually thought he loved me. But as soon as I let my guard down, he'd ruin everything I'd worked so hard for, the way Hedy had shredded my curtains.

I couldn't let him do that to my heart.

31

PHOSPHATE-BUFFERED SALINE

Phosphate-buffered saline (PBS). A solution used in biological research to maintain a constant pH.

OLIVER

I wished we were in my car. Then I'd feel more in control of the argument I was about to ignite.

It was a win that Tessa had agreed to drive to work together. Up until now, she'd insisted on driving separately although we started and ended our days at her place. But her environmentalist, tree-hugging, electric vehicle–loving heart finally caved to my suggestion that we carpool.

So I gripped the armrest instead of the steering wheel and said, "I think we should go public."

"What are you talking about?" She glanced at me from the driver's seat. "You've got plenty of funding. There's no reason to do an IPO right now. Believe me. Been there, done that, got the crappy T-shirt and fourteen years of nothing but bad press."

"I'm not talking about the company. I'm talking about us. You and me."

"Go...public? With our relationship? That sounds like something a pop star would do. I don't even use ClickClackGo."

"All I'm asking is for us to walk into the office together. Do our jobs. Eat lunch in the cafeteria at the same time. Then walk out together. Nothing major. I promise, I won't kiss you at work."

"You mean you won't kiss me at work *again*." She smirked. "We've already crossed that line."

"Definitely not again. Now that we're officially together."

She shifted her hands on the wheel, and they made a sticky, sucking sound against the leather. "I don't know. It was kind of terrible when I dated a colleague before. The smug looks, the assumptions..."

The last thing I wanted to think about right now was douchebag Harry. "Everyone would support us. Think about it. You don't have to decide today." I couldn't let her make a snap decision to stay secret. It would make it that much easier for her to walk away.

She glanced at me as she slowed to turn into the parking lot. "I'll consider it."

"Thank you." I wanted to slip my arms around her and kiss her, but one, she was driving, and two, we were still a secret.

After she parked at the far end of the lot, I didn't give her a good-bye kiss. I grabbed my satchel and the boxes of donuts we'd picked up, gave her an awkward wave, and trudged toward the building. Once I was inside, she'd drive up to her reserved spot and breeze into the lab like we hadn't spent the weekend at the spa or last night cuddled up in her bed. I hated the dishonesty of it, but with Tessa, I'd take what she'd give me, and so far, this was it.

Once I'd set down my laptop in my office and the donuts in the breakroom, I walked into the lab and shrugged into my coat. The lab was the same as any other Monday morning, quiet and sleepy until everyone's second cup of coffee. I rolled my shoulders while mentally organizing my to-do list.

Sadie walked in. When she saw me, her eyes narrowed. Then, like every other Monday, she said, "Hey, Ollie. Did you have a good weekend?"

"It was excellent," I said. "How was yours?"

Instead of reaching for her lab coat, she grabbed the sleeve of mine. "Come with me." She pulled me out into the hallway. "No, really. *How was your weekend?*" Her eyebrows disappeared into her blond bangs.

"Very relaxing. Why are we standing in the hallway?"

"Because of *this.*" She pulled her phone from the back pocket of her jeans and tapped it a few times. Then she turned the screen to face me.

It was one of those social media sites, not one I used. ClickClackGo, if I wasn't mistaken. On it was a photo of Tessa, an old one, her red hair scraped back into a ponytail, and dark circles shadowing her eyes. I missed the faint smile lines around her mouth and eyes and the sparkling silver threads in her hair. She looked young, exhausted, and scared.

I tapped to read the caption: *She's done it again. Tessa Bond is fucking her colleague, according to a credible source. Like it wasn't bad enough when she was too busy fucking her number-two to keep Red Rover afloat, now she's getting cozy with the founder of Discovery Diagnostics, where she's currently working. I hope those poor saps know what they're in for...*

My heart hammered, and I shoved the phone back at her. "It's not true."

"You're not with Tessa?" she asked. "Because you didn't fool anyone by walking in separately. You can see the parking lot from practically every window in the building, and no one else drives a car as expensive as hers, not even you."

"No, it's true we're together. I meant that she's going to destroy Discovery. That's false."

"Of course it's false. She's helping us kick ass. But this"—she waved her phone—"isn't the best way for the lab to find out about you two."

"What." Tessa's voice didn't rise on the question. It whispered out of her like her last breath.

Neither Sadie nor I had heard her approach in her soft-soled boots. She had her hand on the latch to enter the lab, and her green eyes were wide and wild as the thunderstorm I'd seen rolling in one spring break in Fort Myers.

"What did you say?"

32

IT'S ONLY A PROJECTION

From Barry Wright's manifesto:
The Earth is flat. Everyone knows it. The moon is an image projected onto a hollow sphere surrounding the plane of our existence.

TESSA

I went still as a statue. Even my heart stopped beating, and my lungs seized.

"What did you say?"

When Sadie turned her innocent blue eyes on me, they were shadowed with betrayal. "Why'd we have to find out from Click-ClackGo? Why couldn't you be, like, cool about it?"

"We—" I glanced at Oliver, but there was no help there. He stared at his loafers as if to keep from reminding me that he'd wanted to tell our colleagues weeks ago. "I wanted to keep my private life private."

"Really?" The mournful tip of her lips was a reminder that she'd shared her hopes, dreams, and secrets with me.

"Look, I'm sorry, I—"

"Tessa. Oliver. Just the *couple* I wanted to see." Judgment sharpened the already crisp consonants in Maya's voice. "My office, please."

"Of...of course, Dr. Perrell," Oliver said. "We'll be there in five."

A sour taste formed on my tongue. Despite his ownership of a large portion of the company's shares, Oliver deferred to Maya like she was his professor and he was some shivering undergrad.

"Walk with me now," she said. "West is waiting." She turned and marched down the hallway.

Oliver's face was pale, but he steeled his jaw. "It's fine. We knew eventually—"

"It's not fine," I growled. "This is the opposite of fine." Without a backward glance at him or Sadie, I followed the CEO.

As she'd said, West was already in her office. He lounged on her sofa, one ankle crossed over his other knee. A sheaf of papers lay on the coffee table in front of him.

At Red Rover, our HR policies had been lax. Common sense, I'd called them. I'd taken the stance that we were all adults, so why make rules? That was why it looked so incriminating when I ignored the ethical boundaries I should have obeyed. Of course Discovery Diagnostics had a policy. And papers. Maybe that was my employment contract that I'd blithely signed so many months ago. Maybe it had a morality clause I'd missed because I'd never intended to sleep with the chief scientist.

Oliver closed the door with a soft snick. Maya planted her sensible heels on the carpet and propped her fists on her hips like a superhero with justice on her side. All she needed was a cape. "Well? Is it true what they're saying on social media?"

"Social media?" My brain was so staticky I hadn't questioned how Sadie had found out.

At the same time, Oliver said, "It's true. And there's nothing wrong with it. Right, West?"

"Wait," I said. "You mean *everyone* knows?"

"It doesn't matter," Oliver said. "We did nothing wrong."

"I don't give a fuck," I said. "Whether or not it's against company policy, it's the perception. I…" My lungs shriveled, and my breath left me.

In a moment, Oliver was at my side, his arm around me. "I've got you."

If he hadn't been the only thing keeping me upright, I'd have stepped away to put some much-needed distance between us. But because all my hard parts had temporarily dissolved, I leaned on the man I'd called my boyfriend all weekend.

Shit. The weekend. Someone who'd seen us at the spa had outed us. And I had one guess who.

"You mean the perception that you engaged in a highly inappropriate affair with a much younger man?" Maya finished my sentence.

I met her gaze, and understanding zipped along it. I'd fucked up, and she was calling me on it.

"Hold on," West said, gesturing at the papers. He was the only one of us sitting. "Tessa and Oliver both report to you. There's no policy that forbids relationships between equals."

"I was the one who initiated it," Oliver said. "If anyone's to blame, it's me."

"Like Tessa said, it's the optics," Maya said. "She should know better."

That sliced right through me, and the pain, like a diamond blade, sharpened everything soft inside me. "I should have." I stepped out of Oliver's hold and stood tall and straight.

Oliver looked like a kicked puppy. For a second, I regretted saying I should have resisted our attraction, that I could have, but I couldn't worry about that now, not while everything we'd worked for hung in the balance.

"It's okay," West said. "I've got some papers for you both to sign and then we'll be good."

Good? Not even close. Before my lungs could empty out again, I said, "I'll review the papers in my office. Are we done here?"

Before anyone could respond, I snatched the papers from the table and fled.

33

CONTRAINDICATION

Contraindication: *A circumstance that makes a treatment more risky or inadvisable for an individual.*

OLIVER

*B*ack in the lab, everything had a kind of haze to it. It wasn't as bad as the day after Simon died, when my eyes—everyone's eyes—had been smeared with tears, and my limbs were too heavy to move, but my stomach had the same hollow feeling. Why was I trying to work, or pretending to, when what I needed was to go to Tessa's office and hug her, or talk to her, or hold her hand, whatever she needed to bring the color back to her cheeks?

But I understood what she meant when she asked if we were done and flew out of Dr. Perrell's office like she was being chased by an orc. She needed space. I couldn't give back her privacy or her gossip-free life, but I'd give her space to think.

I was glad she hadn't come to the lab. The people who hadn't been in Dr. Perrell's office thought it was funny that Tessa and I were together. Some cuffed me on the shoulder like I'd done something great. Others gave me sly smirks as they passed like they'd known all along.

Every time the door opened, I looked up, searching for her. Which made it difficult for me to focus on the trial results I was trying to analyze. They didn't conform to the pattern we'd seen in the other tests, but I knew it was because my mind was hovering outside Tessa's office, hoping she'd rejoin me and we'd be good again.

"Hey," Sadie said sometime after lunch. Not that I'd eaten anything. I sat at my workstation, my phone beside me in case Tessa left her office or texted me.

"What's up?" I looked up from the nonsensical results.

"I'm sorry about earlier," Sadie said. "I should've been more chill about you two. I...you know."

"I know." Of all the people in the lab, only Sadie seemed to have any negative emotions about our outed relationship. As my almost-sister, she'd expected to be in on my secret. "It's okay."

"Is it?" She glanced around the lab. "Or is she feeling some sort of way about it and hiding?"

"She'll come around," I said. She had to. What we had was too special to be ruined by a snarky social media post or censure from the CEO.

"I hope so." She squeezed my forearm. "I was so glad you two were getting along. The lab runs so smoothly now."

"It does, doesn't it?" As COO, Tessa had made positive changes. We no longer ran out of supplies. And communication was better, so we knew what everyone was working on. I'd never wanted Tessa here to begin with, and now I didn't know how I'd live without her.

But thinking about Tessa made me restless, so after Sadie settled at her bench, I went to Yujun's workstation, where he hunched over his laptop.

"Afternoon, Yujun. Are you feeling okay?"

When he snapped up his head, his face was pale. "We need to talk."

"I've got time." I waited.

"In your office."

Shit. Was he upset about the distraction Tessa and I had created? Was he tendering his resignation? I could *not* lose him. Not when we were so close to successfully finishing our clinical trials and getting the cancer test on its way to approvals. My mind spun with worst-case scenarios. The lab would be chaos. No one would know where to find microtiter plates. Or the buffers and reagents we used on a daily basis. Work would stop. Dr. Perrell would be *pissed.* Numb, I led the way to the door, took off my lab coat, and held the door for Yujun. We walked to my office in silence.

Yujun waited for me to close the door but didn't bother to sit. "We screwed up, Oliver."

A chill dribbled down my chest to my stomach. "What happened?"

"The samples were mislabeled. We accidentally used the endometriosis patients' samples in the ovarian cancer patients' tests. The test results are invalid."

"Wait. *All* of them?"

"No, only the batch from last week."

No wonder I couldn't make sense of the results today. I had a moment of relief before my shoulders tensed again. We were supposed to finish the analysis this week, and now we wouldn't.

Things had been going so well that I'd gotten overconfident. I'd spent last week planning our spa weekend and then actually abandoning the lab on Thursday and Friday while I should've been double-checking the samples. This was my fault.

"It's my fault," Yujun said. "I let myself get complacent and didn't validate the samples."

"It's not your fault," I said. "I should've checked too. But we can salvage this. It's only a week's worth of samples. We can invalidate those tests and use the spare samples."

He winced. "The fridge shorted out over the weekend. We lost the samples that were in there. It wouldn't have been a big deal since we were so close to the end, but..." He held out his hands, empty.

"Without those samples, the test is incomplete. Can you call the study coordinator and see if she can get the participants to come back in? Or else make some calls to see if anyone has samples they can lend us?"

"I'll do that. I'm really sorry. I—"

"It's not your fault." I patted his shoulder. "We'll figure it out." Even I knew it was a lie.

After Yujun walked out, I paced my office. We'd gotten too ambitious. We'd taken on too much risk by sending two products to clinical trials at the same time. We'd sown the seeds for our own failure. And now we had no results to show.

Best case, we could get more samples and extend the trial to get the volume of data we needed. Worst case, we'd have to regroup and start over. We'd miss Dr. Perrell's deadline. The one I'd agreed to. And she'd have a case for whatever action she needed to take to salvage the company. Layoffs. Or selling the company.

If Simon was looking down on me, he'd be flipping me off. I'd ruined what he'd built.

34

THE BLACK KNIGHT

From Barry Wright's manifesto:
A satellite commonly known as the Black Knight *has been orbiting
Earth for thirteen thousand years, ever since it was launched by
extraterrestrial beings.*

TESSA

Fucking Harry.

It took me hours to gain some perspective on the whole shit show. But eventually, I realized that a social media post, one obviously planted by my ex, about how I was sleeping with my coworker wasn't nearly as bad as what had happened to my employees after I sold Red Rover. And despite what the post implied, I'd never let that happen here.

So what if Maya was upset? According to West, our relationship wasn't a violation of HR policy, so she couldn't fire me over it. Suddenly, I realized I desperately wanted to stay. I loved working at Discovery because of the important and creative work we did. I loved working with Oliver, too, though I wasn't ready to delve too deeply into the reasons why.

When I finally got over myself and emerged from my office, Oliver wasn't in the lab. I knew exactly where to find him.

Still, I was surprised when I entered the game room and he wasn't staring moodily at Simon's framed photo. Instead, he was playing *Galaxian,* a true classic and far rarer than its successor, *Galaga.* I'd played it for hours on the ancient machine at the gas station where I worked in the tiny town where we lived when I was fifteen. He didn't turn as I approached—probably couldn't hear me over the hum of the spaceship and the bleeps of the alien attacks.

He played with his whole body, yanking the joystick like he was furious at it. Finally, when he was hit and there was a muffled explosion, he smacked his hand on the console and shouted, "Fuck!"

I crossed my arms. "Annoying little buggers, aren't they?"

He whirled to face me. His skin was pale, and his brown eyes were wild and naked with his glasses tucked into his shirt pocket. "What—hi."

"Hi." I stepped closer. Now that everyone knew about us, how intimate we'd become, I could stand as close as I wanted. I whispered, "What's wrong?"

Gently, he clasped my hand. "I'm sorry. The trial is fucked."

"Are you serious?" A tiny part of me suspected he was catastrophizing, but I said, "Tell me."

He was right to worry. As he told me about the mix-up, my skin went clammy and pale. All that work, all those promising results wasted over a mistake anyone could have made. When he finished, I wrenched my hand out of his. "You can't seriously mean that our entire trial is ruined over a few missing results."

"Yujun checked. The study coordinator can't get us replacement samples for another month. And no one in the whole state has the kind of samples we need to finish it by the deadline. We're going to miss it. All our hard work has gone to shit."

"That's just…just…ridiculous," I sputtered. "We can fix anything with time and money."

His voice went softer. "That's exactly what we don't have. We're out of money. And time."

That was why they'd brought me on, because they were dangerously low on resources. And in the end, I hadn't been able to fix it. But this couldn't be the end. We could think our way out of this mess.

"I shouldn't have gone away last weekend. Not when the trial was on the line." He was spiraling.

"It's not your fault. There was no way for you to anticipate a mistake like this." The words sounded hollow, even to me. I'd been a company founder. I'd made disastrous mistakes. Every one had been my fault.

"I was getting a goddamn massage while our company was swirling into the toilet! And now we're—" He clutched at his hair.

I checked that we were still alone. Then, I gently disentangled his fingers from his hair and held his hand. "We're going to fix this."

When he looked at me, his eyes were glassy. "Can we?"

"Of course we can." I hadn't been able to save my employees, not after I'd made the tragic mistake of selling to people who didn't care about other humans, but I was older and wiser now. We'd find a way.

And that was exactly what we did. Oliver and I sat at the table where people sometimes played *Settlers of Catan* and reached out to every contact we had, trying to rescue the project.

Half an hour later, my phone buzzed. I didn't have to look to know what it meant. "It's time for my weekly meeting with Maya. Come with me. She's pissed, but we'll show her we're professionals. That we have ideas to fix this. We'll figure it out together."

I didn't think it was possible for him to get paler, but he managed it. "Are you okay?" I asked. "Do you need a snack?"

"I think we should devise a more concrete strategy before we take this to Dr. Perrell," he said. "Otherwise—"

"Who founded this company? You or her?"

"I did. Well, Simon and I did."

"Don't give away your power. I wish someone had told me that when I was your age." I squeezed his hand, then released it. "Come on."

Upstairs in Maya's office, she greeted us with a furrowed brow. "I didn't realize we were meeting with Oliver today. Or do you two go everywhere together now?"

Okay. She was still pissed. I shut the door. "We've encountered a complication with the clinical trials and wanted you to be aware."

"A complication?" Her eyebrows rose.

I sat in the chair on the other side of her desk and waited for Oliver to take his seat beside me. "The clinical trial ran into a snag, but we have a solution. You're the expert, Oliver. Why don't you tell her what happened?"

Haltingly, he explained the mix-up with the samples. Maya immediately understood the implications, and she scowled. Her intelligent eyes went unfocused, like she was calculating whether this year's bonus would cover her daughters' weddings. And I regretted that it might not, even if we did our best.

"But we have a solution," I said. I told her about the Indian supplier we'd reached out to. They could ship us samples that would allow us to complete the trial.

"Unfortunately," Oliver said, "it's possible they'll be delayed in customs for up to a week, maybe longer if we're unlucky, so we won't meet our end-of-month goal." He watched Maya's expression. It went from angry to resigned.

"It'll be close enough," I added.

Maya's jaw tightened. "There's no such thing as 'close enough.' This will delay the regulatory approvals, which, as you know, are public information. Greenwich will find out."

"Greenwich?" I repeated. "Greenwich Biomedical? Why the hell do we care about them?"

"The company will be worth less to them if we don't have a product on track to release to the market."

My heart stopped, then skipped. "Worth...less? What are you talking about?" I glanced at Oliver. He sucked in a breath and grasped my hand, despite our boss's judgmental gaze.

"We're in talks for a merger with Greenwich," she said. "The board is very enthusiastic about the potential return on investment, but we need the ovarian cancer test to be on track for approvals to maximize the company's value."

I knew what all those words meant, but together, they didn't make sense. "You're selling the company?" When the CEO didn't deny it, I turned to Oliver. "Did you know this?"

"I did." He stroked the back of my hand with his thumb. "But I thought we could avoid it."

I ripped my hand away. Of course he knew. He'd get a significant payout for his founder's shares.

"You've been sleeping together," Maya said, leaning forward, "and he didn't tell you?"

"You made me promise not to!" he yelped.

Ice washed through me.

"Tessa." He turned pleading eyes on me. "I wanted to, but—"

"Shit!" I rocketed to my feet. How had I let this happen *again*? How had I not seen what was happening? "Shit!"

"Calm down, Tessa," Maya said. "It's simply business. You'll get your equity share as outlined in your contract."

"Fuck my contract." My blood turned to lava, and my face burned with it. "And fuck you."

Maya stood. "There's no cause for unprofessionalism—"

I spoke over her. "Oliver, I trusted you."

He launched to his feet. "I didn't think it would come to this. I thought with the cancer test, we'd earn enough to keep the company independent."

My anger cooled to chilly realization. "It seems that the board doesn't agree." I glanced at Maya, who pursed her lips. "They're looking for an exit strategy."

"Something you should know all about," she said.

"Unfortunately, I do. And I don't want any part of this one. Consider my contract terminated." Oliver slumped into the chair like he'd been hit with a sorcerer's enervation spell. I towered over him. "I never want to see you again."

He jerked his head up, his eyes creased with a plea.

The caresses, the kind words, even the sex, had all been fake, exactly like Harry. He and Maya had used me. After I'd sworn never to be used again, I'd fallen for the same tricks.

Disgusted with myself, I stormed out.

I stopped in my former office to pick up my bag and keys, but I left everything else. They could keep the cardigan I wore when the office was too cold. The prickly cactus Sadie and the rest of the endometriosis team had given me as a gift when we sent the test to trials. Even my favorite coffee mug with a drawing of a black cat on it. I could replace all those things.

What I couldn't replace was my integrity, which I'd lost without even knowing it this time. How could I have missed the signs that Discovery was headed for a buyout? That Maya and Oliver were simply marking time until the tests were on the way to market and a buyer could swoop in, scoop up all the assets, and skip away, leaving destroyed lives behind like an old-fashioned game of jacks?

I slunk downstairs, bypassing the lab. I couldn't look any of those people in the eye, knowing they were headed for a future where they had to train their replacements before they were laid off with a severance package that wouldn't begin to cover the lengthy job searches ahead of them.

I kept my head down and gave Ramla, the security guard, one last pained smile as I slapped my badge on her desk. Then I walked out of the building into what I knew would be a lonely, uncertain future. Because I'd been here before.

35

STRAIN

Strain: *A genetically distinct variety of an organism.*

OLIVER

*Y*ujun cringed as he watched me slit open the cardboard box with my pocketknife. "You know, we have people for that."

Inside the box was the documentation, and I set it aside carefully. Shipment and customs had taken only four days, not the week or two we'd feared, and I refused to waste our luck. There would be no fuckups this time. We'd run these final tests ourselves, then we'd have enough data to present a strong regulatory filing.

I lifted out the Styrofoam case and set it on the lab table. "I know, but these are precious. Nothing can go wrong." I poked my tongue out between my teeth as I slipped the knife into the joint and cut through the tape.

"It's the techs' full-time job to process samples," he said. "They're much less likely to slice open their palms or burn their fingertips with dry ice."

Right. I slipped on my insulated gloves and waggled my fingers at him before I lifted the lid. A few tendrils of carbon dioxide vapor sublimated from the remaining dry ice pellets in the container. Underneath were the sealed plastic bags containing the blood vials.

"My precious," I hissed.

Sadie plunked herself down on the stool across the table from me. "Let me help. You can read out the numbers, and I'll catalog them."

"Sure. Less chance I'll make a transcription error that way. Wait." I looked up. She'd already taken off her lab coat and replaced it with her raincoat. Her satchel was slung over her shoulder, and a thick hardcover textbook poked out of it. "It's Thursday. You have class."

"I'll skip it. This is important." She shrugged off her satchel.

"No," I said. "School is more important. You're a scientist, Sadie. You should have the credentials to prove it. Yujun will help me. Or I can dictate the numbers and transcribe them after."

"I'll help you," Yujun said, pulling my laptop toward himself. "Go to school, Sadie. Be a scientist, not a lab rat."

"Lab techs are equally as important as scientists," I said. "We need everyone here." Especially when the whole company was on the line.

"Especially when you're doing it wrong," Yujun grumbled. "Switch with me." He pushed my laptop back toward me and put on his gloves before tugging the sample container toward himself.

Still staring wistfully at the box of samples, Sadie picked up her satchel. "If you're sure you don't need me..."

"Go to school," Yujun and I said at the same time.

"Fine." She turned and flounced out, holding the door for West as he entered.

"I should've known I'd find you in here," he said. He held up a manila envelope. "I've got extra copies of those papers we talked about."

"Papers?" I repeated. Tessa used to take care of the hiring paperwork. Now that she was gone, I supposed it fell to me, but we hadn't hired anyone in the three days since she'd stormed out, believing the worst of me. When had I ever given her reason to believe I'd betray her like that? Since she left, I'd wrapped my heart in bubble wrap to keep it together.

"The CRA? Consensual relationship agreement. My team says you and Tessa haven't returned it yet."

There was a pop in my ribcage like my heart was trying to beat out of its protective wrap. I'd called her and texted her a dozen times like a pathetic jerk, but she didn't respond. I suspected she'd blocked me. I wished I'd been able to do anything more than stammer weak excuses in Dr. Perrell's office, but I'd been frozen by the fear of what would happen to everyone who worked here because of my stupid mistake.

Tessa saw it too, that I'd fucked everything up. I wasn't worthy of her.

I stared at my laptop's screen, the spreadsheet blurring. "Don't need that anymore. It's over."

"Shit, I'm sorry," West said. "What..." He glanced at Yujun. "Never mind. I'll come see you in your office tomorrow, and we'll talk."

"Nothing to talk about," I muttered. When she walked out, it proved she didn't believe in me. She was right. From the beginning, I'd doubted we could meet our aggressive target for finishing the clinical trials and getting the tests approved. With this delay, time was slipping through my fingers, along with my chance to save the company from a buyout...or worse.

Still, it hurt that someone I thought cared about me had lost faith.

"Are you okay, man?" West asked, leaning a hand on the lab table.

"Lab coat," I barked.

"Gloves," Yujun said at the same time.

"Sorry, sorry." West stepped back, holding his ungloved hands in the air. "Is there anything I can do to help?"

I looked up from the spreadsheet and saw the concern on his face. As a human resources professional, he understood that if the company failed, our lab technicians had to compete for jobs not only against all the other qualified workers in the Peninsula and Silicon Valley but also against robots and overseas labs who didn't need health insurance and a 401(k) plan.

"Can you try to keep Dr. Perrell from rushing into any decisions? We need time. Maybe another week or two. Then we'll call in every favor we can to get through the approval process quickly. If we can hold off a little longer..." I shrugged, unable to say my hope out loud. Everything would have to go exactly right.

"I'm so sorry," Yujun said for, like, the fiftieth time this week. "I should have caught the error."

"Hey." I waited until he looked up at me. "It's not your fault. I should have been here, instead of..." I blinked away images of Tessa in that spa shower. I could almost smell the sea sage and my regret.

If she'd never come to work here, I could have focused on the cancer test and never added the endometriosis test to our workload, then we wouldn't have fucked up the samples. I'd have been here to ensure we didn't.

"Read it out," I said, my voice stony.

Yujun read the code on the first sample, and I keyed it in.

"If you need anything..." West's hand landed on my shoulder.

I shrugged it off. "I've got this." And that's when I realized I'd become a leader. Simon might have done most of the work in the beginning, schmoozing with investors to get our funding, bringing on board members to advise us, and shielding me from distractions, but he was gone. And I'd stepped up.

It was my company now. I'd do whatever it took to keep it.

36

A CRYPTID COVER-UP

From Barry Wright's manifesto:
Sasquatch, also known as Bigfoot, is the result of a failed human experiment to create giant warriors.

TESSA

*P*arking was always a bitch in Rincon Hill, even on a Wednesday night in mid-May. I made a wider circle this time, looking for one of those expensive lots with the faded stripes and the dude who looked just as likely to steal your car as to watch it.

Perhaps if I'd ever lived in San Francisco, I wouldn't mind it so much. I'd accept the parking struggle as a way of life, but as someone who'd grown up in the suburbs, then the forests, then Berkeley, then wide-open Silicon Valley, I minded. A lot.

"There's a spot!" Savannah shouted. "On the right! You can parallel park, right? I could never," she said as I pulled up to the front car and turned on my blinker. "Not in my minivan."

"You could do it in this." I hit the button, and the car took over, easing itself into the spot.

"Omigosh." She gripped the door handle. "How does it do that?"

The car finished its maneuvers and put itself into park. "Technology is pretty amazing," I said.

Savannah met me on the sidewalk. "It's why you went into it, right? Even though not many women our age did? Even though your dad's kind of a Luddite?"

"It seemed like magic to me," I admitted. "I wanted to learn the secrets so I could harness it."

"You did. And now you can do anything." She slipped her hand around my elbow and walked toward Danny's bar. "Software, biotech...what's next, space travel?"

I huffed. "That's a dick-measuring contest if I've ever seen one. No, I think I'll focus my energy here on earth." Once I was done licking my wounds. Three weeks wasn't enough time to get over a betrayal like Oliver's. But I didn't want to think about him or the half-dozen desperate texts he sent me before I blocked his number. If I'd listened to the voicemails, I'm sure they'd have said the same thing: *I love you. I'm sorry. I should have told you. Please call me.*

I'd done too much thinking about Discovery Diagnostics lately. And Oliver. Tonight was about Savannah. "Speaking of dicks, tell me what your ex wants now. What problem is the Goddess Gang tackling tonight?"

"Um..." She sped up, tugging me toward the old-fashioned neon sign that still read *Barb's Bar.* "You know, divorce stuff."

I wasn't surprised when we went inside and Justine's was the first face I recognized. It was a little unorthodox for a divorce lawyer to hang out socially with a client, but Justine followed her own rules. She sat next to Carly at Lucie's favorite booth. Lucie stood beside it, bouncing her seven-month-old, Mia, in her arms. On the other side of the booth, her back to us but her petite size and shiny, dark bun unmistakable—

"What's Bridget doing here?" The truth started to dawn on me, and I didn't like it. "We're not here to talk about your divorce, are we?" Bridget was *my* friend. We were here to talk about *my* problems. Ice swept out to my extremities.

"Not exactly." Savannah's grip turned to steel as she towed me toward the booth.

I'd been perfectly fine with having a come-to-Jesus conversation when Carly had her head in her ass about Andrew. But this was different. It was business, despite the fact that Oliver and I had been fucking. "I don't want—"

"Tessa." She pulled me to a stop. "This is what friends do. We talk. And you need to talk."

"No, I don't." But I let her tug me toward the booth.

Carly stood and held out her arms. I gave her a small nod, and she folded me into her embrace. "Sorry about this," she whispered in my ear, "but you need us."

"Do I? Or is it time to find new friends?"

Lucie snorted. "Like you could find friends as awesome as us. I'm going to hand off Mia to her grandma and get us a pitcher of margaritas. Don't start without me." She walked away.

Justine scooted out of the booth and touched my shoulder. "Savannah said you need all your friends right now. I'm glad you called on us."

"I didn't," I grumbled. "But I'm glad you came. You can inject some logic into the conversation." She'd be on my side.

Bridget clenched my hand. "Et tu, Brute?" I said.

"I feel bad about being the one to introduce you to Maya Perrell. I'm so sorry it all went to shit." Her blue eyes shone.

"You had no way of knowing it was a setup. But I can't believe you agreed to be part of this." I waved at the circle of women.

She tipped her head. "I'm always going to show up when you

need me. That's what friends do. I wish you called for help more often."

"I didn't. I don't need this."

"Don't you?" Lucie thumped a heavy tray on the table. It held a pitcher of margaritas, a stack of lowball glasses, a bottle of top-shelf tequila, a bowl of lime wedges, and a saltshaker.

I leaned a hip against the booth's worn upholstery. "My god. Are we going to need all that?"

"I'm being prepared." She splashed tequila into six glasses and handed me the saltshaker. "Let's get started."

I waved off the salt. "I'm driving."

"Danny's brother Leo will drive you home in your car. Now drink."

Once Lucie had an idea, there was no stopping her. So I tossed back the shot and chased it with a squeeze of lime. My friends did the same.

"Sit," Lucie said, "and tell us what happened."

Despite my attempts to position myself so I could flee, I ended up wedged between Bridget and Savannah in the center of the booth. "You all know what happened. Oliver and Maya Perrell lured me in and let me think I could save the company, but they'd been planning to sell all along."

Lucie tipped her head. "Why did that bother you so much? You helped the company grow to a stronger position. Maybe selling is the right next step for it."

My stomach hollowed out. "I had a bad experience before."

I'd thought I could shut down the conversation with that, but five pairs of eyes watched me, waiting for more. Bridget knew the story, and she leaned her shoulder against mine, supporting me. I supposed it was time they knew what I'd foolishly done when I was younger and why what Oliver had done hurt so much. Then they wouldn't try to talk me into forgiving him.

So I told them all about Harry, how he'd used our sexual

connection, my emotional one, and my pain to convince me to sell Red Rover. How he'd leveraged my trust to hide that the buyer, MuskOx Tech, planned to change the employment model to cut costs and all of our people would become independent contractors and lose their health benefits. And after, he'd let me take the fall in the media.

"So that's why those women were so rude in Target that day?" Savannah asked.

"One of them lost her sister. Because of me."

"It wasn't only you," Justine said. "Your board of directors and Harry all agreed to the deal."

"Red Rover was a family—*my* family. I made promises to my people. Which I broke. I deserved everything that happened."

"You tried your best to make it right," Bridget said. "Your foundation helped. And your philanthropy is unmatched. If only everyone knew—"

"No one needs to know," I interrupted her. "I should have stayed hidden. Now when everyone at Discovery loses their jobs, they'll hate me because I was complicit."

"But you weren't," Carly said. "You didn't know what they had planned."

"I should have seen it. Bringing me in was their attempt to buff up the company. They probably positioned me to the buyer as some sort of exit-strategy specialist." I gripped my glass to hide the tremble in my fingers.

Lucie poured more tequila into my glass and topped it with a splash of margarita. "If Oliver did that, he's truly a dick. Danny's got some beefy cousins who can go to his place and—"

"He's not like that," Carly said. "He loves his company. He was trying to save it."

"You talked to him?" I asked, my voice low.

"He came over the other night to get some advice from Andrew. He's all alone," she said, "now that you've left."

Something cracked in my chest. I remembered the feeling of Red Rover slipping out of my hands like sand. Of feeling abandoned by everyone I'd cared about. Now he was going through it too. Despite how he'd broken my trust, I felt sorry for him and the pain he was experiencing. Only a little sorry. He was still a lying douchebag.

"He thought he could prevent the sale from happening," Carly said. "If it helps, he regrets keeping it from you."

"Regret doesn't help anyone," I said. "I should know, since I was holed up with mine for years. Only action helps."

"Maybe you should take some action," Carly said, "and try to help him."

"At least help the people you worked with," Bridget said. "Before it's too late."

"I don't know." I shifted in my seat, but stuck between Bridget and Savannah, escape was impossible.

Savannah put her hand over mine. "I think you feel conflicted because you love him and he hurt you."

I drained my glass and held it out to Lucie for a refill. "I don't love him. I learned my lesson with Harry. And my dad."

"Your dad," Lucie said darkly. "Now *there's* a major dick."

"You told them about your dad?" Bridget asked.

"Oliver did. I should've known then not to trust him."

"You told *Oliver* about your dad?" Bridget's eyes went wide.

"Couldn't help it. He showed up at the lab."

"But you'd have told him," Savannah said. "Because you're in love."

"Am not." I swigged the tequila and held out my glass again.

"Aren't you?" Savannah asked. "What were all those long walks about last week?"

"Wait." Lucie stopped mid-pour. "Are you saying you've been wandering the streets of San Jose like some kind of bleak-moment movie montage?"

"I...I guess?" Was that what I'd done? I'd thought getting away from my house, where I'd so many happy hours with him, would take my mind off everything. All I'd done was replay those good times in my mind. His caretaking. His whispered *I love yous.*

Savannah clapped her hands. "You know what comes next, right?"

"A hangover and a killer headache?" I tossed back the half a shot in my glass.

"No. A grand gesture. You have to go back to him and grovel. Or let him grovel. I'm not sure which of you is more to blame in this love story."

"Him," I said.

"You," Lucie said at the same time.

"I thought you were my friend," I said, gazing into her brown eyes. All four of them. How had she grown an extra pair?

"I'm always honest, especially with my friends," she said. "Yes, he was wrong to keep the truth from you, but you abandoned him when he needed you most. Go back, tell him you were wrong to leave, and help him. That is, if you care about him."

Suddenly, my head was too heavy. I dropped my chin into my hand. "Fuck me. I do. What if he doesn't want my help? I'm only good at wrecking things, not building them."

"That's not true." Bridget nudged me, and I rested my sloshy head against her shoulder. "You built Red Rover from nothing. And you spearheaded that endometriosis project at Discovery. You can build things. And rebuild them. All you need is the courage to try."

"Courage." I huffed. "Something I haven't had in a long, long, long, long time."

"What are you talking about?" Justine asked. "It took courage to defy your dad and go away to college. To leave college and start Red Rover. To start your foundation. And to go to work at Discovery."

"And most of all, to let yourself love someone," Savannah said.

"I don't—"

"Don't try to tell us again that you don't love him." My eyes were closed, but I could hear Lucie rolling her eyes.

"Wasn't." My tongue was thick in my mouth. "Was going to say I don't think I can drive over there. Who can drive me to Oliver'sss?"

My world went black before anyone answered.

~

*I*t was red outside my eyelids, which meant I'd slept through my alarm.

Let's face it, it was probably red inside my eyelids too. *Why* had I insisted on that foolish fourth tequila shot? Party Tessa had forgotten she was a forty-three-year-old woman with endometriosis. Next-day Tessa couldn't forget.

I groaned as I tried to analyze the pain. Was it worse in my head or in my abdomen?

Abdomen.

I curled around the sharp stabs to cushion them. One more minute, then I'd open my eyes and get up. Today was the board meeting, and I owed it to Oliver to show up. Maybe he'd let me stand beside him, or maybe he'd still be too pissed off. Either way, I'd show him I was willing to try.

The dull pain in my head clamored to compete with the inflammation in my belly. Excellent.

Next time I saw Savannah, I'd ask her to activate her mom mode the next time we went to Danny's. She'd ensure I had no more than one tequila shot. Okay, two. *Definitely* never four again.

"Rise and shine, sleepyhead." Savannah's too-chipper voice was accompanied by the clink of a glass. "I want you to drink this whole glass of water."

I blinked open my eyes. The light was weird, slicing through the west window. I propped myself up against the pillows. "Is there coffee?"

"There was," she said, setting the glass of water on my bedside table, "but I tossed it out a few minutes ago, at noon. Want me to brew some more?"

I blinked my burning eyes wide. "It's afternoon?"

"You were tired. I let you sleep in. But if you don't get up now, you won't sleep tonight."

"The board meeting is today. This afternoon. I have to get there." I threw back the covers. "Oof." I groaned as I stood. Standing stretched muscles that wanted to stay curled up. I picked up my phone, then forced my feet to shuffle toward my closet.

Savannah followed me. "Drink this water. We can't have you showing up for your grand gesture rough as a cob."

I glugged the water, not sure what to ask about first. I went with, "My what?" as I scanned my closet for a pair of black stretchy pants that wouldn't cut into my sore abdomen.

"Your grand gesture. It's when the hero in the rom-com goes running through the airport to stop the heroine from getting on her plane."

"I have so many questions." I tugged on the pants. Thank god for spandex. "Why would the hero have to run through the airport? Isn't he on the same flight?"

"No, I guess that one wouldn't work in a post-9/11 world. In the old days, you didn't have to have a ticket to roam the airport."

"Really?" I turned my back to pull off my sleep shirt, blushing when I realized it was Oliver's Dartmouth one he'd left behind.

"Yeah, did you not fly before that?"

I strapped on a bra. "No, Dad didn't believe in airplanes. The Earth is flat, air travel is fake, etcetera."

"Wait. Air travel is *fake?* What about cross-continental flights?"

"Wind to slow things down. Or the passengers' perception of time is sped up by drugs piped through the air vents. There's always an explanation."

"Goodness gracious."

"Exactly." I slipped on a black tunic. "Second question, am I the hero in this scenario?"

"You're the one who walked out, right?"

I slumped, cringing at the memory of slinking out of the building, not bothering to say goodbye to any of my former coworkers. "Yeah."

"Then you're the one who has to grovel. I don't make the rules."

I walked into the bathroom and brushed my teeth. My hair was a nest of tangles, but I didn't have time to evict any woodland creatures who'd made their way in while I slept. I pulled it up into a ponytail and twined it into a bun.

"Do I look ready to disrupt a board meeting, then grovel?" I held my hands out.

"Let's put on a dab of lip gloss so you don't look so hungover."

I rolled my eyes. "Fine." I found a tube and handed it to Savannah. She carefully patted it onto my lips.

"Now you're ready. Go grovel."

37

———

DISEASE RISK ASSESSMENT

Disease risk assessment: *An evaluation of an individual's genetic, lifestyle, and environmental factors to determine a quantitative or qualitative risk of developing specific diseases.*

OLIVER
One hour earlier

I opened my laptop and checked my presentation.

When I pulled my notes out of my satchel, the papers fluttered in my trembling fingers. Quickly, I set them on the shiny glass surface of the boardroom table.

Who was I kidding? Everyone would know from one glance at my greenish face how nervous I was.

God, I missed Simon. He used to run these meetings like a pro. Then he'd text me when it was time for the science, and I'd scurry in to give my prepared presentation. On more than one occasion, one of the members had started to snore in the middle of it. At first, I was offended, but Simon told me a boring presentation was a successful one: people hated to be surprised.

They were going to hate me today.

Dr. Perrell's assistant walked in, her steps silent on the thick carpet. She carried a tray of sandwiches, and I wondered if Savannah had made them. Gemma froze when she saw me but recovered after a few blinks. "Dr. Bond! I didn't expect you to be in here. You know the meeting doesn't start for another thirty minutes, right?"

"Is it a problem that I'm early?"

"Of course not." She set the bagels on a credenza. "The coffee's on the way, but would you like me to bring you a cup?"

I rubbed my sweaty hands on my pants. "No, thank you, Gemma. Maybe a glass of water when you have a minute. Please."

"Sure. Good luck today." She smiled.

"Thanks." Gemma's position would be eliminated if we sold to Greenwich. And she didn't have a life raft of stock options to keep her afloat during her job search.

I scanned the paper that listed my key points. I had to succeed. Everyone's future was riding on it.

"Well, well." I looked up at the familiar voice. "Look who's an eager beaver today."

I stood and held out my hand. "Sir."

My grandfather took it. "It's good to see you engaged in the company. I was worried for a while."

"I prefer the science," I said, "but today's vote is important."

"And which way do you intend to vote?" He lifted his white eyebrows.

"Against," I said with all the confidence I could muster.

"Really? I'd have thought you'd prefer to let someone else be in charge while you focus on the science, like you said."

"I'd much rather." Simon, and even Tessa, had allowed me to do that. Now they'd abandoned me. "But I care about this company, and that means I have to step up and lead. How do you intend to vote?"

"It was a risk to invest in a couple of college kids, but the returns have been good—except for this year."

I winced. Six months ago, Dr. Perrell had reminded me that we hadn't launched a new product in almost a year, but I hadn't thought about how it might affect our investors.

He spread his hands. "I'm getting too old to be traipsing across the country every quarter. I—"

Gemma pushed in a utility cart of bottled water and a couple of large carafes. "Good morning, Mr. Bond. Coffee?"

"Decaf, please," my grandfather said. "With the time change, I've been up since four. I've already had two cups of the leaded stuff."

While Gemma and my grandfather exchanged pleasantries, I worried. Was he planning to vote for the sale? I'd hoped at least my blood relative would stand with me.

I didn't get a chance to ask him as the other board members entered, each one of them surprised to see me. Every raised eyebrow was a dagger to my heart. Had I really been that disengaged? I vowed to dedicate myself to leadership at every opportunity, especially at future board meetings—if I got the chance.

"Good morning, everyone." Dr. Perrell glided into the room, modeling a confidence I'd never feel. She took a few minutes to greet each board member with a warm smile and a hearty handshake. I wished I'd done that instead of hunching in my chair, sweating.

The secretary called us to order and took us through a few housekeeping items before turning to me. "Next on the agenda is an update on research and development."

For a few seconds, I fumbled to get my presentation up on the screen. Carefully, I talked through my prepared points on the ovarian cancer test, reviewing the importance of the first-of-its-kind test and showing how it had finished its clinical trials with strong results, despite running a few weeks late.

"We're on track for approvals by early next year," I concluded.

"Weren't we targeting late this year?" a board member asked.

"Yes, and we'll do everything we can to accelerate the schedule, but these processes take time. Some steps are out of our control. We might not make it."

There were murmurs around the table. My grandfather bent to listen to the board member on his left.

"And," I said, trying to wrench back their attention, "I have more exciting news. Another first: a biomarker test for endometriosis." I segued into the second half of my presentation, wrapping up with, "An inexpensive, accessible test for endometriosis will help people get the treatments they need for better quality of life."

"Discovery Diagnostics fights cancer," a board member said. "Why are we losing our focus?"

"I wouldn't say we're losing our focus. We're leveraging our expertise to combat another condition," I said, "one that affects ten percent of reproductive-age people with uteruses. Studies have shown that more than two thirds of patients with the condition have missed school or work due to it." I remembered Tessa suffering on her couch, reaching for her laptop when what she needed was a nap and a more flexible work schedule. I recalled the sick days Sadie took almost every month. "Think of the productivity lost, the earnings missed. With a diagnosis and better understanding of the condition, more effective treatments are possible."

Dr. Perrell interrupted the new murmurs by standing. "The effort was a pet project of our former COO, Tessa Wright. I think we can all agree, Oliver, that the test could have a significant impact on women's health. I'm not convinced it makes Discovery Diagnostics more valuable in the marketplace, but a potential buyer can decide if they want to move forward."

I stiffened. *If* they wanted to move forward? If our board voted to sell, would the endometriosis test be locked away, never to be made available to people with endometriosis? That sounded a hell of a lot like one of Tessa's dad's wild theories.

"Now," she said, "let's move on to the next order of business. We've been approached by Greenwich Biomedical with a purchase offer."

She named the sum, and it was big. Assuming each of the investors was bought out according to the payout plan, my share would mean I'd never have to work again. Like Tessa, though I was a few years older than she was when she got her life-changing payout. For her, it hadn't been a change for the better.

I glanced around the table. These were all wealthy people. Take my grandfather, for example. He'd retired early and comfortably from his bank president career. When Simon and I approached him for funds to start up Discovery, he listened to our pitch and then wrote us a check, likely thinking he'd never see that money again. He was more of a risk-taker than my father, but he'd never risk more than he could afford to lose. His equity share wasn't the largest, but because he'd been our first, it was significant.

Still, he didn't need a payout. None of these people did. Well, except maybe Dr. Perrell for her daughters' lavish weddings. Briefly, I regretted taking the girls' dreams away before I blurted, "Why?"

"Excuse me?" she asked, an irritated crease between her eyebrows.

"Why should we sell now?"

"As you all know"—she made a slow circuit of the board members with her gaze—"we've struggled to release product to market on a regular basis. This year, our investors haven't received dividends as promised. It's time to seek help, not only for ourselves but for the patients we're looking to serve. The science will be stronger with the backing of Greenwich." She stared directly into my eyes. "We'll be stronger together."

I hadn't thought of it like that. I leaned back in my chair. We'd have access to more resources. I wouldn't be forced to beg Dr. Perrell every time I needed a new PCR machine.

On the other hand, I doubted Greenwich would test as rigorously as I wanted. Like Tessa and Dr. Perrell, they'd focus on profit and loss. I doubted they'd take the time to understand the intricacies of my research the way Tessa had.

"I like it," the secretary said. "It reduces our risk."

Those were my four favorite words. Yet I couldn't ignore the heavy feeling in my stomach. "But—"

Dr. Perrell spoke over me. "Our founder, Simon Grimstone, wanted strong growth for Discovery Diagnostics. He wanted not only for the company to make a scientific difference but"—she chuckled—"a few weeks before he died, he told me his wish was for the company to be listed on the Buzz Bizz 1000. With Greenwich, we can get there. Simon would be thrilled about this opportunity."

Would he? I wished I could pause the meeting like one of Simon's console games and go commune with his spirit in the game room. Maybe I'd hear his voice in the pings of *Space Invaders,* and he'd tell me what he really wanted.

"Not to mention," Dr. Perrell continued, "the benefits to the employees a merger with Greenwich would bring. A larger company can ensure job safety for our staff."

"Would it?"

I turned at the achingly unexpected voice. Tessa leaned against the doorframe, a neon-yellow visitor badge glowing against her black shirt. Her eyes were red and puffy, and her russet hair was scraped back from her pale face the way she used to wear it in the lab. "How—" I began.

Dr. Perrell spoke over me again. "Tessa, since you tendered

your resignation, you don't have a place in this meeting. I'm going to have to ask you to leave."

She lifted her chin. "I know I forfeited my right to have an opinion about this when I left, but I want everyone here"—her gaze connected with mine—"to understand the implications of a buyout. From personal experience, I can tell you that what a company might promise is different from what happens after a merger."

My brain was overloaded, like my laptop when I gave it a large volume of data to analyze. I couldn't get over the fact that Tessa was fighting for my company like an avenging Valkyrie. Would she fight for me too? For us?

"You took your payout from Red Rover," Dr. Perrell said, "so I hardly see how—"

"It was a mistake," Tessa said. "One I don't want to see you make, Oliver."

My name in her mouth was music. She'd come because she cared about me. I pushed back my chair and stood. "Can we break for five minutes?"

"No, Oliver," Dr. Perrell said, "we can't stop this meeting because your *girlfriend* is here." Murmurs erupted from the other board members. "Yes, unfortunately, it's true. Ms. Wright left because she was having an inappropriate relationship with Dr. Bond. Sadly, it's not the first time she's slept with a colleague."

"Hold on just a minute!" I ripped my gaze from Tessa's chalk-white face to Dr. Perrell. "Our relationship is not up for discussion. This merger offer is. And Tessa raises a valid question."

Dr. Perrell crossed her arms. "She shouldn't be here. Whoever let her in today will be disciplined."

"This is almost as entertaining as that show where everyone fights in the mansion." My grandfather levered himself up. "But my grandson is right. We need to focus. Tessa, it's good to see you again." He shook her hand. "I was sorry you left. But Maya is right. You don't have a vote. I don't mind if you stay and listen since it seems that you have some unfinished business." He winked at me. "But I'm going to ask you to be silent. Agreed?"

Tessa's jaw twitched. I sensed the waves of frustration rolling off her. "Agreed, Mr. Bond." She sank into one of the chairs against the wall.

Dr. Perrell's dark eyes flashed. "As I was saying, a buyout could mean higher salaries and more affordable health insurance to those employees who remain."

"To those who remain?" I repeated. "And how many will be let go?"

"That's to be determined," Dr. Perrell said.

"By who?" My glasses had started to steam.

"By leadership. Anyone let go will receive our standard severance package."

Severance wouldn't go far with the Bay Area's high cost of living. Especially for our newest employees, who wouldn't receive much. Sadie's face swam into my vision.

"Does Greenwich offer tuition reimbursement?"

Dr. Perrell's brow furrowed. "I don't know. Our discussions haven't gotten to that level of detail."

Tuition reimbursement might be a detail, but it was an important one. And even if they did offer it, it wouldn't help Sadie if she were laid off. I thought of West and his department. The people in accounting who were so patient with me and my messy expense reports. And our marketing department, who sponsored a costume contest every Halloween and ran the Earth Day recycling drive. My thoughts circled back to the lab.

"What amount of control will they have over our research projects?" Out of the corner of my eye, I saw Tessa nod.

Dr. Perrell lowered her chin. "They made the offer because

they're interested in the ovarian cancer test. I'm sure they'll support that."

Leaving the endometriosis test to gather dust, when it could help patients. With its large portfolio of projects, Greenwich would never let a determined group of lab employees spin up a test that wasn't in the annual plan.

"What if we're stronger without them?" I asked.

"You're opposing the deal over tuition reimbursement?" Dr. Perrell folded her arms. "Think what our ovarian cancer test can do with the power of Greenwich's marketing resources."

"It's not only the tuition reimbursement. It's our people. This company is *nothing* without them. We owe them the respect and care they deserve." That awareness of Tessa I always had? Although I kept my eyes on the people at the table, I knew she'd gone absolutely still.

"Our people have worked incredibly hard to get us to this point," I continued. "We might not have the distributed risk of a larger organization, but we're more nimble. We pivot when needed. Like how we got those samples we needed from the university in India. If I'd had to go through levels of approval, I might not have been able to get them in time to finish the clinical trials. There are benefits to being small." *Sorry, Simon.*

"Are you saying you want to go this alone?" Dr. Perrell asked. "With Greenwich, you'll be able to focus on the science and ignore everything you don't care about. With Greenwich, we'll all have security."

For a second, I let myself imagine what a relief it would be not to have to worry constantly about the company, not to have to think about quarterly numbers or budgets, and to bury my head in the lab.

I glanced at Tessa. Her eyes shone with something like confidence in me. Or could it be love? She'd come here to warn me and to support me. And now she'd stepped aside so I could make my own decision. She'd experienced what could happen when you sold out. How everything could go to shit. If Dr. Perrell hadn't asked questions about tuition reimbursement, what other details had she ignored?

"I know what I want," I said, "and I vote no." I glanced around the table. "I understand if you feel differently, and I'll buy your shares if you want a payout now." My breathing quickened. With most of my wealth tied up in the company, I couldn't afford to buy too many shares. I might have to sell my house to do it. "But I won't vote to sell. Not now, maybe not ever. We can achieve greater success on our own. I'm confident in us. In myself."

I felt a phantom pat on my back, right in the spot Simon would grip my shoulder when he was proud of me. Warm peace washed through me. I glanced around the table at the other investors. Then I looked at Tessa. Her cheeks had pinked, and she flashed me a rare grin.

I'd done the right thing, assuming I survived this vote.

38

A STRATEGY TO INCREASE SOBRIETY

From Barry Wright's manifesto:
*During Prohibition, the US government gave tax breaks to industrial
alcohol manufacturers who added poison to their product. When
people drank the alcohol, they died.*

TESSA

*O*liver's grandfather was the last board member to file
out. Although I'd met him at my first and only
Discovery Diagnostics board meeting as COO, I didn't know the
exact size and weight of his grandson's penis then. My cheeks
went hot as I shook his hand.

"So you're the one who made my grandson a leader." His
eyes were the same color as Oliver's, and they sparkled with
mischief.

"Respectfully, Mr. Bond, he was already a leader. I only
shared my experience with him."

His white eyebrows lifted, and I winced at whatever innu-
endo lurked in those intelligent eyes. But he simply turned to
Oliver, who was frantically cleaning the mess he'd made of the

conference table when he'd yanked his laptop out of the video cable, and the speakerphone had knocked into the coffee carafe.

"I'm proud of you, Oliver," he said.

Oliver turned to face him, leaving Gemma to her much more effective cleanup efforts.

"Thank you," he said. "And thanks for voting with me."

"You presented a compelling argument. Now you need to deliver on those promises you made."

"I will, sir." He glanced at me.

"All right, all right." Mr. Bond chuckled. "I know where I'm not wanted. Come on, Gemma. We'll leave these two to…discuss next steps."

Gemma threw the wad of soggy paper towels into the trash, snatched up the carafe as if to protect it from any further clumsiness, then walked out ahead of Mr. Bond, who shut the door.

I met Oliver at the head of the conference table. We didn't touch, but we stood closer than was appropriate in a boardroom.

"Sorry I barged in on your meeting. I should've called to make sure you wanted to see me after I walked out on you." I didn't know what to do with my face, caught between my happiness for his victory and guilt over what I'd done.

"Sorry? I'm glad you're here." His fingertips teased mine like he wanted to grasp my hands but couldn't forget the glass wall of the room. "I missed you. And I'm sorry about everything Dr. Perrell said about you."

"Why? It was all true. Our relationship *was* inappropriate."

"No, it wasn't. West's paperwork would've made it board-sanctioned."

I snorted. "What I've always wanted, a board-sanctioned relationship."

"When you say it, it sounds sexy." He'd edged close enough that it was *definitely* improper. I filled my nostrils with his aftershave and remembered burying my nose in his skin.

I glanced through glass wall. "Better step back before someone sees."

"I'm not stepping back," he growled. "Are you?"

I lifted my chin. "No."

"Then I guess we're doing this." His lips crashed onto mine. I hesitated only briefly—my reputation was already in tatters—before I relaxed and let his tongue invade my mouth. He'd gone from mild-mannered scientist to corporate raider during the course of that hour-long meeting. Power tasted good on him.

After a few seconds, I reluctantly broke the kiss and stepped away.

The line was back between his eyebrows. "Second thoughts?"

"None. But you still work here. You should keep some semblance of respectability."

"With Dr. Perrell leaving—"

"My god," I interrupted, "did you expect her to have already secured a position at Greenwich?"

He shook his head. "Contingency plans are her superpower. But that means we have an opening for a CEO. We need someone with operational experience, since we're also down a COO. Know anyone?"

"Are you offering me a job, Dr. Bond?"

"I'm absolutely offering you a job."

"Wait," I said. "How will that work if we're, you know, sleeping together?"

"I'm giving myself a promotion. As Chief Scientific Officer, I'll report directly to the board. We'll be peers again. Partners. Will you do it?"

If I were anyone else, I'd have played coy, made him beg for it. But I wanted this. I believed in the employees, the science, and most of all, him. And us. "I will."

"Good."

"But first, I need to apologize for walking out on you and for not returning your calls. I was triggered, and I couldn't be rational."

"I hid the truth from you," he said. "I'm sor—"

"No." I stopped him. "This is my grovel. Don't fuck it up."

"Your what?"

"Yeah, I know. I don't watch rom-coms either. But apparently, when the hero has done something terrible, she has to apologize and make amends."

"Wait, are you the hero or am I?"

I threw up my hands. "I don't fucking know! All I know is that it was terrible of me to desert you when you needed me. I didn't like that you didn't tell me about the potential sale, but I should've trusted you to make the right decision. I respect you." I lowered my voice. "I love you."

He stepped into my space and cupped my elbows in his palms. "You love me?"

"I do. I didn't mean to. I'm sorry."

"Sorry for loving me?" He scrunched his nose.

"Sorry I didn't admit it sooner. To you or to myself. Then I would've understood why I was so angry about the sale. We could have talked about it. I could've been reasonable."

"Please stop apologizing. I fucked up too. Let's promise to love each other today and tomorrow and all the next days. Everything else will work itself out. Okay?"

"Okay." My knees trembled.

"Did you eat lunch?"

My stomach flipped over. "Let's not talk about food. The tequila would only kick it back out."

"Tequila?"

"There may have been an intervention last night. It helped me pull my head out of my ass, but today has been rough."

He grasped my elbows. "You should rest. Want to get out of here?"

"What's this?" I flashed him a flirty smile. "Dr. Oliver Bond is leaving work early?"

"I think I deserve it after saving the company from a takeover. Besides." He leaned down to whisper in my ear, "I want to fuck my girlfriend *now*."

My skin tingled from my scalp to my toes. "I can get on board with that plan."

39

CULTURE

Culture: *In biology, the growth of microorganisms in a laboratory.*

OLIVER
Six months later

"Six months for regulatory approval is almost unheard of, but when the science is solid, when the results are astounding, and when you've got a firecracker like Tessa Wright pushing things along, you can do almost anything." Standing on the sturdiest table in the game room, I gazed out over the crowd of employees, investors, and friends. With my slippery dress shoes on the polished wood of the table, my perch on the table was a definite safety violation. It didn't seem that terrible compared to all we'd risked to get to this moment.

"We're here, tonight, celebrating approvals for our ovarian cancer biomarker test, thanks to your dedication, your brilliance, and your hard work. Thank you, everyone." I raised my glass of sparkling water. "To us."

My grandfather winked at me. A chorus of whoops rose

from the employees and guests as they raised their glasses of champagne.

Like always, my eyes went immediately to the mane of red hair across the room. Next to *Ms. Pac-Man,* Tessa held my gaze, grinned, and raised her glass. She tipped back her head and drank, the long column of her throat bobbing. If I were standing closer and we weren't in our workplace, I'd trace my finger down her neck and watch the goosebumps rise on her skin. Later.

Right now, I had to mingle. It wasn't my favorite activity since I'd much rather talk to my friends than to the journalists, potential investors, and partners invited to celebrate with us. But, Tessa had reminded me, it was something a company founder did.

Still, there was nothing wrong with starting slow. I grasped Andrew's hand as I stepped from the table to a chair, then down to the floor and joined my friend and his fiancée.

"Good speech." Andrew shook my hand.

Carly leaned in to kiss my cheek. "We're so excited for you."

"I wish we could've gotten both tests through approvals." I glanced over Carly's head toward where Tessa had been, but she was gone.

From behind me, she whispered in my ear. "Greedy." She draped her freckled arm over my shoulder then, louder, said, "We can't expect the feds to fast-track *two* women's health products."

I hated that she covered her frustration and disappointment with snark, but her friends and I saw past it. Carly grasped her hand. Andrew, always the optimist, said, "I bet you get the approval in January."

"Thanks." She pressed her palm into my shoulder in a gesture I knew grounded her. Over the past six months since she'd first told me she loved me, she'd used my body as a kind of touchstone. I loved it. I reached up and held her hand to me.

"Snacks!" Savannah sang out. She held out a plate loaded with antipasto skewers. Carly took one, bit into it, and moaned. "Oh my god. Why can't Audrey get these at the events she makes us attend?"

"Because she hasn't hired Savannah," Tessa said. When Savannah offered us the plate, we waved it off. Earlier, we'd stuffed ourselves on the ones that hadn't passed Savannah's rigorous quality checks.

"Wait. You *made* these?" Carly asked.

Savannah seemed an inch taller. "I've expanded beyond breakfasts and lunches to evening events. Tessa helped me with the waitstaff and the logistics." She lowered her voice. "Don't tell anyone, but this is my first one."

"And it's perfect," Tessa said. "You've found your calling."

West stepped up beside me, and Tessa tensed. I held her hand firmly in mine. We'd filled out all the paperwork he wanted, and as long as no one walked in on us banging in the supply closet, there was no issue with our being a couple. Fortunately, we didn't need to bang in the supply closet since we had a big, comfortable bed at Tessa's house. And a shower, and a couch, and a kitchen counter (only when Savannah wasn't there). My dick stiffened, so I shifted and mentally listed the amino acids in alphabetical order.

"Introduce me to your friends?" West's voice sounded strange, low and rumbly. Did he have an upper respiratory infection? I nudged Tessa a few inches away from him.

I gestured around the circle. "This is Andrew Jones and his fiancée, Carly Rose. Andrew and I have been friends since college, and Carly, Tessa, and Savannah have been friends for a couple years. Savannah catered the event. Everyone, this is Asher Weston."

"Everyone calls me West." He held out his hand to Savannah first.

Her hands were occupied with the plate and napkins. Her face went pink. "Sorry, I…"

"Sorry." West rubbed his hand on his jeans. "You made the food?"

"Yes. Here, try some." She held out the plate to him, and he took a skewer.

He bit into it, and his eyes rolled back. "Delicious."

"I'll give you her card on Monday," Tessa said. "We should use her for more events here."

West's gaze didn't leave Savannah. "We should."

"Excuse me." A Black woman I didn't know appeared at Tessa's side. "You're Tessa Wright."

I released Tessa's hand but stood close beside her as she squared up to the other woman. I wished she didn't have to fear unpleasant encounters, but we'd occasionally met her former employees who didn't know that Tessa was as hurt by what had happened at Red Rover as they were.

"I'm Niobe Haines. I'm a healthcare blogger. I understand you've got a biomarker test for endometriosis in the approval pipeline?"

"We do. I can't comment on the approval status—"

"That's okay," Niobe said. "I'm excited about the test, and I wanted to thank you for developing it. I've always suspected I have endometriosis, but I haven't wanted to get the surgery for a proper diagnosis."

Tessa's shoulders dropped. "I'm sorry about your condition. I have it too. I know how important the test will be to millions of people."

I set my hand on her back, offering her my support. She didn't often talk about her condition, and I was so proud of her every time she did.

"Thank you for what you're doing for women's health," Niobe said. "I'm a big fan."

Tessa grinned. "Thanks."

When the blogger walked away, I whispered, "You're an inspiration."

She turned to face me. "I'm just doing my job. We all are."

I rested my hands on her hips and pressed a kiss to her lips. "Your job is important. *You're* important. You're a role model."

"So are you." She circled her arms around my neck and curled her fingers into my hair. "I admire you. I love you."

"I love you too," I murmured.

West cleared his throat. "Still in the workplace. Let's ease off the PDA."

Tessa took a step back but trailed her hand down my arm to lace our fingers together. "I think someone's jealous."

"Maybe I am," he said evenly, with another glance at Savannah. "Still, let's keep kissing to a minimum in the office."

"Fine," she huffed.

My heart expanded in my chest. Tessa and I were together, and she wanted to kiss me in the office—and everywhere else. Life was pretty good. And I was glad to be living mine at last.

EPILOGUE 1

BRIDGET

"Some party, huh?" I tipped my glass of sparkling wine to Justine. She clinked hers against it. "We used to have parties like this, years ago. Now we're lucky if we get a couple of drink tickets and a taco bar. I guess all the money's in biotech now, huh?" Oliver and Tessa's party to celebrate their test's approval was enough of a big deal to merit free-flowing beer and wine, plus the best hors d'oeuvres I'd ever tasted.

"Margins are higher on drugs than on technology services," she said. As a divorce lawyer, Justine had no business knowing as much about corporations as she did, but she'd taught herself to manage her own investment portfolio. "Still, events like these can help build morale. When you're CEO, you can bring them back."

It was the kind of throwaway comment we often made. I'd been strategizing to earn the top job at my company for my entire career. Now it hit different, like popping candy packed inside a bowling ball in my belly.

"What?" she asked. It was her job to interpret microexpressions. I was afraid there was nothing micro about the face I'd just made. "What's wrong?"

"Nothing...exactly." I wavered. I'd resolved not to say anything tonight since we were celebrating Tessa, but Justine was one of my best friends.

"Now I'm worried. Did that dick, Cole, do something freshly shitty?"

"I—no. Not exactly."

"Then what happened?"

I drained my wineglass. "The board met today and announced the new CEO."

"Oh god. They brought in an outsider. Those *fuckers!*" Fire erupted in her eyes. "Look, we'll zhuzh up your résumé and mine our networks. We'll find you that CEO role you deserve."

"Hold on." I set a hand on hers. "I got it."

"You...got it? *It,* as in, you're CEO? That's amazing!" She set down her glass and grabbed my shoulders. "Why are you making a face like you're about to puke up a canape?"

"Because I have to share it." I closed my eyes, remembering his stony expression when he walked out of that conference room. "With Cole. Until one of us proves we deserve the position more than the other." *He* hadn't looked like someone had taken his blown-glass dreams and smashed them with a sledgehammer. He'd looked calm and confident after. Like he knew he'd win the Hunger Games they'd set up for us. He was young and on the rise. No one would ever write off a harsh word from him as *that time of the month.* He had every reason to be confident.

"What the absolute fuckery?"

I couldn't help the smile that teased at my lips. "You talk like that in front of judges?"

"No, I save it for when my friend gets screwed over at her job. That guy's been at the company for, like, a minute, right?"

"Ten or eleven months. I've worked there for *fifteen years.* Where's the justice in that?"

"Seriously. We'll work our contacts. We'll find a company that actually deserves you."

"Wait." I might not have earned the CEO position outright, but that didn't mean I wouldn't get it eventually. I had cultivated my network at the company for years, I knew exactly how everything worked there, and I was clearly the best candidate. Besides, I had the beginnings of a plan to prove myself. "I think I want to give it a chance, see how it goes."

"If you're sure?" Justine's eyebrows lifted.

"I'm sure. Let's talk about something else. What's going on with you?"

"Oh, you know." She flapped her hand. "Same old stuff. New day, new divorce. Why do people get married, anyway?"

I snorted. "No idea. I mean, I guess if you want kids, it makes sense, but who has the time? I'd never have made it to even co-CEO"—god, why had I brought that up *again?*—"if I had babies to raise. With five girls, my mom never had time for a career. And now my sisters with kids have, you know, respectable jobs, but..."

"But nothing like ours. Or Tessa's. Having it all is the biggest lie they ever told us."

"Yeah. I don't miss it, though." Maybe it was a lie. But it was something I'd told myself so often it sounded like the truth. "I have enough nieces and nephews to satisfy that maternal itch."

"Or to stifle it entirely. Miss me with the diaper changing and tantrums in the grocery store, am I right?"

"Absolutely." Though I loved the curl of little fingers around mine. The ten minutes spent chatting as I brushed out and braided my niece's hair.

"Savannah's got kids." Justine tipped her chin at our friend, who held a platter of hors d'oeuvres out to a tall guy wearing jeans and a checked shirt.

"Yeah, and see what it got her. A twenty-year hiatus from the workforce that means she's got no résumé and no retirement fund. I'm glad she's found her calling in catering, but you'd better get her enough money from her ex to give her decades of security."

"Don't worry." Justine's eyes blazed. "That fucker climbed the corporate ladder while she raised his babies. He's going to pay."

"Good." I watched checked-shirt guy take another prosciutto-wrapped fig. "What's going on there?"

"There?" Justine snorted. "That's just Savannah feeding some guy who likes to eat. Believe me, she's never dating again. She tells me that every time we meet."

"That guy looks like he's into more than her cooking. His face looks like he swallowed a light bulb."

"Could be just the glow of youth? He can't be over thirty-five."

I sighed along with my friend. "I just dropped two hundred bucks on a new moisturizer that promises to restore my dewy skin. As hard as it is to rise in the ranks in tech, it's even harder for a woman with wrinkles."

"Let me know if it works. My cream isn't cutting it anymore. And it's four hundred dollars."

"Yikes. Fucking patriarchy."

"Fucking patriarchy," she agreed.

"*She* looks happy," I said, tipping my chin at Tessa.

"Incandescent. And I don't think it's her face cream."

"Or even the good D," I sipped my chardonnay. "She's actually in love."

"Yeah." Justine wrinkled her nose. "I hope it lasts."

"I have faith. I know you only see the dying relationships, but my parents are still married."

"Or they just can't afford to get divorced. Fucking patriarchy."

"They're in love!" I insisted. "They still kiss every morning before they go off to work."

"Okay, sure. But the only reason to get married these days is for the financial benefits."

"Wow." I stared at my friend over my wineglass. "That's bleak."

"You wouldn't believe in love, either, if you'd seen what I have."

"Maybe not. Still, I know it's not for me." Tessa and Oliver looked so damned happy. I was thrilled for them and only a little jealous. I certainly wouldn't sacrifice my career for it the way Savannah, my mother, and my sisters had done.

"Me neither." She slipped her arm through mine, locking our elbows together. "Spinsters forever?"

"Spinsters forever," I agreed. "Come on. Let's get more wine, then you can help me strategize about how I'm going to win this thing at work."

"Help you beat some dude who got a promotion just because he's got a penis? I'm so in."

Warm affection rushed through me. With my friends, I could do anything, even beat Cole Campion.

❧

I hope you enjoyed this tease of Bridget's story, which is next in the series. When Bridget and her nemesis, Cole, are temporarily assigned as co-CEOs and given the chance to compete for the solo job at a corporate retreat in Costa Rica, they encounter crocodiles, sabotage, and—possibly—love. Be sure to get your copy of *Advances and Retreats,* available at all retailers.

EPILOGUE 2

FALSE VICTORY OVER THE SOVIETS

From Barry Wright's manifesto:
The Apollo 11 "moon landing" was faked by actors on a secret NASA sound stage. Everyone knows the moon is a projection onto the celestial dome, but during the Cold War, the US was desperate for a win against the Soviets. So they pretended to travel to the moon. Only suckers believed them.

TESSA
Late December

"Look." Standing in my—our—kitchen, I kissed Oliver to take back a little of the hurt. "We'll be fine. Better than fine..."

He set a hand on my lower back and kept me from pulling away. "As long as I leave you alone."

"It's a girls' thing." My cheeks heated, partly because I'd claimed, at age forty-four, to be a *girl,* and partly because of the way I wanted to stay with him in the kitchen and keep rubbing up against his body to chase the tingles that had started with that touch on my back.

"I'm cool with that," he rumbled. "I'll serve you snacks and hang out in the bedroom, and when you need a break…" His hand slid up my side, his thumb brushing the underside of my breast over my sweater. "I'll serve you something special."

I moaned. "I want something special *now.*"

His chuckle was dark as the shadows overtaking the room at twilight. "Do you?"

"Cut it out, you two," Savannah said, bursting into the kitchen. "The girls are demanding snacks, and we can't wait for you two to finish canoodling."

"Canoodling?" Oliver wrinkled his nose.

"It's a Y2K thing," Savannah said. "You wouldn't understand."

"I was around during Y2K," he protested.

"Stop teasing him, Savannah," I said. Taking a step back, I smoothed the front of his charcoal-gray sweater. "Go on. Tell Andrew hi for me."

"Game night won't be the same without you."

"Maybe you'll win for a change." I kissed his cheek.

"I've already won," he whispered in my ear.

"Seriously, you two," Savannah said. "Before I throw a bucket of ice water on you."

With one last, longing look, he turned away and grabbed his keys from the hook. "Okay if I'm back around midnight?"

"Sounds perfect," I purred.

Savannah groaned.

I waited for Oliver to walk out, then I turned to my friend. "You *seriously* need to get laid."

"What?" She went pink all the way to the open collar of her cranberry velvet tracksuit. "I won't even be officially divorced until next week."

"I'm not telling you to get married. I'm saying you could use an orgasm or ten."

"Ten?" Her eyes bugged.

I waved away her shock. "It's not difficult. Take the weekend. Pace yourself. And be sure to hydrate."

My phone buzzed on the counter with a security system notification. I hit the button to let in Bridget, glad she'd actually made it this time. I hated how demanding her job had become. She'd taken on too much in her desperation to prove herself in the CEO position. Still, I tried to be supportive. We all did.

"Right. Snacks," I said. "What do we need?"

Savannah shook off her fog. "There's homemade hummus in the fridge, and some Buffalo chicken dip, which you should avoid because it's got cheese in it. And grab the veggie platter. I'll get the crackers."

I set the platter on the island as Bridget let herself in through the kitchen door, scowling.

I still wasn't a hugger, but I walked over and squeezed my friend's shoulder. "Rough day?"

"The worst. Some days, I want to give up."

"That's life as a CEO," I said, not unsympathetically. I remembered the long, difficult days, agonizing over decisions, but also the highs of knowing my company succeeded because of me. I wouldn't exactly call it easy now, but having Oliver a few doors down the hall helped.

"As a *co*-CEO, you mean."

"Hasn't that been resolved yet?" I asked.

Savannah folded her into a hug. "What did he do this time, honey?"

Bridget bit her lip. "It's more what I found out—"

She stopped when the door opened. Oliver stood in it, his eyebrows drawn together.

"What's wrong?" I asked, striding toward him.

"Nothing? But your dad's here." He winced. "Surprise?"

Cold prickles erupted in my belly. Why had he shown up tonight, when I had friends over? "Shit."

My father pushed past Oliver. "Happy solstice."

"The solstice isn't until next week. And I didn't think you were coming this year. Not after last year."

He looked down at his socks. (Fortunately, he had enough manners to toe off his muddy boots at the door.) "About that. I might not agree with how you've decided to use your talents, but you're my daughter, and I shouldn't have protested at your place of employment." He looked me in the eye. "I'm sorry."

I couldn't recall that he'd ever apologized to me before. Had one of his conspiracies come true? Had the chemtrails tamed him? Had aliens flipped on the obedience chip he claimed they'd installed? "Um. Okay. Still, you could've let me know you were coming."

"I try not to alert the G-men of my whereabouts." And now he was back to the father I recognized.

"Right, right. I've got guests, so—"

Lucie walked into the kitchen, shielding her eyes. "I can't wait any longer. I'm coming to get my own snacks. You guys better not be having a threesome in here." Dropping her hand, she took in my dad's worn jeans, his Army-surplus jacket, and his scruffy white beard. "Oh. Hello."

"Hi, Mr. Wright." Bridget stepped up to him and extended her hand. She was clearly still in work mode with her heels and black sheath dress. "Remember me? I'm Bridget."

"Tessa's friend, the corporate sellout," he growled, not taking her hand.

"You do remember," she said brightly. Her hand fell to her side.

"Stop, Dad," I said, trying to keep the frustration out of my voice. "Bridget is not only very successful but also serves on the board of several philanthropic organizations."

"Your dad?" Lucie waved. "Hi. I'm Tessa's friend Lucie Knox."

"Holden Caulfield."

"Dad." I glared at him. "This is my father, Barry Wright."

Lucie surveyed him like she was memorizing the buzz cut he gave himself. Maybe she hoped to interview him later. His mind *was* kind of fascinating.

"What've you got going on here, Tessa?" he asked gruffly.

"My girlfriends are here. We're having a party."

"Party?" He narrowed his eyes. "That doesn't sound like you."

"No." I huffed out a laugh. "It doesn't. Still, I invited my friends over tonight."

Lucie and Savannah stepped closer, bracketing me between them. Bridget crossed her arms and flashed Dad a challenging stare.

"Mhm. But *he* isn't a girlfriend." Dad jerked a thumb at Oliver. Bless him, Oliver hadn't taken the opportunity to slink out the way I might have. He stood staunchly in the corner, arms folded, watching my dad's every gesture.

"No, Dad." I took a deep breath. "Oliver lives here. He's my boyfriend."

"Boyfriend?" he scoffed. He trailed his gaze over Oliver, from his too-long hair, which I loved to bury my fingers in, to his soft cashmere sweater and polished loafers. "You're that fella from the fake cancer laboratory."

Oliver pushed away from the wall. "It's not fake. We do very real science there. Tessa's the CEO and has made some significant contributions herself."

"She bought into their lies when she went off to college." Dad spat the last word like he always did, even though he and my mom had gone. "Still, it's a good idea to have a man around here. Do you know how to shoot?"

Oliver chuckled. "Does skeet count? I went out a few times with my dad and grandpa. I got pretty good at archery at summer camp."

My dad pierced him with a stony gaze. "Your summer-camp

bow and arrows aren't going to protect anyone when the lizard people come for us. Neither is Tessa's flimsy security system."

"Yikes," Lucie said. "Mr. Wright, you've got to tell me more about these lizard people. Do they walk on two legs or four? And what do they eat?" She stepped closer and tentatively took his arm. "I'm a writer and a former journalist."

"A journalist, huh?" He nodded. "Girlie, I could tell you stories that'd straighten your hair."

"Dad," I said, "it's girls' night. Why don't you eat something and rest? We can talk in the morning."

"We could take some snacks outside," Oliver said, "and have a couple of beers by the fire pit."

When I went with Oliver to a conference in Boston and his parents met us for dinner, his dad had pestered him about keeping Discovery independent. Instead of sitting quietly and eating my lobster, I argued that he'd taken a good risk that I thought would pay off. We'd sat shoulder to shoulder, a united front. Now, Oliver was offering to take one for the team? Because, I realized, that's what we were. A team.

I leaned in and kissed him. "Thanks," I murmured against his lips.

"Of course. I'll tell you about it later when we're in bed."

I nuzzled his ear. "I can think of a lot better things to do in bed than talk about my dad."

He held me to him. "Is that a promise?"

"You know it is. Now I'm going to entertain these people for a couple hours, then kick them out."

"And I'll argue with your dad until I wear him out."

I pecked his lips. "Good luck with that." Pulling away, I said, "Why don't you tell my dad about the company's new product?" We'd made a press release, so it was all public knowledge.

"You've developed a cure?" My dad narrowed his eyes at Oliver.

"Not a cure. A test."

As I turned back toward my friends and picked up the platter of cheese I wouldn't eat, my dad growled, "What good is a test, when the government is sitting on a cure?"

I smiled. They could argue medical conspiracies all night while I entertained my friends. "Bridget," I said, passing her the tray of cheese, "tell us what your nemesis did this week."

"Oh my god." She popped a cube of Jarlsberg into her mouth, then took the platter from me. "You won't believe it."

I turned my head to wink at Oliver, then I hustled my friends out of the room.

Hours later, when we were in bed, I told Oliver about the dickish thing Bridget's co-CEO had done and he told me about my dad's latest theory, then I cuddled against his chest. "Tonight was perfect."

He chuckled into my hair, his warm breath a massage against my scalp. "Because we spent it apart?"

I twisted a lock of his hair around my finger. "Because even though we weren't in the same room, we were a team. Thank you for entertaining my dad."

"Of course." He pressed his head into my hand. "I'm glad you had fun with your friends."

"You know, if we tear down the fake apartment building at the front of the property, we could build a better entrance, something more welcoming." My heart raced at the thought of strangers being able to enter the property, but I breathed through it. My friends would feel welcome, and I liked that.

He kissed my forehead. "If you want. There might be room for a pool and an outdoor kitchen. An entertaining oasis."

I shuddered with anticipation, not horror. I pushed him to his back. "What do I need an outdoor kitchen for? I don't cook."

"*I* cook. You'd love my grilled scallops."

"Mmm." I kissed his lips, then the tip of his chin, then the hollow between his collarbones. "Tell you what else I'd love…"

"Hey." He stopped me before I slid lower. "You know I love you just as you are. We don't have to entertain. You don't have to change anything about this place."

A thrill sped through my body. "I know." And I did. "But I'm ready to open things up again." The way I'd already opened my heart.

He knew what I meant. "I love you." He traced my cheekbone with his finger. "I love how brave you are."

"You're brave too." I leaned into his touch. "I love you. I love that you took a risk on me.

"Best risk I ever took."

I grinned. "Same."

~

Thank you so much for reading *Conspiracies and Chemistry*. Please consider posting a review on your favorite retailer's site, BookBub, or Goodreads.

Members of my VIP Reader List get a free bonus epilogue showing Tessa, Oliver, and the Goddess Gang. Go to michellemccraw.com/CACBonus or scan the code below to grab it!

ACKNOWLEDGMENTS

Thank you, reader, for spending your time with Tessa and Oliver and the Goddess Gang. Your support means the world to me.

Thanks to my beta readers and writing pals, Carla Luna and Karen Grey. Your feedback made this book so much better. Also, Karen, thanks for being my Atlanta book event and bookstore buddy. Buying books I don't have time to read is always more fun with a conspirator.

Thanks, as always, to Melanie Rose Clarke for getting up early to write with me. Your encouragement and accountability help so much!

Finally, thanks to my daughter, P, who helped me make sense of all the biotechnology and laboratory research. I so appreciate your talking through it with me! Of course, all errors are my own, and I'll chalk it up to Romance Reasons.

ABOUT MICHELLE

Michelle McCraw loves reading kissing books and working in tech. One day, she decided to combine her two interests, and now she writes steamy, nerdy contemporary romance that just might make you laugh. Her books feature characters who unashamedly love science, engineering, and technology.

A native Texan, Michelle has shoveled snow during nor'easters and knows the proper response when someone yells, "O-H." She now calls Georgia home, where she doesn't miss snow AT ALL. She enjoys reading, travel, drinking bourbon, and spoiling her extraordinarily ill-behaved but adorable dog. She has been a finalist in the RWA Vivian Contest, the Contemporary Romance Writers' Stiletto Contest, and the Windy City Romance Writers' Four Seasons Contest.

For updates about upcoming books and more free reads—plus guaranteed puppy pics—subscribe to Michelle's newsletter at michellemccraw.com. You can also follow the author on Facebook and Instagram.

facebook.com/MichelleMcCrawAuthor

instagram.com/MMOWriter

amazon.com/author/michellemccraw

goodreads.com/MichelleMcCraw

bookbub.com/authors/michelle-mccraw

BOOKS IN THE 40 AND FABULOUS SERIES

Fashion and Passion

After a disastrous self-help seminar, Carly finds friendship, empowerment, and maybe love with a younger admirer. Get swept away by sparkling banter, new besties, and spicy seduction, perfect for a bubbly escape.

Frenemies and Lovers

When Carly needs a date to her ex's wedding, she agrees to a deal with Andrew, a devilishly handsome younger man. Her frenemy's son. Who happens to be her one-night stand. What could go wrong? Who says you can't be fabulous over forty?

"Total catnip" (5-star review)

Books and Hookups

Writer Lucie's life is looking up: she has a new book deal, fabulous friends, and a bar where everyone knows her name. The last thing she needs is a surprise (geriatric?) pregnancy with her much-younger neighbor.

Conspiracies and Chemistry

Secretive billionaire Tessa seeks redemption from the biggest mistake of her life by betting it all on a groundbreaking biotechnology company, which happens to be run by her younger nemesis. Who knew lab coats were so sexy?

Advances and Retreats

When Bridget and her nemesis, Cole, are temporarily assigned as co-CEOs and given the chance to compete for the solo job at a corporate retreat in Costa Rica, they encounter crocodiles, sabotage, and—possibly—love.

Marriage and Trouble

After an accident, everyone mistakes woozy animal-loving cyclist Pax for Justine's fiancé. She needs a husband, and he needs cash to keep his animal rescue afloat. When real feelings start to develop, their marriage is anything but convenient.

Sugar and Spice

Invisibility is Savannah's superpower. West is the one person it doesn't work on. Inconveniently, he's also her (younger) roommate.

BOOKS IN THE SYNERGY SERIES
CAN BE READ IN ANY ORDER

Work with Me

She's got a checklist for every occasion. He's never met a bad decision he didn't make. Can straitlaced single mom Alicia find a way to work with billionaire tech genius Jackson and save her business—without falling for him first?

"Slow burn magic!" (5-star review)

Friend Me

Romance-obsessed executive assistant Marlee has a plan to woo her crush, icy and aloof San Francisco tech executive Cooper Fallon. But it all goes wrong when her fake date, instead of making her crush jealous, sparks more-than-friends feelings. Kissing the wrong guy? Not in her plan. Neither is falling for her best friend.

"Un-put-down-able" (5-star review)

Trip Me Up

Nerdy computer scientist Samantha Jones didn't mean to end up on a book tour trying to pass off her artificial intelligence-written novel as one written the old-fashioned way. And she certainly didn't mean to fall for her flannel-wearing, poetic tour partner. Opposites attract in this road-trip romance.

"This book had me hooked right from the start and up until the wee hours devouring their story!" (5-star review)

Boss Me

Frosty billionaire philanthropist Cooper Fallon would never start a fling with his off-limits assistant, Ben...or would he?

"OMG...If you like forbidden romance this is the book for you!!!" (5-star review)

Forget Me

She doesn't remember their night together. He can't forget it. When Mimi's prospective boss mistakes Mateo for her boyfriend, she's shocked when he rolls with it. But when their fake romance becomes real, will buttoned-up Mimi let down her guard for love?

"I absolutely love this twist on the grumpy sunshine trope." (5-star review)

Tempt Me

When a gaffe caught on camera threatens her company, a no-nonsense tech CEO calls on her bestie's little sister for help. But falling for her sunshiny public relations assistant could get her into even more hot water.

"THIS WAS FUN!!" (5-star review)

CREDITS

Edits and Proofreading

E&A Editing Services

Cover Design

Kari March

www.ingramcontent.com/pod-product-compliance
Lightning Source LLC
Chambersburg PA
CBHW021033310726
48969CB00006B/1630